True Love
& Real Romance

Fiction by Lynda Schor

APPETITES

TRUE LOVE & REAL ROMANCE

True Love
& Real Romance

Lynda Schor

Coward, McCann & Geoghegan ✳ New York

"The Tooth Fairy" appeared in *Ms. Magazine.*

"Class Outing," "Another Great Love That Could Not Be" and "The Highest Grader of All"
were written while the author was part of the CCF Artist Project, on time sponsored by the
foundation with funds provided by the New York City Department of Employment under
CETA Title VI.

Library of Congress Cataloging in Publication Data

Schor, Lynda
    True love & real romance.

    CONTENTS: The Tooth Fairy.—The pest.—Irrevocable.
[etc.]
    I. Title.
PZ4.S3737Tr [PS3569.C5262]   813.'.5'4   79-13135
ISBN 0-698-11004-8

Printed in the United States of America

For Alexandra, Timothy and Zachary

With gratitude to The MacDowell Colony, the Allegro School in Claverack, my parents, and my sister Isobel, for all kinds of support.

The Stories

True Love
& Real Romance

The Tooth Fairy

He lies on the couch, slacks down around his upper thighs, his navel a small sump which his finger falls into as his hand slowly crawls to the volcanic protrusion pushing up his Jockey shorts. Blindly, his eyes engaged in the magazine in his other hand, he searches for the incomprehensible ingredients that really excite. Carola, Georgina, Augusta, satin-bloused, braceleted, pass through his riffling fingers, until Sari, reclining on multicushioned carpets, ankles, wrists, arms and waist encircled in silver and gems, abundant red hair falling across vanilla-junket furrows. Head demurely down, she stares up through thick lashes, daringly.

"Sari," he whispers, imagining the tip of his tongue touching her breast. He can smell the musk, hear her bracelets jungle, as, Turkish and Arabic orientalia rampaging sensuously, she shows him, in various poses, on this double spread and that, other tantalizing portions of her anatomy.

Practiced, he can fondle himself with one hand and hold the magazine and turn pages with the other. In one last motion, knees up, he presses the magazine against his upraised thighs and impresses himself on glossy stock.

"OOooooHhhhhh!!" he bellows, eyes squinting, buttocks taut, raised two feet above the couch cover. As he feels the rhythmic spasms of his entire body surging, he hears a deep, sepulchral voice.

"Whoo hass rubbed the lamp?" Saul opened his eyes in time to see, in a puff of smoke, a woman squeezing out of his penis, attempting to push away the magazine, which was blocking her exit.

"Jesus Christ," she said, fanning away the smoke with one hand and fluffing out her pressed-down hair with the other, "It's like being born again." Saul closed his eyes, this time in fear, as he searched for a rational explanation other than that he'd given birth to a full-grown person. He recalled the words, "Whoo hass rubbed the lamp?" I get it, he thought, grasping at straws, it's the Arabian Nights scene from the magazine come true. Of course he wasn't rubbing a lamp, but what the hell, here was a genie all his own.

The woman sat on the floor a moment to orient herself. Saul smiled to himself and watched her thick auburn hair shiver as she shook her head dazedly.

"You're supposed to be asleep," she said, covering her knee with her white gauzy dress, nervously fingering the hem where it met the top of her combat boot.

"Is your name really Sari, or is it made up for the magazine?" he asked.

"I don't understand. Do we speak a different language?" she asked, shaking out something that must have been crumpled behind her. A pair of wrinkled and slightly damp giant translucent white wings unfurled, convulsively at first, staccato, then completely, with a double pop.

"What the hell are those?" screamed Saul, pressing himself against the couch cushions.

"Those are my wings," she said, looking behind herself, not at first aware what he meant. "What do they look like to you?"

"First thing you'll have to do as my genie," said Saul, "is get rid of the tacky costume." Raising his body as little as possible, he gingerly pulled her wing.

"Ouch," she said. "Okay, I've wasted enough time. Let's have it." She lifted the side of the cushion smartly, throwing his head off, and felt under it with her other hand.

"Where's the tooth? You were supposed to leave it under the pillow. If you don't follow the rules, I don't have to leave the money. You weren't even supposed to be awake."

"You're cracked," said Saul. "Who on earth do you think you are? The Tooth Fairy?"

"That's right. I am the Tooth Fairy." Saul was silent for a moment.

"Look, you're my genie. There's no such thing as a Tooth Fairy."

"Are you kidding? You mentioned it first."

"I was trying to be facetious and that was the most ridiculous thing I could think of."

"I wonder," said the woman, "that you don't question the reality of a genie." Silence for a moment.

"Because it's only logical. It fits. I was fantasizing Arabian Nights and you appeared in a puff of smoke. Besides, I need a genie, not a Tooth Fairy. This apartment is a mess, I'm tired of frozen dinners and jerking off."

"Then why don't you get married?"

"Ha, ha," laughed Saul, attempting to hide his terror. "I just never loved anyone who loved me and vice versa. A practical arrangement with no emotional involvement is perfect."

"I think," she said, her green eyes irritatingly lucid, "when people become interdependent they become emotionally involved, even without infatuation."

"I'm not interested in interdependence. You're my little slave, my little genie . . . mine . . . mine . . . you're mine. He grabbed her and held her arms behind her back, which contracted with pain. Suddenly he drew back and doubled over himself as her heavy leather boot shot swiftly out from under her skirt. His unsuccessful attempts to hide his pain moved her. She twisted the tip of her forefinger in her mouth. As soon as Saul could breathe he said, "Oh, my balls!—" He opened his eyes wide to keep the tears from falling out.

"At least you could say you're sorry," he whined.

"I'm not sorry," she whispered. "You hurt me first."

"You're not sorry," he murmured in disbelief, suddenly surprising her in a grip similar to the previous one. This time, feeling him pressed tight against her smooth flank, she made no attempt to struggle.

"I have to leave. I have a job to do and you're holding me against my will."

"I'm only fighting for what belongs to me," said Saul.

The Tooth Fairy decided not to argue, just to escape as soon as possible.

"A woman can't go anywhere alone at night without coming across some creep who imagines he has the right to possess her," she murmured.

"Wait a minute," said Saul. "Whose apartment is this? Who's intruding and trespassing? Besides, giving children money for their teeth is nonsense. I'll bet my taxes pay for it." An evil look appeared in his eyes. "You were sent to me and despite your own confusion about your identity, you're going to be my genie." He twisted her arms behind her. "What do you say?"

"Yes," she whispered, wincing.

"Yes, Master," he corrected. The Tooth Fairy remained silent and immobile, only her eyes shifting back and forth slightly as if they would escape. "I want you to dress like a genie," he said. "This cloth isn't bad," he continued, grabbing a piece of her skirt between a thumb and forefinger, "but the style is *yucchh.*" He spat on the floor for emphasis. "And boots with a dress like this? You could be pretty, but you lack chic."

"These clothes are practical. The boots are heavy-duty because I often travel long distances and traverse unknown terrain. And this dress isn't a dress." She spread her legs to show that they could separate and each was still surrounded by cloth.

"Those wide pants aren't bad," mused Saul. "but only an angel fetishist would go for those wings."

That reminded her. She felt a surge of urgency.

"I'm going now. I promise I'll come back here later."

"Do you think I believe you?" Saul asked, rummaging in his closet. He emerged, swinging strips of patterned cloth, and before the Tooth Fairy could struggle, he tackled her and tied her to a chair with the bright strips, which were four gaudy ties.

"How can you say anything about my clothes when you have ties like these," said the Tooth Fairy, who then realized that perhaps she'd better say nothing as she seemed to be in the hands of a madman.

"These ties are the height of fashion now," said Saul.

"Just to make sure you don't escape, I'm going to tie you like this." He showed her a photograph of a woman on a chair, naked, bound with twine in an intricate and symmetrical pattern.

"This is a Japanese bondage magazine," he said, proudly.

After searching in his closet, he emerged triumphantly with a neat ball of heavy twine, which he proceeded to wrap and knot across and around her body and the chair, carefully referring to the picture, which he placed conveniently on the floor.

"Why can't you simply tie it?"

"This is more aesthetic, don't you think? Those Japanese sure can wrap," he said admiringly, in the center of a complicated maze of cord somewhere between her knees and ankles. "I've always fantasized doing this."

"I think you have sexual problems," said the Tooth Fairy, tearful, tired, and losing hope of escape.

"Of course I don't, I just like to try everything," said Saul, but not until he'd paused and looked at her for a moment, one eyebrow raised in a forehead high, pale, and delicate as a baby's under the hair that covered it, which he brushed back in puzzlement. This flash of vulnerable forehead left the Tooth Fairy flushed, her heart beating hard.

"If you don't untie me I can't be your genie."

"I'd rather keep you this way till you lose your compulsiveness about your work."

"But there's no one else to do it. Besides, I'm not meant to be here and I don't want to do genie's work."

Saul looked at her coldly. "Did you choose your work, which you seem to love so much, or does your whole sense of personal identity derive from your job?" She burst into tears.

"You make me so unhappy," she moaned, "from the moment I mistakenly arrived." Saul looked at her, his face a compassionate reflection on her own, but the look immediately dispersed.

"I bet you're using tears to manipulate me into feeling sorry for you so that I'll let you go."

She felt hurt and powerless since he insisted on misunderstanding her, and remained quiet for a while, exhausted.

"Okay," she said softly, "I'll stay with you without trying to escape until I can convince you that I should go. When you understand you'll be joyful, and kiss me good-bye."

"That's smart," said Saul in his old cold voice, apparently reveling in victory. Hearing that, the Tooth Fairy decided to escape anyway.

"You don't hear me," she complained.

"That's why I'm not married. In case I forgot, one evening with you is enough to remind me. I don't have to hear you. I don't want to hear you." He tried to rip open the rope without success.

"Try that piece," said the Tooth Fairy, pointing with her chin at a portion of knot that extended a bit. "If you free my hands I can help you."

"I can't free your hands. Should I call an ambulance?" There was a deep chime.

I'm about to be saved, thought the Tooth Fairy. The doorbell rang again. Saul became frantic, clawing ineffectually at the knots.

"The way you respond to pressure, you must be a great lawyer," she laughed, but then found herself empathizing with his anxiety. "If you don't answer it, no one will know you're home," she whispered.

"Saulie, answer the door. I know you're in there, Saulie." Saul froze. "Saulie—hurry up!" Mobilizing himself, Saul ran to the door.

*

Mrs. Rauschenberg stood in the doorway a moment and sniffed, as if she could smell trouble. Entering peripatetically, her legs surrounded by shopping bags, she saw the Tooth Fairy, her dress ripped, tied in a complicated oriental bondage pattern to her son's antique kitchen chair, her wings, which had been dejectedly drooping down the back of the chair onto the rug now perking up behind her in radiant translucence.

"Saulie, are you a pervert or something? And in the antique ladderback I got for you at the East Hempstead flea market."

"Don't worry, Mother. We were just practicing some knots. Actually she's a genie. She's going to do everything I say."

"You always were spoiled," said Mrs. Rauschenberg, eyeing him suspiciously. "At least you're not a homosexual. So, I suppose you rubbed a magic lamp?" she said, looking at the Tooth Fairy.

"Really," said the Tooth Fairy, trying to be supportive, "he was just rubbing himself and I popped out by mistake."

"Saulie, remember what I told you about excessive masturbation? Why can't you be normal and get married? You think this genie will live with you out of wedlock?"

"You mean, Tooth Fairy," corrected the Tooth Fairy.

"So what else is new?" asked Mrs. Rauschenberg, removing some jars from her shopping bags.

"Mother," said Saul placatingly, "I know you don't believe me, so I'll tell you the truth," he lied. "Mother, we're going to be married. I'd like you to meet—" Saul looked at the Tooth Fairy blankly.

"Antoinette," said the Tooth Fairy. "Antoinette Tooth Fairy."

Saul's mother, easily untying Antoinette, says, "Sounds like a *shiksa* to me."

Suddenly Saul realized that he could never make his mother happy.

"Actually, Saulie, with me around you don't have to get married." She handed him jars of homemade food, and displayed the interior of a whole bagful of breads and cakes. "What can a wife do for you that I can't, besides indulge your perversions."

"What about normal sex, Mother? Everyone needs normal sex."

"Your father and I haven't made love for fifteen years, since he became impotent. But that doesn't mean we don't love each other," she said from between clenched teeth. "What can a genie do that I couldn't?" she shrieked. "Can a genie clean as good as me?" She took a sponge and began wiping up. "Can a genie cook as good as me?" Her fat arms encompassed the pile of food. Saul said nothing. He stood immobile, a jar of gefilte fish in his hand as his mother recaptured some reusable shopping bags and departed.

*

"If you just let me go do my tooth-fairy work tonight I swear I'll be right back. I must do my job when the children are in their deepest sleep."

"Who's going to clean this mess?"

"Why don't you try again for a real genie while I'm gone?"

"I'm getting attached to you," said Saul. "What if I try again and get Cinderella?"

"At least Cinderella can cook and clean," said Antoinette.

She wasn't lying when she said she'd be back, but seeing the moon, feeling the gentle breeze roiling around her, she couldn't conceive of returning. She flew easily into the open window, easing gently onto the sill. She rose, took a step and opened her mouth in a silent scream. While balancing on the other foot, that one also stepped on something sharp. She stood immobile until her eyes became accustomed to the darkness. In a moment she saw that the entire floor of the child's room was cluttered with clothing, toys, and papers. Damn, I forgot my boots, she thought, tiptoeing through the junk to the side of the bed. This child was lying absolutely stiff in the center of the bed, up and down, not a limb bent, his head straight. The covers were also arranged perfectly, only his feet were exposed, and those too straight up, heels against the sheet, like a corpse in rigor mortis. She peered fearfully over to look at his face. Two dots of light glowed from the eyes. She drew back suddenly. Then she saw the reflected dots of light flicker and she realized that, though open, his eyes had moved and he wasn't dead.

"How come you're still awake?" His head didn't move. "I'm the Tooth Fairy."

"I know," the child whispered. "What did you think I took you for? A genie?"

"I thought that, holding your head like that, perhaps you weren't able to see me."

"I have excellent peripheral vision. My vision in the front is not so hot. In order to avoid getting glasses I memorize the eye charts."

"Why do you lie like this?"

"If I don't keep my head straight I won't be able to see all sides of the room at once, and if I have my feet covered I'll smother."

"You're afraid of something?"

"I'm afraid of everything lately. I'm riddled with fear ever since I saw that movie about those giant plovers. And another where a quail hypnotizes nannies into committing suicide."

"You know it's impossible for a giant plover to get up this far," she told him. "Plovers can't fly or climb seven stories."

"I tell myself it's not rational, but it doesn't help the fear. Personally, I'm in favor of sex in the movies for kids instead of horror and violence."

"I guess I have to make this transaction while you're awake then," sighed the Tooth Fairy. "Everything's been going wrong lately."

"How much will you leave?"

"Twenty-five cents."

"Haven't you heard of inflation?" asked the boy. "Look, it's an eyetooth. Don't I get a little more for an eyetooth? I got a quarter for my front upper. Now I'm older. Shouldn't I get a raise?"

"I'm sorry, it's a fixed rate, not decided by me."

"Please," whined the child, "please. I'm saving for a tape deck and a deluxe skateboard, which is on sale right now."

"You really are an obnoxious kid, aren't you?"

"Yes," he laughed proudly. "Well, if you can't leave more than a quarter, could you lie with me for a while? Maybe then I'd fall asleep."

"Well, maybe for a few minutes if it will really comfort you."

The child moved for the first time and opened the cover for Antoinette, who slipped into his warm and slightly indented place. Before she even relaxed she heard a shrill shout.

"Brett. What's going on in your room?" A light flashed on somewhere and then diminished as a black form stood in the doorway of the child's room, blocking it. A glow backlit the form as it made its way toward the bed.

"Who are you and what are you doing here?" Brett's mother demanded.

"It's the Tooth Fairy, Mother. She was just lying with me for a moment because you won't."

"Tooth Fairy, my eye. She looks more like a winged whore to me. Of course I'll lie with you, darling," she said as the Tooth Fairy flew unobtrusively out the window. Antoinette opened her hand in which she held the tooth and looked at the minute luminous object, so cute, so pearly. Then suddenly she threw it and watched it fall. It was no more to her than a tiny trajectory, not quite as pretty as a shooting star.

*

"I knew you'd be back," said Saul.

"I didn't," said Antoinette, dejectedly slumping into the couch.

"What's wrong?"

"I don't know. I just feel depressed." He supported her body and brought her into the bedroom. She lay listlessly across the bed staring into space.

"Do you imagine that is seductive?" asked Saul.

"I'm just resting."

"But I waited for you, you promised you'd be in the mood."

"Do things always turn out exactly as you expect?"

"Mostly," said Saul. "I usually put myself in situations where they do."

"Well, they don't for me," said Antoinette, envious of him. "But I'm more able to take unforeseen circumstances so I'll end up having a more exciting life, and learning more, even if it's not as comfortable."

"*Na-na, ne-na-na,*" said Saul. "Since you don't know what it feels like you wouldn't understand that what really feels best is power and control." He lay down beside her.

"You don't look very tempting," he said. "You look as if you're about to cry." She closed her eyes wearily.

"I guess I want you to be tender with me. Especially as I've never done this before."

"You're kidding!"

"No. Tooth Fairies never do that. But I'm willing to try. I'm not as rigid as you and it looks interesting."

"'Interesting' is the key word; forget about tenderness," said Saul nervously. He rummaged in the drawer and returned with a giant box containing row upon row of small metallic packets.

"These are to prevent you from getting pregnant."

Antoinette pictured the box full of rows and rows of women which Saul would take out and blow up as he did with this milky balloon.

"Do you feel anything?" he asked.

"Am I supposed to? You haven't touched me yet."

"Just looking at these condoms gets me excited," he said, pulling off his clothing, then hers. From his vantage point, kneeling between her golden upraised calves, her lovely face back along an imaginary horizon line, she didn't look much different from a woman in a magazine.

Antoinette giggled nervously. Suddenly she felt a rush of joy seeing him perched over her, naked and powerful, gleaming with sensuality. Feeling a sudden rush of pleasure, she wondered whether that was love.

He lay across her limp and sweating. His weight felt good.

"Twenty minutes!" he said, turning the clock to face him. "That's fantastic! Isn't that fantastic?" He looked down. "Where on earth is the condom?" he asked, frantically searching his body and the bed.

"Is this it?" Antoinette held up a limp moist thing resembling a portion of umbilical cord.

"Where did you find it?" Saul asked. Antoinette pointed between her thighs. Saul's face was blank with panic.

"Listen," he said, "I'm not kidding. Stay here as my genie and you'll never have to go back to work. You'll never have to work again," he reiterated, turning on the TV at the foot of the bed. "Would you mind getting something to eat?"

He looks so handsome, she thought, watching the light from the TV reflected on his vapid face. He grabbed at the dish of grapes and peanut butter sandwiches on the bed between them without removing his eyes from the screen. Antoinette put her arms around his head and blew on his ear.

"We'll do it again when *Baretta* is over," he said. "It'll be even better next time."

"You're so virile," she said when *Baretta* was over. She pulled the blanket off playfully. Her green eyes gazed up, glowing with passion and desire to please. He felt a sudden oppression at her sweet and so earnest efforts, and his penis became soft.

"I knew it. I knew I'd become impotent like my father, but at least he was in his forties when it happened and I'm only thirty-five," he groaned.

"Don't worry," said Antoinette. "I don't think it's possible to become impotent for good in one second."

"I can't explain it." He shook his head in wonder. "Suddenly I saw you as you, and then it happened," he said.

"Let's get married," he said to her one night two months later, as she vomited into the toilet.

"Uuhggg, aarrgh," she said. Saliva dripped from her lips into the bowl. "Why do you want to mention that?"

"I think you're pregnant. I want a baby now. Let's get married. I love you."

"Pregnant from that one time?"

"It's possible," he said smiling proudly.

"I'm getting an abortion, then, and I'm leaving you," said Antoinette, still on her knees. He was on his knees beside her as if they were both worshiping the toilet bowl.

"Let me up." She swayed weakly. "I want to brush my teeth. Oh, teeth, teeth, when teeth were my life—white ones, yellow ones, filled ones—just the word 'teeth' makes me shiver with joy." Saul followed her into the bedroom and sat down next to her limp body.

"That's because you feel sick," he explained. "It's glandular." His face was directly above hers and she felt as if she wouldn't be able to breathe if he didn't move it aside.

"I have to escape," she said.

"You can't escape your destiny," he said ominously. "Even my mother thinks we should have a baby. She says if it's born with wings we can always give it plastic surgery."

"I hate it here. I forgot what it feels like to be myself."

"Yourself? Who's that?"

"A Tooth Fairy."

"I thought you got over that," spat Saul scornfully.

"Why should I want to stay here with an impotent lawyer to cook and keep his house clean?"

"Many women before you did." He paused. "My shrink says I won't be impotent forever. Listen," he cajoled, "if you have the baby I'll let you be liberated. You can earn one third of the income and do two thirds of the housework. And I won't say anything about your boots."

"Go fuck yourself," she said, and wept because he wasn't trying to be mean.

"Okay, go. It's your fault I'm impotent anyway. I never was before, not even once."

*

Antoinette's anger propelled her through the air like a jet. She felt the wind rush past her as she flew, colder on the two wet rivulets running down her cheeks. One for sorrow, one for joy, she thought, readjusting her flight for the internal burden she now carried. She flew higher, hair streaming behind her like a comet. When she flew joyously in through the beautiful large window on the seventeenth floor, in her unbalanced condition, she was unable to avoid the gymnasium equipment that she saw too late, hanging from the ceiling.

The fresh light of early morning shone ingenuously through the large uncurtained window. The little boy walked dubiously and silently, in his pale green flannel Dr. Denton's, to where the Tooth Fairy hung, head back, toes pointing downward as if she were trying to reach the floor. She swung gently.

"Mom, the Tooth Fairy's here," he called tentatively.

"What did she leave?" called a voice from the other room. The small boy ran back to the bed. He rummaged under his pillow and extracted an envelope. Feeling his own little tooth still inside, he removed it and looked at it dejectedly.

"Nothing," he answered, tears falling down his fat rosy cheeks as rapidly as rain.

The Pest

Roger, poised over Arlene with his elbows straight, felt as if he were the George Washington Bridge spanning the Hudson River, his toes in New York, his face in New Jersey. The substance beneath his body ran by with a swift and even current no matter how much he attempted to stab it into remaining in some kind of reality by swiftly jabbing his prick in and out. Suddenly, staring at one of her round molded junket breasts, strawberry nippled, vaguely trembling with every thrust but never losing its shape, he surrounded the strawberry with his moist mouth and bit, hard.

"Ouch," screamed Arlene, tears of pain and surprise pooling spontaneously, drowning her small blue eyes, overflowing and rolling down the wide, suddenly reddened sides of her face, symmetrically and at exactly the same speed, noted Roger absently, as if observing a stock car race. Rubbing her breast, she scrutinized him, searching for evidence that she'd been bitten accidentally in an excess of passion.

"I was attempting to grasp your essence," said Roger.

"With your teeth?" Arlene elevated her upper torso, throwing

Roger off, her tears falling forward like light rain onto his hairy thigh. He wiped them off absently. "You aren't the first man who thought my essence was in my breast. And now you're wiping my tears off as if they were birdshit. You know what?" she asked, not waiting for him to answer, "you hate women. You're trying to get even with me for the pain your wife caused you. Why don't you go and bite your wife's tit?" Roger didn't answer. His head was lowered as he searched for some delinquent dust in his navel. Arlene pinched his leg. "Answer me."

"I wasn't aware that you asked a question," said Roger, brushing off the pinch as if it were a mosquito. "She's not my wife any more. She already lives with someone else. I couldn't just ring their bell, walk in, refuse her lover's invitation to dinner, stand there watching as he sits at the table, until Edith, holding a casserole with both hands, like an offering, a bright ruffled potholder sticking up around each handle decoratively, places the casserole ceremoniously in front of Dick the Prick, whose eyes have been worshipfully following her, until at this climax, they smile at each other exclusively. The moment his eyes transfer their affectionate gaze to the casserole, and Edith straightens her body, I, who have been waiting silently, lift one side of her sweater and bite her breast."

"You make a joke out of everything," said Arlene, both pleased and disappointed that Roger was so detached from Edith.

"It is a joke that you imagine that Edith caused me pain. The reason we're not together now is that I had absolutely no feelings for her."

"I thought it was because she had a lover," said Arlene, searching Roger's whole body desperately for the minutest indication that she had some effect on him.

Roger sat there with perfect equanimity remembering how he'd found himself sneaking through the dried rushes of the Lees carpet like a Comanche, his heart beating a drum signal to his limbs, but he made it to the bedroom door, which was slightly ajar. That was the first time Edith had ever really excited him.

"Why did you faint when you discovered them if you didn't feel anything?" asked Arlene.

"My past has nothing to do with you, so why bring it up? Whenever I tell you something you save it up to use against me later," Roger said angrily. "I fainted from anger, not because she was having sex with someone else, but that she had emotions without me when I had remained faithful to her despite my lack of feeling. It was very easy for me to leave her. I never even think about her."

"It's frightening that two people can live together intimately for years, then split and never think about each other," said Arlene, "but I don't believe it. You just don't allow yourself to have feelings."

"Well why should I?" asked Roger, rising. "I don't want to get hurt. Imagine how hurt I'd be if I had feelings," he said, his voice becoming louder to compensate for the distance he put between them as he walked to the bathroom.

Arlene followed, naked and crying loudly, as she watched Roger lay his limp prick over the clean white edge of the porcelain sink like a dead eel and turn on the water.

"Why are you crying now?"

"I'm crying because now I know for sure that I'll never be able to reach you," whined Arlene, groping for Roger's toothbrush, purblind with tears.

"You're only crying to get me to sympathize with you," he said, cockily throwing water over his prick, which was still hanging over the side of the sink.

"So what? What's wrong with my wanting your sympathy? Is that a crime?" she shrieked, trembling, squeezing the toothpaste all over her hand, the edge of the sink and the floor. They looked at each other in the medicine chest mirror. Her mouth reminded Roger of "The Scream" by Edvard Munch.

"Would you please clean that up?" he said, his chin indicating the Dionysian application of toothpaste.

"Ohh, I invested so much in this relationship and it's all wasted. I can't bear it, I tried so hard for nothing."

Roger was calmly soaping his prick now, with pleasure and concentration, like a small boy washing a pet.

Arlene, hiccuping, watched malevolently. "You don't want a

trace of anyone else to remain on you," she said.

Roger didn't answer. He felt it would be best to ignore her until her outburst was over. He thought he saw her on her hands and knees, cleaning up the toothpaste, but when he finally turned he saw an enormous bug, at least as large as a kneeling person, light brown, one feeler up and one dragging on the floor, eating toothpaste.

"Oh God," said Roger to himself, "how am I going to get out of here? I warned her about being unclean." I may as well urinate now, he thought, since the entrance was blocked, hoping that the bug wouldn't decide to move toward him. He ignored it until, shaking off the last drop of piss, he looked around trepidatiously. It was gone. Thank God, he thought, trembling, as he warily peeked outside to see whether it was in his large clean studio room. He was afraid he'd find it sitting on his queen-size bed, sullying the Scintilla satin spread with bug stains, but all was clear.

Arlene wasn't there either. She hadn't even said goodbye. While Roger detested incomplete and prematurely truncated affairs, he couldn't deny that he was relieved that both Arlene and the bug had disappeared. Walking toward his drafting table, he now noticed, written in magenta lipstick on his kelly green satin bedspread, the message, "My essence and I have flowed out of your life with a swift and even current," each distinctive character framed with a greasy border of maroon. Despite his commercial-artist's appreciation of the color combination, anger at the destruction of his spread overrode a sudden regret he felt that he was missing something, that he'd let something go that he didn't have the ability to recognize as special, having interred Arlene with his own boring personality.

Well, that was the cleverest thing she ever said anyway, he thought, as he settled into his swivel seat and leaned his elbows on his drafting table, lining them up along the clean edge of his metal T square, and absently looked out of the window he faced. Carefully, he lifted a sheet of tracing paper between his forefinger and thumb, and before he could place it on the white Bristol board already on his desk, the images that had been stirring in his neighbors' window across the courtyard achieved the clarity of recognizable forms, naked ones in fact: a woman's buttocks being pressed against the glass, forming two whitish circlets, flat, but not too flat to disguise their anatomical origins; the manner in which they were pressed alternately larger and flatter then smaller, rhythmically, was an indication of the activity they were engaged in, which caused Roger's breath to catch, even before he perused more explicitly, noticing how two bodies intertwined, how strong arms folded around a willowy back, how straight blond hair swung back and forth, one tendril stuck to the side of the face with sweat, Roger imagined, imbuing what he could see with a multitude of romantic and passionate details, even imagining that he heard the faint echo of grunts and moans across the courtyard.

He overrode an impulse to duck down and hide, deciding that he had a right to look out his window into his courtyard. He could scarcely comprehend an intensity of passion that could obliterate self-consciousness and the whole outside world, and had an uneasy feeling resembling jealousy and anxiety, which he attributed to his not having had an orgasm with Arlene that morning. Still seated, he leaned forward and pulled his curtain closed and, with anticipation, leaned back as far as his swivel would allow and pulled out his prick, carefully, so that it wouldn't get scratched by his zipper, wrapped his now-hot hand around his member, already hard enough to allow the full five-digit grip, and closed his eyes, pictures of the scene he'd just witnessed fleeting from zoom-lens distance to closeup with many added attractions. He was about to come. He squinted hard, gasped, bit his tongue between his teeth, ceasing all motion in order to prolong his pleasure, when the doorbell rang loudly. He rapidly, and with some effort, stuffed his prick away, which luckily, due to the shock of the buzzer, could bend somewhat, and, attempting to breathe normally, he opened the door. An attractive and glamorously attired woman stood there.

"Roger, I just stopped by to ask you whether you could possibly have that mechanical done by this afternoon," she said, slipping under his arm, which leaned on the carved lintel. Roger, slightly surprised, followed her into his apartment.

"You could have called to ask me that," he said impatiently, feeling her presence an imposition. "You may be the art director, but you don't own me."

"That's not very hospitable," she said, removing her coat and sitting on the edge of the bed. "If I were a male art director you'd never speak to me that way. I need that work. Not every one could be trusted to work as well as you and get it in on time."

"It isn't fair for you to drop in here without calling first, as if I have no identity other than worker," he said, refusing her flattery. "Perhaps I was busy with something personal. Work isn't everything."

"Work is everything," she said reassuringly. "You don't seem to have much of a life, either." She glanced at the writing in lipstick with which she shared the bedspread. "Good color," she said, appreciatively. "I'm glad your girlfriend's gone. She caused two of your projects to be late."

"Don't be silly," said Roger, smiling. "I think you're jealous. Maybe you really came here for something else," he said lasciviously, prey to the sudden feeling that if he fucked her hard, himself on top, he'd be able to retain that position in all their dealings.

"I have a policy of retaining a work relationship with those who work with me. Does being in an environment with a bed change our whole relationship?"

"Why not be flexible? We learned in art school that environments affect people."

"Well, we don't want to let environments tell us what to do either. It's just like you to blame the bed for your own impulses," said the art director, replacing her hat. "By the way, you need an exterminator," she said, peering at the enormous bug, which watched her from behind the partially open door, in the gloomy interior of the closet.

Roger, staring horrified at the bug, had a revelation.

"Arlene. Arlene," he called, not daring to approach, "will you take off that costume?" The bug looked back at him, its glance partially obscured by the Bloomingdale's sport jacket hanging directly over his head. Fearful of a closer confrontation, Roger lifted his Trimline telephone receiver.

"Arlene, you're there," he said. "How could you do this to me? You always had a grotesque sense of humor, but I thought you were above revenge."

"What are you talking about, Roger?" asked Arlene.

"How could you put this awful bug in my apartment, Arlene?"

"What bug?" asked Arlene.

"For all I know, that bug is you," said Roger triumphantly.

"What bug? Did you call me just to blame me for something again? I bet you miss that aspect of our relationship. Perhaps we can continue just that one aspect. Every day you can call me just to blame me for something. Otherwise we'll never talk to each other."

"That kind of sarcasm is ugly, Arlene. I have the most enormous roach in New York City right here in my apartment and I'm sure it has something to do with you. It is you. The moment you left, it was here."

"Roger, if I left, how could I be there? You're calling me at my home."

Roger was too upset to figure that out, and Arlene was beginning to hope that Roger's irrationality was caused by regret.

"It definitely isn't me. Maybe it's Gregor Samsa."

"Who's Gregor Samsa?"

"The man who turned into a roach in 'Metamorphosis,' who really symbolizes Kafka's own feeling about himself."

There was a pause. "Are you saying, Arlene, that this bug is Kafka, or are you really implying," he said, emphasizing his words in an ugly way, "that the bug is me?! You would say or do anything to see me get upset. I'd hoped you were too big to need this kind of revenge."

"There's no real revenge possible for the person in love on the one who isn't," said Arlene, her voice trembling. "You need an exterminator, not a lover."

*

Roger absently pushed the door of the exterminator nearest his brownstone whom he'd carefully looked up in his Yellow Pages, but it only pressed his shoulder back. Puzzled, he checked the name. "Exterminating Angels." Encouraged by this concrete confirmation, he pushed again, equally impotently, then, noticing a small pink buzzer, pushed it. He waited impatiently as footsteps became louder and louder, the number not in conjunction with the size of the store, which was only about six feet wide. He attempted to peer through the louvered window but couldn't see anything despite the thin, tantalizing cracks. Every time it seemed that if he just moved his head a little further to one side, something would come into view, the moment he moved it even just a fraction of a millimeter everything was lost.

"See anything?"

Roger swiveled and was blinded by an unexpected patch of sunlight falling on a flat pendant of blond hair which swung out from the doorway, eclipsing the white gleam of a bare chest, which sank not a moment too soon into the dim reaches of a flowing kimono. When the woman shrugged her head, motioning him to follow, her hair flew back into the gloomy interior and the yellow brightness vanished.

"I wanted the exterminator," said Roger, fearfully, after they'd covered what appeared to be a lot of distance in a dark corridor, no sign of store or office.

The woman employed a subtle motion of her shoulders without even turning, to reassure Roger that he should follow, as he kept his eyes on her white heels, rhythmically rising and falling with a sharp slap as they alternately met the sole of her high-heeled satin scuffs. Some light began filtering out into the corridor, which soon dilated to a surprisingly elegant foyer and in turn, through an Arabian arched doorway, burgeoned into an enormous lounge.

"I'm in the wrong place," mumbled Roger hoarsely. "I only wanted an exterminator," he repeated.

I'll buy a drink and leave, he thought, noticing a bar in the rear. He was led across a deep white carpet, so thick that each step sent him slightly askew, and deposited on a maroon satin couch brocaded with tiny pink roses. It wasn't the furniture he stared at while accepting a drink that was offered him, it was the erotic sumptuousness of the place combined with the fact that it was fully populated with women half undressed, or some other fraction, the remainder in various scanty erotica. In another setting he might have laughed at these costumes; here he found himself quite flustered. Although he was the only one fully clothed, he felt defenseless. Roger couldn't deny the fact that this exterminator looked exactly like a brothel, a combination of Wild West and Italian Bordello, and he wondered whether anything would be required of him.

"I'll have Johnnie Walker Red and water on the rocks," he called to his retreating guide, in an attempt to compose himself.

Left alone, sipping his drink, he perspired, oppressed by his fear of VD, and mulled the question of whether or not it might be communicated by promiscuous use of drinking glasses when he suddenly raised his drinkless arm across his face to protect himself from what seemed to be a group of women stampeding toward him.

They were merely glad to see him, however, and Roger was able to examine them more closely as they arranged themselves around him.

"My name is Chryssa," said the person at his knee, while he observed one creamy buttock draped over the arm of his couch, within licking distance. "What's yours?"

"Roger," he said. They all laughed.

"It's not that funny," said Roger.

"It's just that it's a pun," explained Chryssa, "you know, Roger?"

Roger told himself that these people and he were on different wavelengths.

"Knock, knock," said Chryssa, banging his knee with her pink fist.

"Who's there," said Roger.

"Wet."

"Wet who?"

"Wet out the water, I'm dwowning." They all burst out laughing again.

This time Roger joined in. The more he drank, the funnier

everything seemed. "Knock, knock," he said, "but this time you say, 'Wait a minute, I'm putting on my coat.'"

"Knock, knock."

"I'm putting on my coat."

"No, no," laughed Roger hysterically, "I did something wrong. First say, 'Who's there?,' then say, 'I'm putting on my coat,' and then repeat the name I say."

"Knock, knock."

"Who's there?"

"Jim."

"I'm putting on my coat, Jim."

"Knock, knock."

"Who's there?"

"Ernie."

"I'm putting on my coat, Ernie."

When Roger said "knock, knock" again, he heard an impatient murmur, so he began to speak double time, indicating with his nodding head that they shouldn't let him down.

"Who's there?" they asked in unison.

"Tex."

"Wait a minute, Tex, I'm putting on my coat."

"No," screamed Roger jovially, "you did it wrong. It's, 'I'm putting on my coat, Tex.'" The women roared.

"What wears tiger skin, is yellow and has a pointy head?"

"I give up," said Roger.

"Tarzan the banana."

"Sorry, girls." The woman in the kimono had returned. "I'll have to take him from you." Turning to Roger, "She's ready for you now."

Who's ready? thought Roger, so anxious he could hardly follow. Perhaps he'd drunk too much. He became fearful of losing control. The woman went down another long corridor, stopped at one of many doors, silently pushed it inward and walked away. Roger walked in and looked around. The walls were completely mirrored; there was a baroque sink, plants and a couple of trees which, multiply reflected, appeared almost like a forest, and in the center was an enormous bed, confirming Roger's fears. Luckily the room was also vacant. He sighed, and turning to leave was suddenly face to face with a tall woman with thick blond hair, who wore only a leopardskin sarong and boots.

"Excuse me," he said, "it was so silent I thought no one was here."

"My name is Sheena," said the woman. "Have a seat." She pointed toward the bed and, when Roger remained immobile, swept in front of him with a long stride. Roger followed, dumbfounded. She was really a colossal woman, he thought, as her large round buttocks moved ahead of him almost at eye level, rhythmically. Her long legs appeared to eat the distance to the bed in two large chews, while Roger felt he was running to keep up with her.

"Sheena?" Roger asked, smiling wryly with only one side of his mouth, not actually sure whether or not he was joking. "Any relation to Tarzan?"

"Let's get down to business," said Sheena. "What's your problem?" Roger kept his eyes on the broad expanse of naked shoulder, at his eye level now they were both seated on the bed. For a moment, he thought she was referring to a sexual problem and hesitated.

"We can satisfy you, I'm sure."

He mumbled, confused, at her shoulder, "I'm plagued," he paused, "by a giant roach." The moment he heard his own words he wondered whether everyone weren't speaking in some kind of code that only he wasn't aware of. Perhaps, especially if he was in the wrong place, even the words "giant roach" meant something else, with a sexual connotation.

"Would you say that was an unusual problem?" he asked insecurely.

"Well," she said, "this is the right place, but you may not be the right person."

Roger mulled the meaning of that.

"Why don't you lie down and relax," Sheena suggested, tracing with her fingertips the swollen veins on his hands clasped tightly on his thighs, his thumbs buried securely between closely pressed legs, disturbing the configuration of sand dunes he'd already begun to imagine her shoulder as, as she moved her arm.

"I don't want to lie down," said Roger, now watching her finger on his hand objectively as if it were a fly, the sumptuous spots of her soft, scant leopard covering blurred in his peripheral vision.

"Tell me," she asked softly, "what exactly do you feel that giant roach means to you?"

"Oh no you don't," said Roger. "What are you, a therapist in disguise? Is this a secret place to get people trapped until we become hooked and dependent on therapy for years?"

"Of course I'm not a therapist. Did you ever see a therapist like this?" She pointed to herself.

"No. I never saw an exterminator like this either," said Roger, forced into looking at her, nervously picking up a small paperweight from a nighttable full of them. He shook it up and down, absently observing the tinsel floating around in the fluid like snow. Then he noticed that, instead of tiny plastic figures or miniature buildings, there was, inside, braving the momentary snowstorm, a preserved bug. Seeing the bug alleviated Roger's paranoia, as it was the only nondisorienting object for an exterminator.

"I suspect that the roach is really my girlfriend or former girlfriend Arlene, and that she did it to spite me—or, quite possibly, it is my former wife Edith, for revenge—or it's Arlene for revenge and Edith for spite." He looked at the creamy black leather of her high boot with a silver spike heel in which he could see his own face reflected very tiny.

"Why? Do you feel guilty toward either of them?"

"No, I feel they have a demonic side which, if I let it, will destroy me, or worse, make me look completely ridiculous."

"I've read that Jean-Paul Sartre once had a similar problem. Objects became humanized, or animated, and followed him, nearly driving him crazy with fear," said Sheena.

"You seem really erudite." When she'd stopped looking directly at him, Roger felt himself staring at her eyes, such a pale blue that, from the side, as a light from a lamp shone into them, he could see right through them; they reminded him of a pool in Florida outside a motel, no trees shading it, the merciless sun shining into the blue water through which he could see the bottom clearly.

"Perhaps you fear it's an alter-ego—the ugly, horrible, gross, evil, unattractive aspect of yourself which, in real life, you attempt to suppress, repress, and disguise?"

"I don't think any part of me is as disgusting as all that," said Roger, defensively smoothing back his hair. He gazed deep into her cleavage, which made him feel as if he were very tiny, his whole body perched on her breast. "You know, I read 'Metamorphosis' too. This bug I have may be Kafka's ugly self, but it isn't mine. You want to know what that thing really is? Probably just a plain old bug, and what I think about it is that it's ugly and dirty and I want it killed," he shouted, rising unsteadily.

"If you kiss it, it may turn into a princess. Or if you live with it a while, your awareness of its inner beauty may cause you to reconsider your desire to get rid of it."

Roger moved toward the doorway.

"Maybe it will leave if you ask it nicely," called Sheena coolly from the bed where she sat, one colossal leg crossed over the other, the black of her boots blending into each other, accented by tiny reflections on each silver heel. Her hair, as she moved her head, fell backward in a huge wavy mass, almost reaching the bedspread, her now-exposed breasts rising from a healthy ribcage like tropical fruits in the rainy season. The further he moved from her the better he could view her in her totality. She was really magnificent.

Roger arrived home very drowsy and loped around, warily attempting to ascertain the location of the bug so he could rest as far away as the dimensions of his apartment allowed. He considered staying temporarily with a friend, but his progressive search seemed to indicate the bug's departure, which pleased Roger so much that he repressed any question of how it could possibly have gotten out. He dropped onto his smooth, clean satin sheet in that ecstatic moment of complete relaxation just before sleep, but not before washing his hands and face and brushing his teeth.

He awoke with the feeling that he was struggling to keep from sliding into a declivity. Turning over, he opened his eyes and realized he was staring straight into the beady eyes of the bug. He bellowed and vaulted from the bed. He watched the bug in disbelief, shocked that they'd been sleeping side by side. He thought he remembered going to sleep wearing his underpants. The idea of the bug lying next to him when he didn't have underpants on caused him to retch.

He was crawling over the rug, searching for his undershorts, retching, when he recalled his dream.

He was running from something frightening, and Sheena was running with him, but she said she couldn't protect him. Arlene was with them and Edith had a gun, so he decided to let them come along. Despite the fact that he was terrified, they stopped off at Baskin-Robbins so Arlene could buy a beautiful blue ice cream cone.

"I think it's spoiled," said Arlene, holding it out to Roger. "Try it."

"It isn't spoiled," said Roger, having tasted it. "It's because it's a synthetic flavor. Bubblegum." Roger attempted to choose between bubblegum and two other synthetic flavors, Charleston Chew and Pink Water Lily, each tasting like a different kind of plastic. At the thought of plastic, Roger's mouth watered. Holding out his magnificent magenta ice cream cone, Sheena retreated.

"Don't drip that on me," she said, regretfully. "I can see that we have two different life-styles, because when I have this dream I have it from an entirely different viewpoint."

Roger had the annoying feeling there was something more he needed to recall; he thought if he could put his finger on it, it couldn't disturb him. He realized anyway that, despite the fact he hadn't finished the promised mechanical, he'd still have to call an exterminator. I really do have something more compelling, he thought, picturing his art director.

While watching himself shaving, he had a sudden, unexpected visual recollection of Sheena's eye as he had seen it, light shining through it, so pale, so blue he could almost smell the chlorine. With that image he was hit with desire as palpable as a blow to his chest and lower abdomen; worse, he had to back up immediately so that his sudden erection wouldn't bump into the hard enamel outer edge of the sink. He clenched his teeth hard against his inner pain, which was dispersing and rising, leaving tachycardia, a hot face and red ears. He clenched his teeth again, with the sudden urge to bite her, eat her up. Never before had he had the feeling that fucking wouldn't end the discomfort of his desire. I'm in love, he thought, terrified.

He was considering prolonging and intensifying his love by calling another exterminator as he'd planned and never seeing her again, but in the meantime his desire was too concrete. He jerked off over the sink, enjoying the expression of pain suffusing his face in the mirror. He shot into the porcelain, but although his erection subsided, the desire was not at all assuaged.

Roger desultorily examined the pattern on the couch while waiting for Sheena. This time no one approached him, no one was friendly, everyone appeared rushed and busy. I should have brought a book, he thought, bugged at the wasting of time, until he had the revelation that time spent in any way related to his love was top priority. How different he'd become in one day. Nevertheless, he decided to wait at the bar.

"Where's Sheena?" he asked the barmaid, watching her dextrously spritz his Scotch with a practiced turn of her delicate wrist.

"She's inside with another customer. Can't anyone else help you?"

"Uh-uh," said Roger.

"So. You've got a crush on Sheena?"

Roger didn't hear her. He was attempting to master the nausea which suddenly overpowered him. This must be jealousy, he thought.

"What is she doing?" he asked, attempting to be casual, but the barmaid was busy at the other end of the bar. He slid quietly off his stool and, ducking down, half-ran, half-hopped, chicken-like, into the dim corridor, like a camouflaged soldier in active combat. He realized how silly he looked and the uselessness of his actions, but the part of him that censored irrationalities was obviously out to lunch. He knelt on the floor outside Sheena's door, which was open just a crack, not daring to stand up in case his knees cracked. No light emanated from the room and, at first, no sound. Roger moved his upper torso back and forth in an effort to penetrate the mystery of the room when he began to be aware of muffled voices. His heart pounding, he bravely attempted to analyze the nature of those sounds, not without difficulty, above the din of his own blood coursing through his body with unprecedented speed. The best he could hope for was that she was speaking to herself, but he imagined what he heard to be erotic resonances. His desire to push the door open more was overwhelming, but he hesitated, not knowing whether it would squeak. Just as he was about to faint, the door was pulled open, away from him. Still on his knees, he fell forward in a deep bow, touching the tips of Sheena's boots with his forehead.

"Do you think this is a Japanese movie?" he heard her ask. Her sense of humor gave Roger the courage to raise his head, and as soon as his head was once more outside the threshold, Sheena emerged, shutting the door behind her, through which Roger, although he was dying of curiosity, didn't have the courage to look.

"Why don't you get up?" she invited.

Roger rose, his eyes, adjusting in their sockets to the change in height, never leaving her face. "Is there a man in there?" asked Roger, realizing he had no right to ask but absolutely needing to know for his well-being—the medicine for a terminal illness.

"None of your business," she said, turning and walking down the corridor.

Roger followed the clatter of her silver heels on the floor. He could hardly see; it was all he could do to restrain himself from initiating some form of physical contact, like clutching her from behind.

"Do you have to be so secretive?" he whined. "Isn't it just as easy to answer openly when you know it'll make me feel better?"

"You're acting inappropriately," Sheena said coldly. "You'd better leave."

"Yes," exhaled Roger, relieved, but, having turned and begun to walk away, he was struck with the realization he would never see her again. He revolved. "Wait," he called, "will you have dinner with me?"

"I never mix work with my social life," she said, as Roger approached her again.

"Then let's just have a social life."

"I don't want to have a social life with you," Sheena said, emphasizing it by stepping on his foot with her boot.

"What about my bug?" he asked desperately. "Please help me get rid of it."

"There are thousands of exterminators you could call," she said calmly, logically. "Not everyone is right for us."

"But I don't want them, I want you," he cried. "Take me, please take me," he implored, grabbing her arm.

She shook herself loose with difficulty, lifted an oversize spray gun and aimed it at him.

An enormous cloud obscured the whole upper portion of Roger. It cleared slowly, like a morning fog, leaving halos around all the lights. For a moment before losing consciousness, Roger felt, for the first time, he belonged to the universe.

"I told you not everyone is right," she whispered to him, as he slowly fell to the floor.

Irrevocable

When Carla opened the door, she felt an incredible heat, an incandescence, suspended in the entranceway, contrasting with the crispness of outdoors. The room was laden with it, light was hanging in it, emanating diffuse and heavy. Remains of dinner and unfinished bottles of wine still on the table increased an atmosphere of abandon.

"Have some wine," said Erica, flushed, a quality of anhelation about her words, which swung quick and light. Her buttocks were exposed, egressing from the bottoms of her cutoff shorts like two halves of a Golden Delicious apple. Warren, seated at the table, leaned back, greasy fingers still around an empty wine glass like a baby's rattle, feet propped on another chair, Henry the Eighth on a bridge chair, face turgid. Marilyn sat next to him, smiling a continuous smile, beginningless and endless, a beneficent beam. Both of them were watching Erica walk to and fro, her buttocks tantalizingly sliding into and out of the bottoms of her shorts. Carla slipped out of her coat standing there, watched, hypnotized.

"Again, again," ordered Warren, waving Erica back and forth on an endless journey, all of them watching closely, eyes plastered on the frayed edges of the shorts, as if they were watching water dripping, waiting for each drop to fall, and when it did it was so fast they missed it. Marilyn looked at Warren and laughed, while Erica complied, pleased with the appreciation of her body but distracted.

"Look what we found in the hall," she said to Carla. "All these goodies." Erica and Marilyn rushed to the closet and urgently pulled stuff out, fabrics flying, held them against themselves for seconds, then flung them aside.

"Try that on," said Warren to Marilyn, who came out of the bedroom in a few moments in a shirt, translucent and shimmery, glued to her breasts like a lubricated condom.

"Look at those breasts," Carla exclaimed. Marilyn smiled proudly, the same beaming smile, chin slightly lowered to her chest in a subtle indication of modesty, but her body perfectly poised, still and suspended like cucumber in aspic. Warren grinned in the sudorific atmosphere as if this were a show for him alone.

"I wish I had breasts like that," said Carla.

"I don't," said Erica. "I like myself the way I am."

"I like myself too, but I'd like myself even better if I had breasts like that." She cups an imaginary breast in an attempt to capture the essence of that kind of body, just as she'd often looked out of the corner of her eye, trying to picture an imaginary pale yellow lock of smooth hair with a whitish glow like dental floss, falling onto a black sweater faintly caught in the quick glance, instead of her own, dark and curly.

"Warren, why don't you try on these pants?" asked Marilyn. Warren, taking part for the first time, came out of the bedroom subtly preening in the pants like an animal responding to another's chemophores, his face beaming with mounting sensuality.

"Doesn't Warren look great with his hair long?" asked Erica, appearing to enjoy Warren's participating and her friends' appreciation of him.

"It looks beautiful. So black and shiny," said Carla.

"Warren will be glad you said that. He's always wanted black hair," said Erica. She looked at Marilyn. "Doesn't Carla have fantastic hair?" she asked.

Carla became aware of the gentle weight of her hair, a wide aureole encompassing a spiteful energy, as she said, "I always wanted hair like that," pointing to Marilyn's long, straight hair, incapable of any suspension, running between her breasts and down her back like dark liquid.

Erica said, "I don't. I like myself now."

Carla looked at Warren. His blue eyes were lubricated, pupils engorged, reflecting everyone's sexuality. She went closer to him, then took great pleasure in giving him a long, exaggerated, burlesqued kiss, protected by the presence of Erica and Marilyn, who watched.

"Are you sure you have to go?"

"I promised Pablo."

*

Carla sat, legs under her in the large chair, watching Pablo through the glass of the soundproof room, four hours later, still fixing his synthesizer. His bass player was asleep on another chair, anger twitching his mouth, nose red and peely from his cold like a shedding snake. She glanced at the clock, which was disproportionately large, like a stage set, and pictured Marilyn in the darkness of Erica's alcove, her friend's patchwork quilt covering her, everything immersed in the pink glow of the sodium lights outside, listening to the sounds of traffic and foggily absorbing the visual images of the gently moving plants, their darks fluctuating in the unnatural pink flush behind them. She can hear the ceaseless restless rustling of the blankets on Erica's and Warren's bed, at the other end of the large room.

Erica's lying on her back, white skin incandescent, legs spread far apart, knees slightly raised, Warren kneeling between them, thin thighs slightly flattened as he rests for a moment on his haunches, his penis orthogonal, purple, pointing within the blanket at the apex of the tent it makes, balustered by Warren's head, from which point the blanket descends, enclosing them both. He grabs the white skin of Erica's stomach with an air of rapt absorption, like a potter kneading clay. Erica giggles, ticklish.

"Sshhh." They both giggle muffled. Warren bends his head and laughs into Erica's abdomen, causing her to giggle even more, then suddenly her expression changes to one more like pain as Warren has his head between her legs, nuzzling to fit better, like a nursing kitten. Trying to keep the bed from moving and making love completely underneath the covers was so exciting to Erica that it was almost impossible for her to keep from crying out.

Marilyn, listening to the stifled sibilation of the bedclothes and muffled murmuring from the bed, already excited from picturing Erica and Warren making love in conjunction with certain sounds, imagining what they were doing, had a sharp sensation of loneliness and pictured Jay in Boston as she gently let her fingers slide over her clitoris already erect and lubricated. She held her hot palm cupped for a moment over her entire vulva, encompassing her clitoris, just feeling the gentle warmth and nonaggressive pressure. Placing one hand under her so that her backside rested on it, she gently traced her fingers around her clitoris, not actually touching the very tip until she couldn't stand not to, then running her finger slowly along it, seeing how slowly she could, measuring each sensation. Breathless, she moved her fingers deeper and deeper, imagining Jay, Jay's lips, Jay's penis, all the time touching her clitoris with the other hand, taking it off to touch her nipple. She put her hand back on her clitoris, her other fingers so deep into her vagina she could feel way behind her cervix and, hips off the couch, she came, silently, with just a catch of her breath. Before her orgasmic contractions were even completed, she had her pants back up trying to recall whether she'd made a sound.

Carla was falling asleep. The music, though loud and wild, was just another part of the atmosphere by now. She woke from her torpor when the music stopped. Pablo, as if his height made it difficult for him to move, was walking slow-motion out of the recording room, still in his leather jacket.

"We have to do that set over."

"I agree that we should do it again, but we only contracted for five hours of recording, it's already three in the morning, and we have no more tapes."

"After all this, I'm not leaving until we do that set again, man," Pablo said, slowly sticking his thumb into the bowl of his pipe, which he'd removed from his mouth, his only outward expression of tension.

"Use Annette's from her last recording. Her last two sets were no good anyway." Carla was flabbergasted that Pablo would erase his former wife's recording without asking her. From his tone she could tell he was still angry at Annette for leaving him.

"I'm sorry," he said to Carla, sitting down on the arm of her chair, an act that, for him, had the magnitude of a loving gesture. Carla wondered whether he was sorry he still felt so much for Annette or sorry that he'd made the session so long and imagines she's upset because he's been forced to ignore her.

"Here's a book I found in the john," he said, removing a small paperback from his pocket. "Maybe it will keep you from being bored." Carla, sleepy but addicted to reading matter, opened the book.

Rose, already beautifully acquainted with the joys of loving, was to discover soon that there were other pleasures such as she'd never imagined. Tiptoeing down the corridor in her heavy, coarse nightgown, her long hair plaited behind her, her newly wakened body, trembling, barely discernible under her childish costume, she opened the door to her mother's room. The light fell on her mother kneeling by the side of the bed as if saying her prayers, arms straight out, head down in an attitude of supplication, her own heavy nightgown raised, hanging around her waist. Facing Rose were her mother's enormous buttocks, which had always seemed to Rose vulgarly heavy, but which now, naked, exuded sensuality. They were

so firm they were almost erect, and between them she could
see the heavy growth of dark hair. Then she saw her uncle,
standing in the corner of the room, slacks down around his
ankles, removing his shirt and tie. He had the most
enormous, blue-veined member Rose had ever seen, and his
balls were like coconuts still hanging in the shade of their tree.
For a moment Rose couldn't take her eyes off her uncle's cock,
which when he walked over toward her mother, defying
gravity in spite of its heaviness, swung widely. He knelt
behind her mother, holding on to her waist. As if that were a
signal, her mother rose onto her knees, raising her backside
high in the air, and held her buttocks apart with her hands.
Her uncle stared glassy-eyed at the incredible sight before
him. Then he lifted his penis with his hands and guided it to
the gaping anus in front of him. With a hard thrust of his hips
he rammed it into her mother, who yelled. For a moment,
Rose, who'd never seen that done before, felt anxious for her
mother, who she thought was undergoing extreme pain, but
she was glad she hadn't revealed her presence, for she soon saw
that it was merely passion, as her mother writhed and
moaned. Clutching the bedclothes, she nearly pulled them all
off the bed as she came, her huge buttocks trembling.

"More, more," she whined. The uncle, who still hadn't
arrived, continued thrusting, her mother's come dripping off
onto the floor, as she came time and time again. Finally unable
to hold back any more, with a great roar, her uncle shot wads
and wads into Rose's mother, causing a renewal of her
orgasms. Rose quietly shut the door, pondering about this
new way of loving she'd just discovered.

Funny that Pablo should give me this book, thought Carla. Did he
really find it in the john? She recalled the night in the country, a
faint light creeping up the stairs, while darkness streamed into the
calid atmosphere through the windows, heavy wooden shutters
open in the immobile air, to let some of it in just in case it stirred.
Pablo's long thin body, which looks as if it could never feel warm

and soft and close, is deceiving. He plays Carla's body as if she's a synthesizer, timing and motifs perfect. They're slippery with perspiration. Pablo, holding Carla round tightly, is gently thrusting his penis in her, again and again, in rhythmic measures, beat by beat, then changing to half-time, short oscillating strokes, Carla gasping counterpoint. He then modulates his strokes, only inserting the tip of his penis, seeming to hold everything in suspension, till he rotates his rhythm, back and forth, faster, then slower, constantly diversifying, Carla's cries chromatically proceeding up the scale, until suddenly, he takes her nipple into his mouth, thrusting in drumming pressure, holding her tighter and tighter, the room filling with their homophonous contrapuntal chants.

After Carla has come, the stillness is vociferous. They're lying there holding each other. Carla's aware of how wet they are. Pablo hasn't come yet, and after lying there a few moments removes his still-hard organ and, kneeling above her, begins turning Carla over, his large hands hot under her hip. She turns for him onto her stomach. Holding her around her hips, Pablo inserts his penis into her vagina from the back, Carla moving toward it at the same time, raising her hips so that her ass, his favorite thing, is raised and rotating for him as he moves, staring at it. Carla can feel his hand under her moving closer to her clitoris and waits for it to touch her there climactically. Pablo, silent for a moment and still, suddenly removes himself and pushes his penis into Carla's anus. As it is so sudden, Carla's muscles contract; it is painful. She cries, "Don't Pablo, don't." In spite of Carla's tightened muscles, Pablo pushes harder and harder, ignoring her pleas, until he comes.

He lay close to Carla, listening to her cry. Then he said, "I'm sorry baby, I really like it better in your cunt. I do. I really like it better in your cunt. Really."

*

"Erica, when Marilyn's sleeping here, so close, do you and Warren make love?"

"Don't call me Erica. I hate that name."

"I thought you love yourself now."

"I do, it's just my name I hate. I hear my mother's voice, calling it."

"Well, Ellen? Do you? Make love with Warren when Marilyn's here?"

"Of course, we almost always do. We do it very quietly." Carla touched the vivid squares of patchwork where Erica told her that Marilyn slept.

"Do you ever want to do it all together? I mean with Marilyn?"

"I wouldn't mind. I've thought of it. But I don't think Warren would want to, even though I know he once tried to kiss Marilyn."

"I think," said Carla, "that it excites you both that Marilyn is there, or else you'd cool it for one or two nights till she went home." She pictured Marilyn, Erica and Warren as they'd been the other night, flushed, expectant, ultimately saying goodnight, and Marilyn climbing onto the narrow couch alone.

"On the other hand," continued Carla, "it isn't fair to leave her out."

*

It was crowded and hot at El Faro's. Carla sat next to Erica, gazing at the long line of people waiting for seats, who stood there holding their coats, shifting from leg to leg, saliva dripping from their mouths as they watched the waiter bring their Marescos in Egg Sauce, Paella Valenciana and Sangria. Warren sat across from them in his purple T-shirt, beads all tangled with his gold ankh chain, his long, dark hair smooth, with white highlights, and John, curled chest hair showing faintly through his red nylon shirt, ears under his new shorter haircut, looking particularly vulnerable and arrogant at the same time. Tonight their rosy nakedness was exceptionally obnoxious to Carla.

Erica was pouring the Sangria. As she began to pour Carla's, John leaned over from the opposite side of the table and took the pitcher from her. He poured Carla's himself.

"Let's go back to Carla's house and read her story out loud," said Erica.

John, his newly shaved long neck also appearing vulnerable under his round head, nodding his own affirmation of all he said: "I told Carla that now that she's made some money on her writing, she should quit her messenger's job and just use the time to write."

Dipping the serving spoon into the savory whitish egg sauce, searching for shrimp and clams, Carla said, "I'm too insecure to quit. I need that little bit of money every week when I get it."

"You probably think that if you give up your last regular low-salary job just to do something you love, that lightning will strike and destroy all," said Warren laughing.

"You seem really happy tonight, Warren," said Carla. "You're usually quieter. More withdrawn."

"What about Erica?" said Warren, deflecting attention from himself. "Look at her."

Erica was wearing a long black gown, given to her by Wendy, and brown vinyl boots. Her outfit, while pretty, was also a bit jocular, an effect always appreciated by Carla. She was animated, moving quickly, always the first to notice when someone needed more Sangria, talking rapidly.

"Erica's always like that," said Carla.

"Well, aside from being stoned, we're excited because Warren's going to quit his job."

"Really?" asked Carla, looking at Warren, a bit surprised that he hadn't mentioned it, yet knowing it was like him.

John was eating rapidly and noisily, head slightly tilted. He seemed excluded from the general ambience, and Carla, angry at him for being unaware of it, excluded him from her field of vision after observing him relating to his food in a patriarchal way, possessive, demolishing it as if it were an inferior.

"I can see you both being so pleased at his quitting, since the job bugged him," Carla said to Erica, then including Warren, "The job bugged you, but," she said looking at Warren, "you were so happy to get that job, and it's your turn to work, and it just appears like partly a lack of commitment." Carla couldn't believe her friend's happiness at her husband's quitting his job when she'd just worked for two years at one she hated equally, and while he was looking for new work would have to do typing at home and absorb most of the money worries. Carla looked at her questioningly, a bit suspiciously, becoming nauseated from overeating, wine and the heat.

"It makes me happy that Warren's happy," said Erica.

*

Later, in Carla's tiny living room, Erica was sitting on the floor, her long, booted legs crossed in front of her like brown vinyl butterfly wings. She's reading Carla's story.

> The girl was moaning because George had his hand up her vagina and every time he jiggled his fingers there was a sucking sound as if the washing machine was going on "wash." She had her hand around his penis, which was limp and yellow, its head peering over her clenched hand like a newborn kitten. Perspiration poured down George's body onto her towel as his body clenched with the effort of obtaining an erection. The girl, moaning louder now, looked down at her hand and opened it, watched the tiny thing drop to one side, and murmured in a frenzy of passion, "George, george, george, george, george."
>
> George removed his hand from her vagina, looked around for a second, and picked up her alto recorder from the floor where it lay beside her music book and shoes. He looked at it for a moment as if he were trying to decide which end would be best, and moved it gently toward her as if it were an extension of himself.

Warren and John were on the couch, facing Erica, Carla sitting between them. John had his arm around Carla, and Carla had her hand crushed between Warren's thighs and her own. Warren, his eyes on Erica, took Carla's hand in his, still crushed between their thighs, while John moved his arm further around Carla, the gesture appearing to her not an excess of warmth, but a gesture of possession, a manifestation of his desire to exclude her from closeness with anyone else. All their eyes were still on Erica as she read:

> She lifted her head, leaned on one elbow and grabbed his wrist. "No, no, George, no." She held his hand toward her, lay down again, and George masterfully inserted the recorder, mouthpiece first, into her vagina.

Erica was laughing so hard she had to stop reading. They all seemed slightly hysterical. It was late when Carla finished the story, and when Warren and Erica left they seemed to take all the hysteria with them. Carla heard their laughter echoing through the halls leaving John and her in a silent room.

Being left alone with him, Carla was suddenly terrified because she felt alone, worse because John was still there. She sat on the couch and stared ahead vacantly, unwilling to acknowledge John's presence.

"That was a good story," he said sincerely, as if complimenting his dog on carrying the newspaper all the way home, looking at her through tortoise-shell glasses with particular concentration, as if he wished he could just throw her under his microscope with his red and white blood cells and there deal with her more easily. Carla looked at John's suspended expression and thought that it was the way she was with John that she'd enjoyed and not John, and that she'd been having a relationship with herself. She knew he was waiting for some sign of affection. Her loft bed was reflected in his glasses. His tentative round face came closer until the mirrored loft beds merged into a large vagina. Carla felt angry with John, but she let him kiss her.

*

"Warren feels so warm toward you. Something happened last night at the restaurant. He told me he really feels you're a friend."

"That's nice," said Carla. "I thought he always felt that way."
She smiled.

"This is different. He's never felt this closeness before with any
man, or woman, or anyone else besides me," said Erica. "It's like he
suddenly opened up toward you. Partly because of the way you are,
and partly he's been sort of ready." Just then Warren came in with
the mail, dropping it into the pocket made by Erica's crossed legs,
where her cup of tea sat protected, steam rising out like a dormant
volcano, and kissed her before he sat down on the couch, an
eruption of patchwork squares emanating from the indentation his
body made.

"Where's mine?" asked Carla.

"I'm too lazy to get up," said Warren, blushing.

"Look what I got in the mail," said Erica. "It's a questionnaire
from the National Women's Caucus on Female Sexuality. It says
that since sexuality has been always defined by men, they're doing
research on female sexuality to discover what we really feel."

"I hope they discover it soon. I don't even know what I really
feel. Anyway, I have one of those. I got it at a man-hating rally I
once went to. I never filled it out."

"It says, 'One. Is having sex important to you? What part does it
play in your life?'" Erica looked up at Carla as if she expected an
answer. Carla thought a moment.

"It isn't easy to answer these. That's probably why I didn't.
Sometimes having sex is unimportant to me. Sometimes I desire it
compulsively, sometimes I'm compulsively lonely and I think, I
must, I must! Sometimes I'm so horny for a while that I walk
around and everything is sexy to me, I'm in love with everything, I
stand up against people in the train, I'll desire someone's forearm,
someone's fingernail will drive me crazy, I'll fantasize thousands of
sex acts a day. Other times, nothing," said Carla, trailing off,
disappointed with the effort of pinning something so diverse into
words. "And it also has a lot to do with who I'm seeing and
whether I am," she added.

"With me it's different," said Erica slowly. "Partly because

Warren's always here. Though sometimes, it's true, we go for long periods not particularly into sex and others heavy with it. And sometimes Warren wants to and I don't and the other way around. When other things or people excite us we go home and make love with each other." Warren, his book on his lap, eyes immersed in it, intent, was smiling. Carla suspected that he was probably listening, gleefully comparing Erica and herself.

"Let's do question twenty-two," said Erica. "'Do you enjoy cunnilingus? Do you have orgasms during cunnilingus usually, sometimes, rarely or never? Do you have them during oral/clitoral contact or oral/vaginal contact or both? Explain what you like or dislike about cunnilingus.'"

"What is it?" laughed Carla.

"Ha, ha," said Erica.

"This time you answer first," said Carla.

"Okay," said Erica, "Yes, yes, marvelously, absolutely, yes, fantastically numerously yes yes yes yes never never, yummy, yummy, yes yes yes. Let's do twenty-four."

"I didn't answer yet," said Carla.

"Is it possible you have an answer other than mine?"

"I like cunnilingus okay, except some men hate it but think they should do it. In that case it's better left undone. I don't particularly like to have orgasms with cunnilingus because when I'm really excited I'd rather be penetrated immediately."

"Twenty-four. Do you enjoy rectal contact? What kind? Do you enjoy rectal penetration?"

"Yummy," said Carla. "My mommy takes my temperature three times a day and an enema before bed."

"I hate it," said Erica. "I can't stand the idea. Warren loves it. He always tries every time even though I've said no for thirteen years."

"I don't mind it," said Carla. "Sometimes I like it, sometimes I don't. When I'm making love I like some finger penetration, sometimes." Carla looks at Warren's beatific expression and pictures him fantasizing sex with her while he pretends to read.

They're on Carla's loft bed and Warren's eating Carla, her thighs crushing his face firmly but softly, her hands running through his hair frantically as his tongue runs over her clitoris first lightly and slowly, then faster and pressing harder and harder. Carla refuses to come because the more excited she becomes the more she wants Warren to raise himself up and penetrate her fully with his organ, his weight on her body, his lips on hers, every part of her covered with him, and he wants her to come without his losing his erection because he can't wait to turn her over, which he does, lifting his face finally from between her thighs, mouth and cheeks shiny with secretions, expression intent as if he's eaten too much of something good and isn't sure he likes it anymore. Carla's still excited, waiting for Warren to insert his penis deeply into her. Warren, watching her raised rump and writhing hips, rubs his penis all along her cunt from front to back, slowly again and again, then gently inserts his cock into her anus and slowly intrudes it, feeling the tightness encompass his organ and push into his body, filling him full of ecstasy. Feeling as if he'll burst, he drops off his arms, holds Carla around her hips and touches her clitoris in rhythm with his own thrusting. She comes when she hears him moan. He lies there, on her back, perspiration between them like icing in a layer cake.

"What are you doing today?" asked Carla, as she left, her coat hanging off one arm.

"Making love," said Warren.

*

"What do you want in your tea?" asked Erica from the kitchen, as Carla threw her coat down on the bed and lay down next to it.

"I've had tea here at least three hundred times and you always want to know what I want in it."

"That's because you always want something different," said Erica.

"I want chicken soup in it," Carla said, laughing.

"You're doing that on purpose because I told you I have something serious to talk about," said Erica, angry, yet smiling. Carla didn't answer. It was probably true. Erica sat down on the bed alongside Carla's feet so that their two bodies made a T on the bed. One large hand cupped around a mug of tea to support it upright on the mattress, Erica began.

"Warren and I have been married for a long time, and for most of that time, although we loved each other and had wonderful sex, we were both afraid, I guess, to open up to other people, especially Warren, who's very jealous, and his jealousy made me afraid to get too friendly with anyone, or look at them too closely or even feel or think I felt anything. Now all of a sudden we don't feel locked-in that way. It all started, I think, with our relationship with Jay and Marilyn, and every time we were all together the atmosphere seemed more and more charged with a deep warmth becoming more and more sexual, and then I'd discuss with Warren where all this was leading. I even wrote a letter to them this week asking whether they'd feel like going any further with it, like into real sex together. And now all of a sudden, Warren, who's been thinking of this with me for all this time, but didn't really know how he felt, has suddenly opened up to you. He says he loves you and desires you. We both love you and we'd like to make love with you." Carla held her tea tightly and sat up. She had an urge to get off the bed but didn't move.

"First of all," she said slowly, "you say you've desired people often, but because of Warren's jealousy you've never done anything. Now when he finally wants someone, it's okay. That bothers me. Then I think you're using me. You know that once Warren's made love with someone else everything will be in a different place. You're using me to bargain for your freedom." Carla moved off the bed. She pictured the three of them there together.

They're having tea, Warren and Carla on the rug and Erica on the bed. Warren and Erica are already naked, Carla feeling shy still has her underpants on and her spangled shirt. Warren and Erica are patiently drinking their tea, but their fangs are out and their mouths watering onto the tweed rug. Feeling that she's already committed herself, but nervous and feeling cornered, Carla can't find the courage to say she'd like to leave, so she finishes undressing instead, shielding her small shriveled breasts with her arms after quickly pulling off her shirt.

"Isn't she sexy, Warren?" asks Erica.

"Isn't she a little beauty?" croons Warren, as if he were talking to a horse.

"When I pictured this scene before," says Erica, "I always wondered what would happen first. I sort of worried about feeling left out." The moment she finishes speaking, Warren is on top of Carla. Then so is Erica.

Carla put on her coat.

"Why doesn't Warren ask me himself?"

*

Carla opened her door. Warren was standing there in his leather jacket with the fur collar, a smile on his face.

"I told her I was coming. She said 'no kissing.'" He followed Carla into the kitchen where she poured him some coffee from the thermos where she kept it hot. He was trembling all over, but he didn't touch her. His eyes popped and ran themselves along her body. He trembled more violently while his hands alone remained rigid.

"What do you think of Erica's body?" he asked. "Don't you like it? I want you so much."

*

Carla could see outside the restaurant's large window that it had begun to rain, which meant that the laundry would get wet. She thought she should be home writing. Erica was measuring the half teaspoon of sugar into her second cup of tea, her freshly washed, wavy hair tendrily around her strong, large face and outlining firmly the edges of her neck. The gentle rain evoked, as it always did in Carla, a lost poignant feeling, a savored loneliness, and she felt trapped inside.

"Why do we always discuss this? There's a sense of urgency here that's unnatural. It isn't something happening, a natural something, it's being pushed. I feel like I'm being manipulated. It's ruining our friendship. It's like a skier already going downhill remembering that he forgot to learn how to stop."

"In a sense it's true," said Erica, her breath blowing hot tea steam toward Carla. "Relationships change. Things usually have to go somewhere."

"You and Warren are still just as locked in as before if you both can only have lovers together and not trust each other unless you're watching each other every moment. I still suspect you're using me."

"How? I don't think it has anything to do with manipulation."

"I sense behind this Warren's sexual urgency. His need to fulfill immediately what he desires. And I think you're helping him because you hope when you let Warren have what he wants you'll be free too."

"I do want Warren to have what he wants so badly. You don't have to, but you certainly have always acted as if you do. What kinds of indications are all the flirtiness and teasing? What does all that kissing and touching mean?"

For a moment Carla felt horrible, that it was true, she'd enjoyed being seductive and now she'd better pay. But she said, "That's just in fun because I like you both so much and partly because you two are so close I felt protected, secure enough to express something without imagining it would ever culminate in anything too heavy. I'm not sure if I don't want to. But even so, I still feel manipulated. And what about you? I don't know anyone who tries this and still remains friends. No one really knows how they'll feel afterward."

"I know how I'll feel. I know I'll be happy."

"Listen," said Carla, folding the wrapper from her Sweet 'N' Low, concentrating on it. "I'll tell you how I felt when Ed and I traded with another couple. It was summertime and these people with a child sublet the apartment upstairs so that he could finish law school. Andrea and I became friendly first, because our kids were the same age, then we all started going places together, to the pier, to ice cream parlors; we spent more time together than apart. Then one day I looked out of our window, and there, hanging from the wrought iron grating, was Michael.

*

"'Michael,' I said, surprised. 'What are you doing there?'

"'Is Ed there?' he whispered, his fingers turning white.

"'No, but he'll be home soon. You'd better go away,' I said fearful that Ed would see him hanging there because Ed was also horribly jealous.

"'Carla,' he said, 'I desire you.'

"I stood there horrified. I could hear Ed's footsteps in the hall. Just in time, Michael let go of the grating.

"The next time, we were upstairs having dessert with them. I was pouring coffee into my blueberry swirl ice cream, and Michael was eating enormous cherries from a paper bag.

"Michael said, handing Ed and me a magazine, 'There's an article in here that's very interesting about group sex.'

"'I'm not interested in group sex,' said Ed. 'I think it's sick. If two people don't like each other any more they should leave. I can only relate to one person at a time with that intensity.' I opened the magazine. There was a picture of five or six people in bed smiling. The article said:

At first I was very nervous, and had no idea what would happen. I felt shy too. But after the initial shyness wore off, it was the most wonderful experience, the most enriching, to be making love to lots of people at the same time and have so many parts of the body touched and filled at the same time, and touching many other bodies was extraordinarily fulfilling. Since then we've enjoyed group sex innumerable times. It's revitalized our sex lives and our marriage. Contrary to the jealousy I expected to feel, it gave me the greatest pleasure to see my husband traveling to the limits of sexual enjoyment and transports.

"'That's ludicrous,' said Ed, as Michael looked at him without raising his head from under his brows, one of which he raised slightly, his mouth suspended with a drop of blood-red cherry juice on his lower lip."

*

"It was one of those heavy summer evenings. Walking home from the pool felt like floating; my body retained a sensation of the motion of the water. It hadn't been dark long, and low in the sky a husky goldfish moon penetrated the atmosphere with a diffuse glow, enormous and edgeless.

"'Come upstairs for some vanilla fudge ice cream,' said Andrea. Still in our damp bathing suits, we went upstairs. The studio couch was unmade and open, nearly filling the small room. I lay on the bed in my nearly dry bathing suit and stirred fudge into vanilla, creating something the consistency of custard.

"Andrea, slender and brown in a blue and white checked bikini, said, 'Doesn't Michael have a beautiful body? He has the most enormous penis I've ever seen, too.'

"I looked at his body, the usual kind, and wondered why he should have such an enormous penis. If anything about him attracted me, it was his face. Andrea went into the other room and emerged wearing a tiny red transparent nightie, its color so rich that even her suntanned skin seemed alabaster.

"'Why don't you wear one too?' asked Andrea, 'your bathing suit can't be that comfortable.'

"'Go pick one out,' said Michael, 'she has lots of them.' I looked over at Ed thinking he'd be terribly upset about my displaying open sensuality in anything other than private, but his face was blank. He was looking at his ice cream with interest. I went with Andrea and picked out a long pale blue nightgown.

"'Do you mind if I take off my bathing trunks?' Michael asked.

"'No,' said Ed. I looked up surprised that Ed didn't seem to mind this. Andrea shut off the lights, and Michael walked back to the bed nude, weird shadows of his body, penis already erect, thrown faintly on the walls.

"'Why don't you get undressed too?' said Michael to Ed, who was sitting on the windowsill. Carla was surprised to see him do it. He sat on the sill again, naked. Andrea walked over and sat down on the same sill with one leg outside the window on the fire escape.

Neither of them spoke, they merely seemed to be a nude audience at a show. Michael began kissing me.

"'Please, I desire you so much,' he said. 'Let's go downstairs.'

"For a moment, I returned his kisses. Then I said, 'Ed and I have to leave.'

"I went into the other room for a moment to get my bathing suit and I looked for Ed. I was tense, expecting a scene when we got downstairs. I was shocked when I perceived Ed already on top of Andrea on the double bed.

"Michael, walking around distraught, said, 'You have to come downstairs now. Let's go.' He ran down first, carrying the package of vanilla fudge ice cream, and I followed swiftly, not daring to glance at the bed.

"'I can't believe it. I desired you more than anyone in my life, yet the first time was disappointing, although the second time was worth it.'

"'Would you like to go upstairs and get your record book so you can put a grade beside my name?'

"I missed Ed. I watched cigarette butts fall from the fire escape upstairs when I wasn't pretending to be asleep, and pictured the two of them, Andrea and Ed, falling in love. They've already made love once and are still lying intertwined, Ed kissing the chlorine around Andrea's hairline tenderly with gentle nips like a carp. 'I'm so hot,' he says, separating a small part of his body from hers, running his fingertips through the perspiration all over his body, then over Andrea's abdomen, where tiny droplets of hers and his have combined. Andrea takes a dish of ice cream from beside the bed and rubs it on his hard stomach, smearing it around his belly button and into the hair that begins below it. Ed lies back, hands under his head, while Andrea scoops out more ice cream, rubbing it first on his chest, then smoothing it around his penis, which, now erect, is squirming in the vanilla fudge on his belly. Seeing that she doesn't have much left, Andrea gobs the rest all around Ed's cock, and tossing the dish aside, kneels down and begins licking him first

on his chest, sucking all the vanilla fudge off his nipples, then, in a
long line down the center of his pectorals, she traces her tongue, all
the while licking off the ice cream, inserts her tongue into his navel
for a moment then, opening her mouth wide around his penis, she
sinks her head down on it with a moan, lips drowning in pubic hair
and vanilla fudge.

"At dawn Michael prepared to leave, but he seemed nervous.

"'You don't mind if I bring the ice cream back upstairs with me,
do you?' he asked.

"'Oh, no,' I said, imagining that since the whole situation had
been engineered by Michael, Andrea would be more than upset. I
pictured him tiptoeing upstairs and opening the door. Ed and
Andrea are lying in bed, still naked, Ed's torso semireclining, head
resting on the wall behind the bed, Andrea lying on top of the
blanket, a cigarette in one hand, Ed's penis in another. When
Michael appears at the side of the bed, Andrea's calm expression
metamorphoses into an angry scowl. Wordlessly, he shoves the
carton of ice cream under her nose. She smiles then, as if the ice
cream contains hallucinogenic fumes. Gratefully he dips his hand
into the softening vanilla fudge and with a dumb smile rubs some
of the sweet brown and white cream over her shoulder and arm
where it catches in the delicate down, the morning sun reflecting
off the fine arcs.

"I felt fine until Ed came downstairs. The sight of him set off a
chemical reaction.

"'Did you like it?' I asked. There was no answer. 'What was it
like? What is her body like? Does she like it? Was she very
excited?'

"'I'm not asking you about you and Michael,' he said. 'Don't
bother me with that kind of questions.'

"'Tell me, please,' I whined, 'What did she do? Is she in love
with you?'

"'I couldn't get an erection until she ate me. She said I had an enormous penis. We made love for hours.'

"'How many times did you do it?'

"'Just once. The rest of the night we spent talking on the fire escape.'

"'But you just said you did it all night. You're lying to me. Tell me anything, but don't lie. I know now. For the first time I realize. It was Andrea and you who planned the whole thing. You're in love. She pretended to be my friend and tricked me. And Michael's in on it.'

"'You're crazy.'

"'Maybe they both planned it to seduce us both. Maybe they always do it with all their friends.' There was a knock at the door. Michael stood there, face lowered, forlorn, but little dots of desire still in his eyes.

"'Andrea would like you to come upstairs for blueberries and ice cream. And home-baked apple pie with currants, still warm, with hot American cheese. And home made prune brandy.' He looked at me, waiting.

"'No thank you,' I said."

*

There was a long silence.

"No, I won't feel that way," said Erica. "I can tell I won't. I just feel so open, so excited, so glad. Maybe you're not ready yet, but if you don't make love with Warren I'll feel personally rejected."

*

"Hello, Carla? This is Christian."

"I recognize your English accent," said Carla. In the middle of making coffee, she was trying to reach the stove with the phone receiver still at her ear, but the wire was too short.

"I thought, since Louisa was at the library, that you were going to come to the co-op meeting early so that we could get in a quick fuck."

"I'm not really interested in a 'quick fuck,'" said Carla.

*

Warren had just come, and Carla was about to also, when he removed his penis, shook the excess sperm from his semilimp member, and started to put on his pants, having speedily climbed down the loftbed.

"Where are you going?" asked Carla, looking over the side.

"I told Erica I'd be home early."

Carla pictured Erica at home, herself picturing Carla and Warren making love.

They're on Carla's loft bed, Warren flushed and trembling, his uncircumcised penis emerging from its foreskin like a cellophane cigar wrapper half pulled down.

"Oh, you're so beautiful, so sensuous. I love Erica, but you're so much more beautiful. Turn over," he says, his hand flattened under her, attempting to turn her like a spatula under a pancake. Carla obliges.

"Oh, what a sexy ass. I love Erica, but your ass is so much more sensuous. Let me put it in please let me please." Carla gets on her elbows and knees to be more readily accessible, her backside raised.

"Ohh, Erica never lets me . . . Ohh God."

Carla stood naked next to the door so she could lock it after Warren left. "Bye, Warren. Give my love to Erica."

Warren gave her a cursory kiss and ran down the stairs. Carla wondered how Erica felt. Warren opens his door. Erica, still awake, but lying on her bed, legs crossed at the ankles, an open book face down next to her tea on the floor.

"Tell me about it," says Erica. "Was it good? Was it everything you thought?"

"I'm sorry I'm so late dear, she made me stay in the bar for at least two hours before, which wasn't on the schedule. Then she wouldn't take off her shirt. Her breasts are okay, a little shriveled, not as nice as yours. Her ass is nice, one buttock is a little larger than the other. She doesn't get that look of loving like you do, she just has an air of abstract concentration. She let me do it in her ass."

Erica, excited, has been removing her clothes and is lying there naked. She begins lifting his T-shirt from the bottom and he raises his arms so she can get it off. She opens his belt, pulls his jeans down nearly to the tops of his cowboy boots, and, grabbing his penis with her fist firmly, leads it into her mouth. Warren lies back with a smile and closed eyes. Erica moves her head slowly up and down, causing his penis to slide in and out of her mouth along its full length, allowing it further in each time. Warren begins moving his hips, grabbing Erica's hair as if it's a life preserver. He groans, then pushes her head down hard over his penis. Erica gags. She lies on her side. Warren, boots on, jeans still bunched around them, lies behind her. For one instant he attempts to lead his penis with one hand into her anus, Erica reflexively turning away. Without a moment's hesitation, he thrusts it into her vagina from the back, one of his knees between Erica's legs, up close to her body.

"Warren, was it this good?"

*

"I was just telling Carla that I finally called Marilyn because she and Jay never answered my letter," Erica told Warren when he came home. "I didn't want them to be upset about the whole thing, but when I spoke to them I was so hurt." Warren, looking at a notebook, seemed impassive.

"What did they say?" asked Carla.

"Well, they said that they'd done that before with someone, and it didn't bode well. They never talk to the people now and they didn't want to destroy our friendship. I told them I was sure we could work it through even if it got heavy. But the thing that hurt the most is they said they didn't feel the loving and sexual direction things were taking."

"Yummy," said Carla, "that asparagus smells good. Is it from the co-op?"

"Erica," said Warren, "why are you cooking the asparagus now? I'm not hungry yet and probably won't be for a while."

"She can cook it any time she wants, and you can eat it when you're hungry," said Carla, unable to keep silent, partly joking. She smiled at Erica whom she thought she was defending, but Erica looked at her disgusted, apparently disturbed at the interference. Since no one thought it was funny, Carla felt compelled to continue.

"For that matter, Warren, why don't you cook it yourself?" Carla put on her coat, smiling, and let herself out.

"Goodnight," she said before the door closed. Nobody answered.

*

They waved to Carla from inside, at a round table. Through the glass doors of the Riviera she can see them, slightly festive, pointing to an empty chair they'd pulled over for her.

"I'll have cheesecake tonight," said Carla, attempting to get her arms out of the sleeves of her coat without standing up.

"I'll share the cheesecake with Carla," said Warren.

Erica smiled. "Let's all share it, and we can all share a salad with bleu cheese dressing too. Well," she said, slightly breathless, "it's really important that we talk about how we feel about all this. It's important that we do it. If we're going to have this kind of relationship, it's going to be difficult, and we'll have to spend a lot of time on it."

"You're right," said Carla. Silence.

"Well?" asked Erica, looking at Carla.

"Well what?"

"Well, how do you feel?"

"Fine."

"It's just that kind of joking when I'm serious that I hate. And you know it. If you cared about me you wouldn't do it."

"But it's my nature," said Carla. "If you cared about me you'd accept the way I am. At least you'd understand and not take it personally."

"Let's not argue," said Warren.

"Warren," said Erica, her chin becoming more apparent with hurt and hostility, "how do you feel? You never say anything, you just sit there."

"I don't know how I feel," said Warren, blushing in pained confusion, pushing a tiny piece of cheesecake back and forth with his fork.

"Well, I'll tell you how I felt," said Erica. "First, after Warren left to go to you, I felt fine, but a little weird, because I was so super-excited like—I don't know—I guess because it was such a change in our lives, or a major change in what we do. So I smoked some grass in order to relax, and then I began to feel better and better. I listened to some records and I almost fell asleep. I think I must have fallen asleep, because something woke me and I felt disoriented, I knew something was happening, but I didn't remember right away. When I saw that Warren wasn't there, I remembered. I felt horrible. But that was just a momentary reaction. Now I feel good about it except for once in a while, and I expect that I'll just go on feeling better and better." She ended on a high, querulous, almost questioning note, then nodded, head sideways, answering her own question as she sliced her fork through the cheesecake.

"Carla," she added, "what do you feel?"

"I don't feel anything," answered Carla uneasily.

"Carla, when are you cooking dinner for me?" asked Warren, laughing, as he put his arm around her and Erica, pretending to have a harem.

"What are you doing tomorrow?" asked Carla.

"Warren's mother is coming over to cook German dinner for us," said Erica.

"She comes to your house and cooks dinner there?"

"Yes," said Erica.

"Well then," said Carla, looking at Warren, "she has to cook dinner at my house too."

*

Hedwig has just finished cooking and she tastes the gravy, blowing it first.

"When it cools, just put it in the fridge," she instructs Erica, licking off the spoon.

She begins doing the dishes but Erica says, "No, Hedwig, don't bother. It's nice enough that you cooked this stuffed cabbage with raisins for us and baked this lovely sweet cake."

"Well, I like to do it, but I must say, in this kind of kitchen it becomes a chore." She opens the apron over her black skirt, sits down, crossing her stockinged legs, spiked heels burrowning into the rug, and opens a small compact in her purse. She applies more lipstick, talking at the same time.

"Well, Warren, walk me to the subway, will you?"

"No, Mama, you have to cook for Carla now."

"Ach, Warren, you're an albatross."

*

She's carrying a pot of water across Carla's kitchen to the stove, her shoes are off and her hair's messy under her black velvet hat. "If I thought Erica's kitchen was bad, this one's the end. It's absolutely disgusting, a half mile with a heavy pot from the sink to the stove, then back and forth. And the filth? This old linoleum, the dust on the cracking plaster, the roach eggs on the counter—disgusting. I don't know how you can live this way. There's plenty nice apartments in Queens."

"Hedwig," says Carla, "how did it feel bringing Warren up alone after your husband died? Isn't it odd that you never had another man?"

"The price of meat," answers Hedwig, "is such that no one will be able to eat it any more. Even these green peppers, these onions, 3½¢ up from the day before yesterday. Potatoes we use to eat when there was nothing nice and cheap. Potatoes. If you are really poor you can't even fall back on potatoes, they're so expensive."

Hedwig, finished cooking her second dinner, falls into Carla's director's chair, exhausted, hair disheveled, hat crooked, stockings rolled around her knees, staring into space. She goes to the door and prepares to leave without her shoes.

"Warren, Warren," she says, "I love to do it, I do it only for you my love. But Warren, it's killing me. I'm dying, Warren."

*

"I think you should pay for me too, Warren," said Carla, buttering the Italian bread. Warren smiled, but Erica didn't.

"What's wrong?" asked Carla.

"Nothing," said Erica, pushing her broccoli in cream sauce around the dish, but smiling now, at Carla.

The restaurant was dark except for the luminous color, reflections from the Tiffany lamps swaying on the walls. Carla slipped the tart white wine and looked at Warren, whose prick was peering out of his eyes. His head moved unconsciously and almost imperceptibly in a come-here gesture. Carla observed that, since she made love with Warren, she did feel closer to him, warmer. It was a physical friendliness now, and she touched his familiar skin, grabbing his hand next to the tossed salad with the Gorgonzola cheese dressing, squeezed it gently, then stroked it up to his wrist and back. Warren returned the pressure, gazing lovingly at Carla, who put her hand under the table to touch his knee.

"I don't know why you're doing that, Carla," said Erica. "I thought it was obvious to you that I feel worse and worse. I thought it was clear that I'd decided that you two can't do anything any more. Warren knows that." Carla was surprised and felt sudden relief, but she pushed aside her creamed chicken and broccoli in disgust, anger making her nauseated and over-heated, suddenly aware that her palms were beginning to sweat.

"I told you you'd feel angry; you said no. You have to take some responsibility for your actions. You can't just take people and manipulate situations the way you like them, first this, then that."

"I don't understand," said Erica slowly, in a low voice, attempting to make the conversation, which had gotten loud, more private again. "If you really loved me you wouldn't want to hurt me. And I'm telling you that I am hurt and jealous, and I can't stand it. You can't do it."

Carla looked at Warren, who said nothing. She tilted her head, incredulous, and, looking into Erica's blue eyes, said in a low voice, "But Erica, it's too late."

Class Outing

Miss Alba was speaking. Bernadette looked across the room at her best friend Sondra Greenhood, who wasn't smiling or looking at her but gazing ahead in a daze. Miss Alba's sentences began to disintegrate into words, then syllables, then insects, the drone of which could still be heard above Bernadette's thoughts.

Bernadette's mouth fell open, her head lolled lethargically on her hand, elbow propped on her desk. Her two large upper teeth became visible, a wide space between them, in a sallow face dotted with freckles. Vaguely oriental eyes peered from under lowered eyelids, a line of white showing between the lower lid and her dark iris. Drool began to collect inside her slack lower lip and suddenly slid down the corner of her mouth, then along the palm of her hand, pooling again at the heel, which her teeth had almost sunk into as her head lowered sleepily, almost imperceptibly, and dripped in small drops on her desk, where, with her other hand, Bernadette drew pictures, the saliva mixing with old ink and carbon from layers of student hieroglyphics.

The desk was covered with Bernadette's drawings, which

included copies of the Sistine Chapel paintings, with mathematical allowances for differences in perspective. She didn't hear Miss Alba walk up the aisle and stop beside her. The teacher studied Bernadette's desk in surprise.

"Bernadette, have you been drawing on your desk? Do you know what that means, Bernadette, defacing public property?"

Bernadette remained silent, knowing that everything meant something different to everyone.

"This is vandalism," shivered Miss Alba.

Two other children in the class listened to the chilling rebuke. One was Sondra Greenhood who, despite the fact that she hadn't come close to puberty, possessed a faint black mustache. Bernadette caught the mixture of joy and sympathy on Sondra's face; joy that she herself wasn't being scolded, sympathy for her best friend. Miss Alba stared into Bernadette's half-open eyes, one of which appeared orange with the sun shining into it. Bernadette attempted to remain locked in the stare without flinching.

"I'm going to have to send a note home to your mother," said Miss Alba, still staring.

Afraid of her mother, Bernadette looked down quickly. There were rustling sounds from the closet. Laura, short and squat, raised her hand.

"Marc is in the closet, Miss Skim Milk."

"I know Marc is in the closet," Miss Alba said. She sneezed. "Tissue monitor, please—Tissue monitor," she said louder, staring at Charles, who was involved in making paper airplanes which he directed around the room from his seat, emitting sound effects consisting of motors, jets, rockets, and beyond-the-speed-of-sound sounds.

"How come you don't yell at Charles?" Bernadette asked.

"Charles is completely out of it," said Miss Alba.

Bernadette wished she had the courage to be completely out of it, yet she admired Marc Ratner's open rebellion even more. Marc spent a good part of every day in the closet, today for standing in the aisle, his thick lips forming a stupid smile, after Miss Alba told everyone to be seated. Bernadette was in love with Marc, though

Marc exhibited no indications of reciprocity. When Miss Alba shouted, "Marc, please sit down, Marc will you sit down, Marc! Marc! I'll give you up to the count of three. One . . . Two . . . Three . . . Okay, Marc! Into the closet!" Bernadette's heart beat fiercely, her face flushed. She felt his resistance with a combination of fear, embarrassment, admiration and envy.

Marc blinked from the light when the closet door was opened, then resumed smiling. He'd never let anyone see whether or not he was upset, but Bernadette felt that she understood his real feelings. He still refused to sit down, though he stood near his seat, in the aisle. Bernadette noticed that he had a slight scratch on his hairless brown muscular forearm. She removed the pink plastic flamingo pin from her blouse and scraped it over the skin of her pale, freckled, hairy little arm in exactly the same place until it bled slightly, imagining that now they were united in some way. She also imagined that Marc not only knew about her feeling for him, but that he possessed an affinity to her which he was only hiding from embarrassment or fear of rejection; that his blank glances and strange smiles meant special things; the doodles on his desk and papers were all messages. Bernadette had no doubt that Marc would notice the scratch on her arm as an unspoken indication of her love for him. She didn't doubt he knew everything she thought, and reciprocated.

"I'm returning your essays," said Miss Alba.

"What essays?" Laura asked.

"Your essays on whether you would die for your beliefs." Miss Alba aspirated deeply, her nostrils flaring slightly, her chest burgeoning somewhere between the neckline and waistband of her gray gabardine dress. Bernadette stared, hoping for a crisp revelation of Miss Alba's physiognomy. "Do any of you know what an essay is?"

The class was silent except for Charles' version of the takeoff of the Boeing 747 jet. Miss Alba began to weep. Bernadette watched, drooling; the class, nonplussed, sat and stared.

"Tissue monitor," whispered Miss Alba, through her stuffed nose. Marc, in the aisle, lowered his head, still smiling. Laura prodded Charles, who rose with Miss Alba's box of Kleenex. He put his hand on Miss Alba's shoulder. "I'm okay," snuffled Miss Alba. "Charles, how come there's only one tissue left in this box? I realize I have sinus trouble, but did I use them all up?" Charles looked at the floor.

"He used them for making airplanes," said Laura.

"Tattletale," spat Sondra.

"Charles, for that you have to go into the closet." Charles began to cry.

"He's afraid of the dark," said Laura with relish.

"I'm sorry about your science trouble, Miss Alba," said Charles, trembling.

"Couldn't we leave the closet door open?" asked Laura, repentant.

"No," said Miss Alba. "Charles has to learn not to deface other people's property." She led a slumped and passive Charles into the closet. "It's your parents' job to teach you morals and manners, but I have to do everything." She pushed Charles slightly, and he slumped down on her boots, near her umbrella.

Bernadette could see his face redden and tears begin to fall as the closet door was shut. For a moment the class was silent. Then a plaintive cry rose eerily from within the metal wardrobe. Miss Alba steeled herself; the others fidgeted.

"Paper monitor," called Miss Alba. Laura rose tentatively, looking questioningly about her. "Yes, Laura, it's you," said Miss Alba, her sarcasm lost on everyone.

Laura couldn't read the names on top of the papers so she stood there with the sheaf in her hand, looking puzzled. Bernadette, who could read, automatically rose to her aid.

"Bernadette," shrieked Miss Alba, "out of order. One more item on your note home." Bernadette was puzzled by her disobedience. Marc knew he was misbehaving; Bernadette, who always meant well, was unfailingly surprised by Miss Alba's adverse reactions.

"Sondra, you give out the papers." Sondra delivered all the papers to the wrong people. It didn't matter much because each paper had a large red D on top, with the exception of Charles, who got an A.

"All of you except Charles wrote a sentence fragment," said Miss Alba. Sondra herself had Charles' paper and thought the A was meant for her, although she did realize that the paper had quite a bit more verbiage than she recalled writing and was, in fact, four papers, stapled together. This sheaf appeared even fatter due to the fact that each page was a recycled, unfolded former paper airplane. The screams from within the closet were now punctuated by the drumming of fists against the metal. Miss Alba gritted her teeth.

"Almost everyone," said Miss Alba, "wrote the sentence fragment 'I woont.'"

Bernadette felt misunderstood. Though she had someone else's paper on her desk, she meticulously recalled having thought the problem out for three hours before writing, "Iwoulddieformybeliefs," an entire sentence, the question inherent in the answer, as she was taught.

"Come up here with your paper," said Miss Alba. Bernadette went up to Miss Alba with her paper quickly, accelerated by the long jump she made tripping on the saddle oxford that Laura had extended into the aisle for that purpose. "This is not your paper." She looked for Bernadette's paper on each desk.

"No one can understand this," explained Miss Alba. "There's no space between each word."

Bernadette stood there stymied. There always seemed to be something wrong that she hadn't thought of. The banging from the closet increased in volume, accompanied by screaming and crying.

"It may be interesting to note," said Miss Alba above the din, thin lips compressed, "that Bernadette is the only person in the entire class with ideals strong enough to die for."

"Bernadette is an asshole," said Marc, smiling.

Bernadette flushed. She covered the cut on her forearm so no one could see it, then rubbed it, wishing it would go away. She felt tears spring into her eyes, regretting her smooth virgin arm.

"Bernadette is an asshole," shrieked Laura.

A sudden barrage of spitballs and paper airplanes came her way. Bernadette ducked, hands over her head, scrunched in her seat, eyes tightly shut. She fantasized Marc coming over to her and sitting next to her at her desk. She can feel his warm, large and slightly sweaty presence. He puts his firm, strong arm around her, his other hand over her hand. His body covers her, his warmth surrounds her. She looks directly into his deep black eyes. She runs her hand through his soft, straight light brown hair. His thick lips, open but not grinning, come closer, closer. She can feel his nose slightly. His lips press ever so gently on hers as his light breath fans over her face. Bernadette opened her eyes and saw Sondra who, having thrown spitballs herself, has, in remorse, come over and wrapped her arms around her.

*

Sondra and Bernadette had been close ever since they met in Miss Mancewicz' first grade class. Sondra fell in love with Bernadette during a get-acquainted story-telling session and was protective of her since. Miss Mancewicz began the story and everyone took a turn continuing it.

"There was once a little boy named Timothy, who lived with his grandfather," began Miss Mancewicz. "He used to watch birds for most of the day. Either from inside the house, through the windows, or outside the house . . . he observed birds. One day he said, 'Grandfather, birds can fly.' 'Yes' said the grandfather, wondering that it took his grandson so much time to formulate that observation. 'Can people fly too, Grandfather?' Timothy asked. Your turn, Charles." Charles was holding aloft a paper airplane, intoning, "Whirrr, whirr." He looked up when he noticed the unnatural silence.

"Of course people can fly, Miss Monkey bitch. In airplanes," said Charles. Marc laughed hysterically and couldn't stop.

"Laura," said Miss Mancewicz, "you continue."

Laura looked attentive. One cheek was larger than the other. She made a garbled sound.

"What's in your mouth?" asked Miss Mancewicz.

Laura spat six marbles onto her desk, where they stuck together spit-soaked, then rolled off, bounced off the edge of her seat and onto the floor. Miss Mancewicz angrily strode up the aisle on heavy legs, aided by tannish orange support hose. Nearing Laura's desk she slid on one of the marbles and swung her arms out and around as in their arm exercises, but both legs flew out despite heavy black Enna-Jetticks, and Miss Mancewicz landed in the aisle on her behind. She attempted to rise, but unsuccessfully, she was so neatly wedged. Marc laughed hysterically, salive dripping down his chin. Bernadette laughed too, hoping Marc would notice.

"Bernadette," cried Miss Mancewicz, "Help me up, you idiot." Bernadette, chastened, and Sondra, who didn't want Bernadette to feel bad, lifted the struggling Miss Mancewicz by her padded armpits to a standing position.

Laura was in her seat, crying.

"Okay, Laura," said Miss Mancewicz, standing forbiddingly over the squat, tear-stained Laura, teeth clenched, eyes bulging and bloodshot. "Continue."

"No . . . hic . . . said the grand . . . hic . . . father . . . I'm sor . . . ry . . . hic . . . peo . . . ple . . . hic . . . Just then . . . hic . . . Super . . . man . . . hic . . . came . . . flying . . . hic . . . down . . ."

Everyone was paying close attention. Miss Mancewicz indicated Marc's turn with her chin.

"'I knew people could fly,' shouted Timothy. 'Superman ain't people,' says de granpa. 'No, I ain't people,' said Superman, 'but me and de Hulk and Vampirella can show you a good time.'"

"You try, Sondra." Sondra stood and looked around from under her brows. She was so tall already that Miss Mancewicz had to look up at her even though her posture resembled a divining rod always in the presence of water. Bernadette could smell Sondra's breath even before she spoke.

"Timothy's grandfather didn't want to just give a quick, cursory yes or no, or don't-bother-me answer, so he decided to. make a big outing of it. 'Tomorrow we'll go into the woods, Timothy, just you and I, together, eat hamburgers we'll take out from McDonald's and discuss the birds and the bees—'"

"Next," said Miss Mancewicz quickly. Sondra, getting involved and nowhere near finished, stood there with her mouth open, her breath wheezing in and out. "Begin, Bernadette."

"Timothy and his grandfather went to Central Park to watch birds and see why they fly. They found a nest with an entire bird family in it, two kids, and a mother and father bird. The bird babies' names were Alice and Jerry. All of a sudden a bluejay swept down and ate them all, spitting out the bones. The grandfather was so upset he turned purple, had a heart attack and died. Timothy, wearing a Fieldcrest towel as a Superman cape, not having had the benefit of his grandfather's lesson, felt that the quickest way to get help would be to fly for it. He jumped off the high rock they were on and smashed into the brambles below. But he didn't die. His eyes were scratched out and he was blinded, but his life was saved by his landing on an enormous pile of horseshit, as it was the bridle path."

"It could be a 'Scratch 'n Sniff' book," suggested Laura.

By the time they opened the closet it was ominously silent. Charles was rigid and had to be lifted out and placed in his seat. Luckily, from crouching, his legs were bent the correct way, but they had a bit of trouble prying Miss Alba's boot out from where it was stuck between Charles' ankle and the back of his thigh.

"Will Charles be able to go to the zoo with us today?" asked Sondra.

*

Miss Alba's class and Miss Halac's class were going together. Miss Halac attempted to direct the herd into line formation two by two, like Noah's Ark, with her blackboard pointer, which she appeared to fantasize into a billard cue, the tip of which she constantly rubbed with chalk, and the heads as billiard balls, only herself comprehending whose head was the eight ball.

It took nearly half an hour for the lining-up arrangements to be completed, after which Miss Alba suggested that it might be too late to go at all. Sondra and Bernadette, always partners, were quick and obedient, fearfully watchful that due to some naughtiness or iniquity on the part of someone else they'd be separated. Someone was absent from Miss Halac's class, but that conveniently left two extra pupils to support the rigid Charles.

They left the classroom, then the school, Miss Halac shouting, "Hup two three four, hup two three four," and keeping them in line with the pointer. "If any one of you dashes out of line and gets hit by an automobile, you shall be painfully punished," she said. "I have a story to tell you that could be amazingly helpful to you in the future. Once, when I was a little girl, I fell off a railway platform. Hup two three four. Do any of you know how I survived?"

"The train wasn't coming," said someone from her own class.

"It was coming, it was," said Miss Halac.

"You were killed and reincarnated, Miss Halitosis," said the boy.

Miss Halac thought for a moment as if that might be a better story. "Not quite," she said, "hup two three four," as they dragged along, the line tight in front, then slackening, Miss Alba keeping the rear up as she assisted with Charles. In a moment's silence she could be heard pleading, "Charles, we're going to see monkeys and elephants. Please put your feet down, Charles."

"I was there on the tracks," continued Miss Halac. "I heard the whistle, then I saw it coming—so fast, so long, so hard—I knew then that I could never get out of its path in time. I lay down directly in the center of the track, my hands at my sides, closed my eyes and sent a prayer up to God. I felt a swoosh of air as the train began to pass over me. Everything became black and there was a great roaring. I counted the cars as each passed over me by the light that came through my eyelids. I counted as many as thirty, waited a moment and sat up. I looked behind me and watched the train going off into the distance."

She looked around. Miss Alba was coming forward, the others

lagging, some looking at something at the curb, others admiring a car, two trying to pick Charles up from the sidewalk. Bernadette gave Sondra a piece of chewing gum she'd scraped carefully from the concrete, and she could hear Sondra's teeth grind the grime embedded in it.

"There's a bum," shouted Laura, pointing to an old man dressed like a woman with bare legs, short skirt, old suit jacket topped with a shawl, and a kerchief on his head held in place with two wodden clothespins.

"Don't point," admonished Miss Alba absently, now walking with Miss Halac, deep in conversation.

"That's no bum," said Marc, "that's what Bernadette's gonna look like when she grows up."

There was almost unanimous agreement, and much giggling. Bernadette smiled as if it were a joke she could take. Sondra put her arm around her. Bernadette was touched and didn't know what to say. She was slightly embarrassed and felt she owed Sondra something for her devotion, yet the first thing she could think of to say was, "You have bad breath." There was silence. Sondra removed her arm from Bernadette.

"I have a friend who's going to beat you up," she said. Bernadette looked puzzled. Not only hadn't she meant to say that, she couldn't understand how she could get beaten up for an immutable fact.

"Wait here," said Sondra, who left her place on line and went to speak with an enormous bruiser from Miss Halac's class, who now moved slowly up in Sondra's place to become Bernadette's line partner. Bernadette looked for Miss Alba, but she and Miss Halac, their backs to the class, were conversing. She thought of running away, just getting out of line and running, but she looked up the vast street, at the enormous buildings and large cars, didn't know where she was and was too terrified.

"Does Sondra Greenhood have bad breath?" asked the large girl, whom Bernadette wouldn't look at, but who whistled her s's. "Answer me," she said, giving Bernadette a punch in the arm that sent her reeling out of line.

"You stay in line," ordered the looming aggressor. "If those teachers see anything, you'll get it worse. I'll be waiting for you every day." She gave Bernadette a pinch that brought tears to her eyes; she nearly screamed. She began weeping silently.

"Crybaby," said the girl, punching her again. Bernadette continued weeping unashamedly as she was pinched and punched repeatedly.

"Does Sondra Greenhood have bad breath?" she asked again. Bernadette didn't answer except to tell herself a silent "yes."

Miss Alba and Miss Halac turned to face them as they reached the zoo.

"My name is Madeline," said the girl. "You're right. Sondra Greenhood has bad breath."

"Bernadette, are you crying?" asked Miss Alba.

"Bernadette's a crybaby, Bernadette's a crybaby," chanted Marc.

"Marc, even though we have no closet here, I can shut you in the monkey house," said Miss Alba.

Giggles. Bernadette's smile crinkled her tear-stiffened face. She hoped Marc was only picking on her to smoke-screen his feelings for her, which appeared obvious due to his lack of indifference to her presence.

"Bernadette's a crybaby, Bernadette's a crybaby," they chanted in unison.

"If you want to sing," said Miss Halac, "Let's sing a song by Joyce Kilmer from the poem you were supposed to memorize. 'I think that I shall never see, a poem lovely as a tree, A tree that looks at God all day, . . .' go on, class," Miss Halac's was the only audible voice as the class stood dumbfounded, mouthing syllables silently after Miss Halac had already sung them.

"I'm hungry," said Laura. "Let's eat."

"We didn't come to the zoo to eat," said Miss Alba.

"We didn't come to the zoo to sing either," said Marc.

They surrounded a small concession, a cart displaying fur monkeys, plastic animals, horns, Cracker Jack. There was a helium tank around which were wrapped many balloon strings. The bright balloons bobbed a few feet above.

"Put him down on the grass gently," said Miss Alba to the two boys who were dragging Charles. "Charles, listen to me. I want you to stretch your legs. Do you hear me, Charles?"

It took a long time for Bernadette to decide what color balloon she wanted. Her quarter smelled metallic in her sweaty palm, as most of the class, more aggressive, made their purchases. Bernadette anxiously watched them line up without her as people crowded in front of her. She finally shouted "White!" and watched her opaque creamy balloon become large and pale. She gave the man her quarter, which he wiped on his pants leg.

"Thirty cents," he said. Bernadette handed him back the balloon.

"You can owe it to me," said the concessionaire when he realized Bernadette didn't have another nickel.

"We're all going to the bathroom now," said Miss Alba. "Miss Halac will take the boys and wait outside and I'll take the girls." Bernadette wondered when she could get the nickel she owed to the balloon man.

*

The public toilet was an enormous building, no different in appearance from the animal houses. The girls filed up the steps of one side of the building into a huge cool tiled room. As Bernadette looked around at the sinks along one wall, and the gray stall doors lining two walls, her balloon flew out of her hand, rapidly making its way to the high ceiling. She was staring upward, dismayed, when Miss Alba pushed her into one of the empty toilet stalls.

"We have no time to worry about your balloon," said Miss Alba, shutting the gray door.

"Don't forget we never sit down on public toilet seats," Miss Alba's voice echoed. "We don't want to catch any disease."

Bernadette remembered the white-haired matron sitting in the corner, her hands folded in her lap. After the girls leave she'll probably help me get my belloon back, she thought. It took Bernadette a long time to unbuckle her suspender, but she was determined not to ask anyone in her class to do it for her. She pulled her pants down and straddled the bowl. Recalling Miss Alba's admonition, she tried to urinate without sitting down. She felt like crying when the liquid merely trickled down her leg into her sock. She stopped and tried again, but she had to go very badly, and it wouldn't stop, wetting her overalls, socks and shoes. She remained in the toilet closet crying, listening to her class emerge from the stalls, Miss Alba helping them wash their hands, their leaving. Though she'd planned to wait there till they left, she somehow never thought they'd completely forget about her.

"I hate them," she cried, angrily pulling pieces of toilet tissue from the holder one by one, trying to place them on the seat without touching it as her mother had shown her, but they fell into the bowl. When it was stuffed, one or two pieces stuck on the seat, Bernadette, overalls pulled up and buckled, sat there and wept.

"Bernadette," she heard someone call suddenly. "Bernadette." It echoed coldly through the enormous tiled room. She so much wanted to run outside, be with her class again, but she sat there very still and in a moment it was silent. She sniffled, left the booth. Her balloon, she could see, was still touching the ceiling like a milky cloud, its dirty string vibrating gently, out of reach.

"Please may I stand on your chair so I can get my balloon?" Bernadette asked the attendant politely, feeling safe in the old woman's presence.

"Don't bother me," said the matron. "Why don't you get out with the rest of your class? Get yourself another balloon." She got up, grabbed a mop and swung it, just barely missing Bernadette's arm.

There were few people around outside. Bernadette heard the lion's roar from a distance. All the animals seemed to be indoors. She looked in vain for her class. She heard monkey chattering and ran into the monkey house. A fat orange orangutan sitting in a tire swing looked at Bernadette impassively. In one of the cages, a wiry black monkey stopped swinging to look at Bernadette. A pink thing between his legs began to swell, and Bernadette became aware that he'd been pulling on it. She watched, fascinated, then realized that the monkey wasn't even looking at her but was staring glassily into space.

She stood in front of the lion house looking in, cold now, and terrified. She could see from the doorway that her class wasn't in there, and she could see the lion pacing, uttering a rhythmic unearthly roar. She began to panic and pictured her class entering the monkey house at the moment of her exit. Suddenly she saw them all on a grassy mall, ran over and slid liquidly in line, but the corners of her mouth pulled uncontrollably downward, and she wept with relief.

"Bernadette," shrieked Miss Alba. "We've been looking all over for you! Where have you been!" She made Bernadette relinquish the line to stand in front of her.

"Do you realize how inconsiderate you are?"

Marc giggled. At first Bernadette was so relieved to be there she didn't mind the yelling, though tears ran again down her streaked filthy face.

"I lost my balloon," she said. She thought of her pale milky balloon floating out of reach, deserted on the cold bathroom ceiling.

"It's all alone," she wailed.

"I don't know what I'm going to do with you," said Miss Alba. Madeline, who had crept forward, took Bernadette's hand.

"I had to call your mother," said Miss Alba spuriously. Madeline felt Bernadette go rigid with fear, but she relaxed as they marched across the grassy mall.

"I'm hungry," said Bernadette.

"We've already eaten," said Miss Alba. "I'm afraid we've spent so much time looking for you, your punishment will have to be no lunch."

Bernadette dreamed of ice cream.

"Miss Skim Milk," said Sondra, "Bernadette wet her pants."

Bernadette remembered. Her overalls, wet, heavy and warm,

were becoming cold, the cuffs going slosh-slosh on the ground.

"Miss Halac, do you believe this?" Miss Halac struggled along, carrying Charles.

"It's your turn now, Miss Alba, he's heavy."

"Bernadette, we went to the bathroom," said Miss Alba, beginning to weep. "There's no logic," she cried. "The best laid plans of mice and men— The world is falling apart. Tissue monitor—" The tissue monitor, draped over Miss Halac's shoulder, didn't respond.

"Use your sleeve," ventured Laura.

"As punishment, you'll be my partner, Bernadette," Miss Alba said when she stopped crying. She held Bernadette's hand tightly, hurting her. Bernadette's fingers attempted to squirm in Miss Alba's dry, rough grasp, but she wouldn't let go. She could hear the class whispering and laughing, super-conscious of the slush-slush of her wet cuffs.

"Bernadette's a retard, Bernadette's a retard," they chanted. "Bernadette's a crybaby, pants-wetting retard, Bernadette's a crybaby pants-wetting retard—" She looked hopefully up at Miss Alba, who seemed to be enjoying the chant.

At the seals, Miss Alba forgot about Bernadette and let go of her. Tired but safe, Bernadette gazed at the deep calm water in a daze of peaceful exhaustion. Suddenly a seal broke through the calm water, nose first, fur glistening, then dove again. Bernadette strove unsuccessfully to see it. It popped up in an unlikely place. A larger seal popped up. They played tag for a while until the large one jumped on the concrete steps to sun, while the small one hopped about, attempting to coerce the other to play.

Small and plump, hair matted and tangled except for the invisible arterial integrity of two braids down her back, clothes filthy and wet, and face streaked in varying values of black and brown, Bernadette swayed in rhythm with the seal, seeing nothing else. She imagined she was a seal, swimming and playing and watched over by the fat mama, whose sleek black coat had become dry and brown like worn velvet movie seats.

"Bernadette," shouted Marc suddenly. "Let's play dodge ball."

Bernadette turned quickly, shocked out of her trance just in time to see Marc throw a tomato at her. She moved slightly, and it hit her on the leg, splashing all over her pants.

*

Bernadette silently decided to leave this class that treated her so badly. She no longer cared what happened to her. She'd become a seal, and they'd have to leave without her. She walked away just as Miss Halac was transferring Charles, knees still bent, to Miss Alba's shoulder. Half the class dumbly watched Bernadette walk into the park.

Bernadette kept walking. Her pants were dry, albeit stiff; she was filthy and starving, but she felt a sense of liberation and adventure, laced with the pleasure of spite. They'll be sorry, she thought, stupid Miss Skim Milk and those horrible kids. She recalled her mother and felt a deep pity for her. Even though she'd probably spank Bernadette if and when she ever got home, she knew her mother would be out of her mind with worry. She wandered up the dark street thinking about food, when she became aware of footsteps behind her.

Heart pounding she ran, but the footsteps also seemed to be running. Terrified, she kept her head down. It wasn't until she was upon it that she saw the small gaudy movie theater.

Bernadette entered quickly and looked around. There were a few people on line near a ticket taker, but she thought she'd eluded her pursuer. Suddenly she saw him enter, breathing hard. She wasn't positive it was he, but she thought so. She sneaked fearfully past the ticket taker, who seemed to see her but allowed her to enter anyway. What a nice man, thought Bernadette. She felt safer in the interior darkness. If her pursuer wished to catch her, he not only had to wait on line, but he'd have to locate her in the dark and drag her out silently. She carefully chose a seat next to a large man who, she felt, though engrossed in the film which flickered shadow-like across his face, would most likely be a fine protector. Soon she relaxed, enjoyed the Technicolor images and tried to figure out what the movie was about. She was almost asleep when she felt the man's hand on her thigh. It was large, warm and comforting. He was fiddling around with his other hand, but she was so sleepy she couldn't even turn her head. He took her hand and put it on his penis, which he'd removed from his pants. It felt smooth and hot.

"Please move your hand up and down," he whispered, placing his large hand over hers and moving it the way he liked.

"But I'm so tired," said Bernadette in a weepy whine.

"Then go to sleep while you do it," said the man. "It's not difficult, and it doesn't mean anything."

The Highest Grader
of All

When I was in college, I had the well-known art historian Professor Dr. Paul Zucker for Art History. We were all terrified of him; if not terrified, at least cowed. He was in his seventies, had thick gray longish hair pushed back behind pendulous hairy ears, which he considered the most intellectual type.

"Geshhtaaldt!" he'd roar. "Most uff you vill neverr unnderr-staandt geshtaaldt, the maagicckh eqvvaashun in vichh the whole isss morre thanze summ of it'zz paardtsz!" The hocking of his heavy German accent, constantly occupied, when not actually teaching, in expressing scorn for us students, infused the air of the Art History room with a tropical humidity into which our thin dry voices disappeared.

Dr. Zucker had a strange method of grading. Though, at the time, the class all laughed at his method and understood the inequity, the arbitrariness, none of us were willing to complain. Who could we complain to? Dr. Zucker himself? Because of the unfairness of his grading method, we never had to speak in class, write any paper or take any exam. Perhaps because we were art students, we may have had something missing from our intellect that is necessary for survival, but we never realized how closely Dr. Zucker's grading method resembled certain Nazi philosophy, particularly the racial superiority theory of Adolf Hitler. While Dr. Zucker didn't seem to discriminate racially (although he might have studied our names in secret, but I doubt it), he graded us solely on our appearance. He would call our names one by one so that each of us could stand up for inspection. Since even by the end of the semester he knew no one except the person who ran the slide machine, he'd look at each of us for about five seconds. If you were short and fat, an endomorphic type, Dr. Zucker would give you a poor grade, anywhere from D to C plus, according to how endomorphic you actually were. Mesomorphs, the athletic type, would receive median grades of C plus and B or B plus, and the thin, intellectual ectomorph received the highest grades, B plus through A plus.

Perhaps we were all used to being graded in subtle ways on our appearance but never so explicitly and according to skeletal type. Dr. Zucker held the theory (which he postulated in class, so it wasn't difficult to make the connection) that the ectomorph was the most intelligent and intellectually endowed of all the humanoids. Therefore our physical structure was proof we deserved the grade we got. Maybe we almost believed he was right, but he had almost all of us searching ourselves for ectomorphic traits. None of us would dare oppose this demagoguery because, not only was Dr. Zucker the archetypal patriarch, he also taught at The New School and Yale.

My friend Helen, although she was really brilliant and got As in everything, always got an A plus from Dr. Zucker because she had the good fortune to resemble exactly Pharaoh Akhenaton, during whose reign in Egypt, Egyptian art and culture reached its apex. I got a C plus and a look of disgust, because, I think, of the difficulty I presented in classification. I think he could sense that I was at a loss about myself. I certainly seemed willing to accept his C plus assessment of my body and mind, not to mention skill in Art History, although Phoebe, short and squat like Henri Rousseau, received a C, only a plus away from myself. Narcissa, Ramona and John, three ectomorphs who always sat together and wore nothing but black, always got As. Lenore rises and sits again so rapidly that she creates a long, thin visual wake, or after-image, and after a moment of tension, during which it is possible she'll be asked to rise again, she's given an A.

*

In another course, three-dimensional design, I stand in front of the class, my body bisected by the heavy slab table I'm leaning my pelvic bones into. The class is silent and expectant. The teacher, Mr. Kratina, rests his thick, spatulate, koala-bear fingers on the slate table top where he's sitting, leaning against the wall. His eyes spin on stalks; the short hair on his wide head looks cruel. Can he be waiting for me to speak? In front of me is my three-dimensional design project made from old mailing tubes and sharp pieces of mirror, gleaned from the garbage of Flatbush, where I am constantly ostracized for wearing paint-covered dungarees and searching in garbage cans. "Go back to the Village" is a common remark. I'm looking forward to moving out of Brooklyn before they mobilize a pogrom against artists.

"Well?" asks Mr. Kratina. I look at him stubbornly, lips sealed.

"If you refuse to describe your work to the class I'll have to give you a C or an incomplete."

Now is the time for an explanation, at least an understanding of my philosophy, but to me my silence is more than complete. Any attempt at explanation would sunder this perfect completeness, drag my project into the realm of the ordinary. I remain silent, stubbornly purist. Lenore slides down into her seat so that it appears as if she'll drip off onto the floor, but she moves her leg under the table and gives me a hard kick. I look at her and read in her face an entire future of practicality. She draws me into another reality, but who is right? Mr. Kratina's pale seaweed-green eyes recede angrily behind his high cheekbones, setting like horrible suns.

"I don't believe in explaining a work of visual art," I say. "Anyone can see that I've done the assignment. But I feel that words will limit and destroy the gestalt."

"Next time, if you don't describe your work orally," says Mr. Kratina, "you'll receive an incomplete."

At the Sagamore Cafeteria with Narcissa, I feel strangely alien, as if either she or I were from outer space. Narcissa, part oriental, is incredibly exotic with her high cheekbones, dark slanted eyes and straight fine hair which moves easily along her long white columnar neck, and her mother's white, white English skin. For me she exuded an aura of sex, romance, adventure and depravity because she came from a bad home, wore only black and hung around with Ramona and John. She's eating Sagamore's greasy potato lotkes, while I, for my skin and weight, stick to black coffee and half a grapefruit with a bleeding cherry in the center as she tells me about her married life.

A wizened man in rags, dark area of fresh urine on his pants demarcating his genital area, sits down at our table to consume the leftovers from our dinner while pouring ketchup, salt, sugar and cream into his cup of boiled water. Does this bother me? No flowing greensward and ivy-covered buildings for me; the Bowery as campus was perfect.

I observe the derelict's real life efforts at survival, a chill of joy running through me, and continue to grapple with my badly cut grapefruit sections and dull spoon, my digestion assisted by the juices set flowing by the smell and sight of Narcissa's greasy potato lotkes, which my grapefruit tastes like as I watch her unselfconsciously and sensuously devour them. Her ingenuous attitude about the caloric content of what she consumes is enviable to me, a kind of innocence I can never recapture. On the other hand, pale lipsticked lips parted, seeming to swallow with only the back of her throat, her black-outlined oriental eyes peering over her white cheekbones, she nonchalantly recounts incredible experiences in areas unknown to me.

"I don't know why I got married," she says. "Maybe I was getting even with Ramona for marrying John. He took her away.

She used to be mine. Anyway, I was making it with all these guys, and I couldn't come with any of them. But Frank, he really made an effort to make me come. He really tried. He's studying psychology. I spent more and more time at his place trying to come. Then I had a fight with my parents and took my valise and stayed at Frank's. He said, 'Why don't we get married? We might as well.' So I said 'O.K.' We went to my house to tell my parents, who didn't give a shit. Frank and I walked over the Brooklyn Bridge to his apartment on Henry Street carrying a lot of pots my mother gave us."

The derelict, not nearly as interested as I was, went off to glean leftovers from another table. I was morbidly fascinated by the monotonously delivered narrative, totally devoid of romance.

"Now that we're married," continues Narcissa in her hoarse voice, "Frank doesn't care whether I have an orgasm or not. He just fucks like a machine and instantly falls asleep. Sometimes I'm so frustrated I could cry. I see if he's asleep and then I masturbate with his soft prick still in me. Frank told me to go to a shrink."

I sip my coffee, trying to be casual. In those days this type of explicit confession was extremely innovative. I pictured the unknown Frank lying partly across the naked Narcissa, his limp prick still interred, as she quietly and surreptitiously masturbates to orgasm. I had no advice to offer. Nor could I identify with this antiromantic tale, except that the more I pictured it, the more romantic it became. I was still starving but tried not to order anything else.

"I think I'll have a Coke," says Narcissa, burping slightly.

*

The model imagines it is cute to pose lasciviously while staring at my painting teacher. Sparks shoot from Mr. Ippolito's velvet eyes. I have to admit he's sexy. Though small and slightly balding, Italian, he resembles, incredibly, Napoleon, with a sharp nose, long dark eyes, soft hair pushed to the side and deliciously molded lips. While he appears extremely arrogant, because this is his first term teaching painting at Cooper, there's still something vulnerable about him that makes me feel protective toward him. At least I'm motivated not to be too obnoxious in his class. During the break Mr. Ippolito follows the model out, but it isn't until now, recalling it, that I can entertain any suspicion that they found a place, the teachers' lounge, the rest room, the darkroom, where he could quickly open her robe and insert himself. At the time I wasn't capable of imagining those things even when they were happening. My consciousness was full of blank spots, which I'd like to fill in now with all the details of the past, but it's too late.

I'm having difficulty finding out how I want to paint the model because actually I don't want to paint the model. I can't think of why I want to paint a nude woman. I'm anxiously seeking a way to see her that would interest me so that I can enjoy expressing my exaggerated vision of it, but I haven't discovered it yet after hours and layers of paint. I want to think about it for days while just looking at the model, but if you don't lift your paint brush for days in painting class, you get an incomplete. I'm beginning to get it now. I'm painting her as a landscape, something like Monument Valley, in various shades of white, taupe, beige, mauve, eggshell, and gray. Taking a break to think, I sit in a corner. Mr. Ippolito comes over.

"Are you having trouble?" he asks.

"Yes," I say, "I can't visualize the total gestalt I'm looking for. I hate painting nudes."

"Don't worry about the nude." He studies my painting thoughtfully. "Don't paint the model," he says slowly, "paint the . . . paint."

"I think I know what you mean," I say from the corner where I'm still sitting. Mr. Ippolito gives me a piercing look. I imagine he's getting ready to ask me to rise. Instead, his delicate eyebrows rise slightly above the bridge of his nose.

"Are you tired?" he asks solicitously. I merely nod, surprised. That one small remark, dealing with the personal, is a catalyst, and I realize suddenly that I'm madly in love with him.

*

Phoebe's and my active antipathy to each other has created a bond between us. We also have in common that we are both dedicated virgins. Nothing can pierce our membranes, which in my case, appears to cover my entire body and mind. We're constantly seeking an adventure that will break through, touch us in some exciting way, but we know no way to achieve this unknown except to display our cold, cute little bodies in places that have an aura of adventure. We've decided to cut Typography class and Advertising Design and seek adventure in the Village. We're still angry that our petition to the Dean stating that students who want to be Fine Artists should be required to take nothing but Painting Class, every period of every day has been denied. Why should we study things we'll never use? we asked him. The Dean's answer was that we are in Cooper Union unconditionally to obtain a well-rounded education and that after we graduate if we wish to do nothing other than paint, we are welcome to do it. "Why should a painter," we asked, "have to take Speech Class, Humanities, Typography, Horseback Riding?" If we did only painting, that would have been the only chance for some us ever to paint that intensively again. On the other hand, I see now that the Dean was right, it is the painting that was the most useless of all the courses, though when I'm in a bad mood I tend to think they were all useless. It only takes the Alumni Fund's semiannual request for money to remind me that I'm still not a success.

Phoebe and I walk through Washington Square Park and sit next to the fountain for a moment, absorbing the sun, but it's autumn and pretty cool. The fountain is preempted by NYU students and people on their lunch hour.

We enter the darkened Cafe Rienzi, with its atmosphere of delicious decadence so infusive I almost faint. Delirious with the possibilities of the unknown, drinking a cappuccino, I see through the window, sitting on the tenement stoop across the street, Ramona Romanovsky and John. Their motorcycle is parked next to them in the gutter in front of John, bisecting him in such a way that if I squint one eye, I see half of him, if I squint the other, I see the other half. Ramona, a tall pale blonde with prominent light blue eyes, reminded me of a Russian princess. She appeared to be in a state of blasé dejection.

"Do they really live there?" I asked, hardly believing that anyone I knew really lived on MacDougal Street. John, with his newly grown moustache, casually put his hand on Ramona's knee, a gesture that indicated to me a kind of possession so complete it was already unconscious, a state between a man and woman I could only imagine. What were their lives like? They'd quit school just to live here and be together, eat together, make love together, and ride the motorcycle, John in front, Ramona behind, her blond hair flying out behind her as they sped through dark lanes. They lived in fantastic poverty together, ecstatically alive, abandoned in a world of sensation and passion, eating toasted Levy's rye bread with butter and jelly, or cooked spaghetti with ketchup-and-butter sauce and drinking stale Gallo with maroon flecks. I'm filled with envy, realizing I'm fated to finish college and travel home to Kings Highway every day, my path in life demarcated by the tracks of the BMT. Gazing searchingly and hungrily around the dark corners of Cafe Rienzi, I see no adventure, only Phoebe's stubby paint-stained hand completely encompassing her coffee cup, ignoring the handle and holding it as if it were a glass, her entire hand attempting to extract every bit of warmth from it, and when it's finished, squeeze it out.

"Isn't that horrible. Just horrendous," says Phoebe.

"What?" I ask.

"It's that John's fault that Ramona quit school just to live with him and cook for him. He could have waited at least till she graduated. Look at the apartment they have to live in."

I stared at Phoebe, her sharp-edged lips turned down bitterly, shocked at her conception of the events.

"Why blame John?" I ask.

"He just wants to possess Ramona and make her his slave."

This idea is so alien to me and my romantic conception, even further out seems the idea of blaming John for Ramona's decision. I said nothing because at that time I listened to everyone but kept my own thoughts secret. Did Phoebe know something about Ramona and John that I didn't? I wondered. Did she know something about life that I didn't?

*

I know that Mr. Ippolito teaches night class on Thursdays, so one Thursday I remain in the photography lab late. I use the painting studio to unroll my blotter and appear to study the still damp photos of all the bums I've taken. Superimposed over their image is what I can see and hear, from the corners of my eyes and ears, of Mr. Ippolito, which runs over the photo images like double exposures.

"Mr. Ippolito, can I come home with you?" I ask toward the end of the class, at a carefully planned moment, a moment watched and waited for for nearly two hours, supposed to appear casually extemporaneous. He seems only faintly shocked.

"I want to see your paintings."

"Okay," he says. "Did you call your mother?"

"Yes," I say, wondering whether that's a sarcastic reference to my age. The thing is, I haven't called my mother, I don't know why. Perhaps I wish to reserve her as a nagging anxiety, a barrier to my complete freedom. Perhaps I just don't know what to tell her. I suspect she might think it odd that after ten P.M. I'm going home with my painting teacher to see his paintings. My mother and I have always had differences about what was odd behavior and what was not. On the other hand, she might think nothing of it because she trusted teachers implicitly, but my own fantasy was too lurid to pull it off. The later it became, the more afraid I was to call home, yet I was compelled to fulfill this fantasy. I still don't know how to integrate the practical with the romantic and fantasy elements of my life. I accompany him as he retrieves his coat from the teachers' lounge, following silently.

"I have to go over to the gallery for a few minutes," he says, "to help hang a show."

I follow him to his gallery, the Tanager on Tenth Street, where I watch him help get ready the exhibit of Theophile Repke. Mr.

Ippolito stands back to make sure a painting is in just the right aesthetic position, while I watch silently, pretending to be experienced and casual.

"Do you like them?" he asks me as we leave.

"They're okay," I say. Why did he ask me anyway? Can he really care? I'm not the critic from *The New York Times* or *Art News*.

I'm smitten with admiration for Mr. Ippolito's top floor loft studio, which faces Tompkins Square Park and is like some European building. It's enormous, its floors well sanded. The scant furniture is also sanded and oiled, each piece an article of perfected aesthetic concern, as are Mr. Ippolito's velour shirts and blazer jackets and imported Italian slacks, each pocket bound with a narrow edge of real leather. This is the first living loft I've ever seen, but I'm even more impressed by the fact that next door lives another famous Abstract Expressionist of the New York School.

I sit on an antique velvet couch, which gives the perfect touch of artistic incongruity with the austerity of the gestalt, and Mr. Ippolito gives me a glass of beer like his own. I must call my mother, I think, but even though the later it becomes the more imperative it is that I do so, the less likely can I, yet it is a gnawing anxiety that undermines my joy, as, I don't realize at the time, it will for the remainder of my life. Mr. Ippolito is not lazy about bringing out one large oil painting after another, placing each, one at a time, under a spotlight for me to view. They are nicely textured, sensitively rendered, lushly colored landscape-like abstracts, constructed with golds, yellows, pinks, oranges, reds, magentas—among various horizon lines. They're tasteful, even sensual, but their gestalt doesn't speak to me.

"How do you know when you're finished?" I ask.

He seems surprised by such a question, but that's a problem which constantly plagued me. Later on I realized that it was because I didn't know well enough what I was saying or wanted to say, so I never knew when I'd finished saying it successfully. It seemed to me I'd never ever known when a nonobjective painting was completed, having to accept its completion on faith or instinct. It seemed too simplistic to think that a painting was a finished work of art just because the design worked.

"I just know when it's finished," he says. He drags out a painting, passionate in deep royal blues and shades of virulent green, a swirling abstraction completely different from his other paintings—its vertiginous movements are definitely, abstract as the painting is, inspired by an enormous palm plant.

"This painting I really love," I said. "I love it. It has all the passion of the plant, the feeling of its movement, without being only the plant; it's a painting of paint too, completely abstract."

"Hummm," says Mr. Ippolito.

Suddenly I feel embarrassed. To nonobjective painters of the New York School of Abstract Expressionism, the idea of retaining any subject matter is considered somewhat backward since, by abolishing subject matter, they've set art free. Even I, though I scorned nonobjective painting, wondered when I'd be able to free myself from the prison of the subject. That painting of Mr. Ippolito's is the only one of his that I've remembered and still recall clearly, though I looked for it in many later shows and exhibits of his work and never saw it. That's how much he was interested in my opinion. On the other hand, there was no frame of reference for it in the body of his work. It was an anomaly, a detriment at this time when the galleries require consistency of a painter from one painting to the next, as if each show is made from one enormous painting cut into many pieces.

Leaving the last painting out, Mr. Ippolito sits next to me on the couch, downs the last of his beer and puts his arm around me. "We're all really alone," he says.

This remark surprises me no less than the fact that his arm is around me; it is in the same dramatic style of unbelieving cynicism as any of my contemporaries' remarks. I felt that it was a personal plea I could satisfy and at the same time it revealed Mr. Ippolito as being unflaggingly lonely, therefore accessible.

He lifts my chin and peers into my eyes, breathing warm breath on my face and slowly, slowly, gently places his lips on mine.

Beginning with the most subtle pressure, as if to acclimate me, he kisses me deeply. My heart pounded violently, but not with sexual excitement. I was simply overwhelmed this was really happening. He put his arms around me, pressed hard against me and stuck his tongue in my mouth. It's really happening, I said to myself so now go ahead and feel something, but I couldn't. Even though this was my greatest fantasy, and initiated by myself, I couldn't believe this thirty-six-year-old professor was kissing me, his eighteen-year-old painting student. I still wonder why. When I was teaching at Pratt, would I accept the advances of even the sexiest freshman? While their external package looked good, upon opening, even the brightest was shockingly immature. And the teacher–student relationship can't easily be ignored. And what about the rest of the semester? Then again, perhaps it's the slight perversity of the relationship that has a certain charm.

Mr. Ippolito kisses harder, his hands moving over my breasts. I must call home, I think. He touches my crotch and runs his hand gently along it, his brow, wrinkling with passion, registering an expression of pain. I wondered whether he could feel my Modess.

"I have to go home," I say.

"Why not sleep over? Please sleep here," he entreats.

"I can't," I say. "I have to go home." I am embarrassed to tell him that at two-thirty in the morning I have to call my mother and am terrified to do it. Also, I don't want to tell him I am a virgin, but I am concerned about my performance. And what about this Modess sanitary pad? How can I discreetly dispose of it? Does he think I have a puffy vagina or does he guess there's a napkin there? Why didn't I think of all this before? My fantasy always ended before this. A little necking was all I came for, a romantic kiss. I only wanted my painting teacher to fall in love with me.

"Please, please," murmurs Mr. Ippolito, putting my hand on his prick.

"I really have to go now," I say.

"Please sleep here," he implores.

"Where will I sleep?"

"I'll let you sleep on my bed, and I'll sleep on the couch." He thinks I'm playing some kind of game and is willing to go along. He doesn't suspect my innocence and fear. "I'll ride back to Brooklyn with you tomorrow," he says. "I have to visit my relatives."

Relatives in Brooklyn! Not Tuscany or Venice. This glimpse of Mr. Ippolito as a real person is tempting, yet all the more frightening. I think of my mother.

"No, I really have to go," I say, pulling away. Mr. Ippolito frowns but says nothing, as I resume my shoes and coat. He silently removes his European duffel coat from the sanded antique coatrack and walks me to the station. Of course he's not going to accompany me into the depths of Brooklyn at three-thirty in the morning if I choose so irrationally to go home. He waits with me for the train and gives me a small kiss goodnight, which goes up in a puff of our breath.

*

"Marilyn," Narcissa asks, "do you like Herbert Plattner?"

"Yeah, he's okay. I hardly know him. Why?"

"Do you think he's sexy?"

"He's okay. Why?"

"I think he's cute. And sexy too. He's always fooling around with me. We're real attracted to each other. I'd love to go to bed with him. I have fantasies about him when I'm masturbating."

"So why don't you go to bed with him?" I ask.

"Because I'm married," says Narcissa. "He's a virgin, too. I love virgins. I love showing them what to do. They're so cute and so touching. After the first time I don't like them any more." Narcissa pauses for a moment. "Listen, Marilyn, would you consider going to bed with Herbert Plattner?"

"I don't know . . . maybe."

"He'd like to go to bed with someone because he's tired of being a virgin. He wanted to go to bed with me, but I couldn't. I suggested you as the next best thing, and he said okay."

"Really?" I said, flattered.

"Come on, Marilyn, he's so sexy. It would be so exciting, and since I can't do it, you could tell me everything. If I know everything about it, it will be almost as if it's happening to me."

"Okay," I say, thinking that perhaps this is the best way to dispose of my own burdensome virginity, in a calculated way, with someone in exactly the same position, arranged and overseen by a matchmaker. There were even romantic possibilities.

"Good," says Narcissa. "I wish I could watch, but if you tell me everything it will be the next best thing."

Herbert Plattner and I met as arranged by Narcissa, on the bench next to the first-floor elevator. We attended class with each other every day but never discussed this meeting. We pretended we were strangers and in a way we were because we were thrown into a completely new context without any foreplay, so to speak.

"Do you think we should have something to eat first, or is it better on an empty stomach?" asks Herbert.

"I think you have to wait half an hour after eating," I said.

"No," says Herbert, "that's swimming."

"Oh, what's the difference? Let's go eat something light."

"Let's get some oysters," says Herbert. "By the way, Narcissa made us sandwiches. She said doing it makes you hungry. Do you think we could eat them now? I'm hungry already."

We go to the Sagamore Cafeteria, where the rule is no sandwiches brought in from the outside, and sneakily open Narcissa's bag after buying coffee.

"What are they?" I ask.

"I think they're hamburger on white," says Herbert, pulling up a flat transparent cover—white bread inundated with ketchup, which looks like a layer of wax paper—to reveal burnt ochre meat lovingly garnished with a marbleized mixture of cadmium red ketchup and yellow ochre mustard.

"What do you think of this color combination?" he asks.

I stare at it for a moment, attempting to abstract the color from the subject matter. "Ugghhh," I say. "It's only good in the gestalt of hamburger." Later on, Claes Oldenburg, who then worked in the Cooper Union Art Library for two dollars an hour, would further abstract it by abstracting the entire hamburger, color and all, out of the realm of food into the realm of art.

"I have a prophylactic," says Herbert. He removes a foil packet from his wallet and opens it.

"Why are you opening it here?" I ask.

"You're supposed to test them for holes," he says, blowing it up.

"Not here, Herbert. How will we carry it?" Herbert keeps blowing it up until it's as large as a mammoth zucchini.

"It has a hole," he says. Everyone looks at us as the prophylactic suddenly begins flapping to and fro, emitting a sharp whistle. Herbert's wallet, lying on the table, has a permanent circle embossed on the leather.

"How long have you had it?" I ask.

"Three years," he says.

On the way to Herbert's tenement apartment, shared by three people, making the twenty-seven dollar a month rent nine dollars a month each, we stop at the drugstore.

"You ask," says Herbert.

"No, you," I say.

"No, you."

"Come on, Herbert!"

"Can I have a package of Trojans?" whispers Herbert to the salesman.

"What?" asks the salesman, leaning over the counter toward Herbert.

"CAN I PLEASE HAVE A PACKAGE OF TROJANS?" Herbert shouts, turning bright red.

"Regular or lubricated?" asks the clerk, leaning back. Herbert looks at me, standing fifteen feet away trying to look inconspicuous.

"REGULAR OR LUBRICATED?" he shouts. Everyone looks at me. I toss my hair.

"Lubricated, of course."

I am immediately turned on by the romanticism of the particular odor exuded by tenements, which makes me gasp for breath the moment I enter their cool and musty halls, smelling like an overgrowth of mold and mushrooms, superseded by the odor of ammoniated cleansers mixed with dirty water, to hold those vegetations in abeyance.

"This is my bed," says Herbert. "This is Cyril's bed. These are my books. This is my desk," he says, trembling, as I look around. "This is my advertising project. These are Cyril's books. This is Cyril's desk. This is my T square. These are my pencils. These are my clothes, these are my shoes." He looks around the clutter desperately, then suddenly begins ripping off his clothes, so quickly that he is in his underpants, as I look on, astonished and fully dressed.

"Don't you think we should kiss a little?" I ask, becoming nervous myself.

"Is that how?" Herbert asks idiotically, relieved to slip into the role of incompetent where nothing is expected of him. He sits down on the bed. As I approach, the pimples on his chest become clearer in focus and more luridly colored.

He looks at me strangely. "Do you like me? Do you like me?" he asks urgently. .

"Of course I like you," I say woodenly, becoming terrified. I had been enjoying our attitude of clinical experimentation, which I didn't want destroyed by any feeling. The atmosphere of feeling and affection that Herbert was rapidly trying to effect, and probably couldn't function without, was exactly what terrified me. Speechless, we listened to the sound of a key in the door, and Cyril enters the room.

"Hi," he says, looking from me to Herbert.

"Hi," says Herbert. "I was just showing her my art supplies."

Cyril looks puzzled as his eyes run over Herbert's body, naked except for his Fruit of the Looms.

Narcissa waits for me in Two-Dimensional Design.

"I thought you'd never get here. How was it?" She looks up at me from her seat with an eagerness only coated with lethargy.

"It was almost very nice," I said, "but nothing happened."

"How come? You mean I got all excited for nothing?"

"Herbert was all undressed, we had the prophylactics, and then Cyril walked in."

Narcissa shook her head slowly, her hair swinging back and forth, tickling her shoulders. "He certainly could have arranged for Cyril not to come home early. I'm sure he subconsciously did this on purpose. I hope you'll try again." Narcissa removes her two-dimensional design project from a plastic bag. It is a collage composed of various textures in subtle shades of brown. She runs her hand over an area composed of short, curly hair.

"This is Frank's pubic hair," she says.

"It is?" I look at it, then look away, not wanting to appear to study it. I can't help picturing this same hair around an imaginary Frank's genitals.

Did Narcissa say to Frank, "Hey, can I have some of your pubic hair for my two-dimensional design assignment?" Did the idea occur to her after they had made love, while Frank lay on their bed, already limp and sweaty? Wow, I think, there's something so intimate about this; it's like Narcissa displaying her relationship, her sexuality to the entire class. Perhaps it's a subtle seduction for the professor, who, when he looks at the collage, will suddenly see Narcissa exposed, naked and sexual. I feel a pang of jealousy at her ability to strip so easily in front of anyone.

"Did you hear?" she says. "Ramona was killed."

A chill ran through me. "What?"

"Ramona was killed. On the motorcycle. She and John were going some place and the motorcycle crashed into something. She was thrown over a hundred feet and her skull was crushed. She died right away."

A small feathery tickle ran across my scalp, and my fingertips became numb. I spent the next moments picturing the motorcycle crashing, Ramona being thrown, arms akimbo, landing, lying limp and white in a puddle of blood, which gushes from her blond hair spread wildly around and frames her hair, making it appear almost white as the wispy tips become submerged and drown. I rerun this picture four or five times and stop in time to avert a knot of nausea.

"Are you upset?" I asked Narcissa.

"Sure I'm upset," she said, opening a chicken sandwich. "But I haven't seen her that much since she quit school. Maybe the fact that John took her away was partly responsible for why I got married too. And now John is fine. That's what disturbs me. Not even a broken finger, and it was all his fault. Did you ever hear of anyone in the front seat getting killed? No. It's always the one who rides in back. And now he's back in school!"

A different interpretation occurred to me: that by riding on the back seat, entrusting her body to the driver, Ramona as good as committed suicide.

"The worst thing is that after I told my shrink about it, all he did was try to seduce me," she said.

*

I've just received a D on my book report on Thomas Mann's *Death in Venice,* even though I've worked on it longer and harder than anything and I really love it. It's slightly unusual—aimed at proving, by citing sections from various of his stories and analyses of their meanings, that Thomas Mann wouldn't approve of having his stories analyzed and book reports written about them. In order to do this I've had to put in a lot of extra effort to prove that I wasn't trying to get out of doing a report, but my efforts were entirely unappreciated by Professor Caldiero, who is, in fact, angry that I've deviated from the assignment. I am devastatingly disappointed.

"How can you be disappointed?" asks Lenore. "You're so incredibly unrealistic. The way to get As is just to do assignments simply, the way they ask, copy most of it from the book, make it simple and use lots of his own ideas from the lessons."

"He says I'll fail if I don't do it over."

"Then do it over," says Lenore. "Do whatever they want."

I understand the meaning and value of what Lenore is saying, but I don't know whether I'm capable of absorbing the information as part of my structure and dispensing suitable practical action.

"Read mine," she suggests.

I take her report, which is short but has a huge red A in the right hand corner, and skim through it. It's simple, like a preview of *Jonathan Livingston Seagull.*

"Lenore, I don't know whether I should do it. Besides, doing it over would implicate the integrity of my first report."

"Marilyn, do it," she implores. "You can practically copy mine. Don't you want to get an A? What do you think we're in school for?"

*

Phoebe and I have climbed the long flights to Mr. Ippolito's loft on Tenth Street East, to which I have retraced my steps. I've much regretted that other time and wish I'd stayed. Mr. Ippolito appears also to regret that time, but in the opposite way: He wishes he'd never said I could come home with him. This I infer from the fact that he never speaks to me about anything other than painting and has never invited me over, though I palpitatingly await that moment, rerunning the events of that night with different endings as often as *Casablanca* with Bogart is reshown. Today, by taking the initiative and visiting him, I hope to see him in his own habitat, perhaps to recapture intercourse of a social, rather than painter-student, nature. But being nervous about it, I asked Phoebe to accompany me. If worse comes to worst, we may have an adventure. We wait for hours on the steps outside his door gossiping, but he never arrives.

"Sue Flack saw him in Provincetown at a beach party," says Phoebe, "and he was chasing Marisol all over the place, but she was angry at him for something." I picture this and become jealous of Marisol, not only a mature attractive woman who has made it in the art world but also from South America. I'm jealous of her for being in a position to reject Mr. Ippolito. From where I am now, it would take enormous fortitude on my part, more than I possess, to reject him.

I've scarcely finished thinking about this when a beautiful, slender woman, thick hair cut straight across like Cleopatra's, a band over the top of her bangs delineating her oval face, climbs over us and rings Mr. Ippolito's bell. There's no answer, of course. We watch her quietly, bug-eyed.

"Marilyn, that's Marisol," whispers Phoebe.

It looks like her, but I've seen her before only in photos. I can't be positive, which I always like to be, but I'm tempted to go along with Phoebe because it's good for the gestalt of the day, after discussing Marisol, actually to see her calling for Mr. Ippolito. When again there's no response, she opens the door anyway, with a key, and disappears inside. My heart sinks. I can't compete with this kind of intimacy. I don't want to see any more. We decide not to wait but to leave a note. Phoebe rummages with her sturdy, apt fingers in her art supply laden bag and pulls out a pencil and paper. "We were here but you were not," she writes.

"Who should I sign?" I'm embarrassed to sign my name and feel that the message is mundane. Perhaps it would be best if he never knew I was here chasing after him, but I still feel like leaving something. I don't want him not to know we were here either.

"I have an idea," says Phoebe. "This is good because he's Italian." She traces her hand on the page and fills it in with charcoal. We write under it "The Black Hand."

*

Phoebe and I walk together to the elevator. We're on our way to Art History class, where we are going to be graded. In the elevator, John is standing next to us. I peruse him, to determine from his features whether or not he's ravaged with sorrow about Ramona's death. He must have controlled his grief or he wouldn't have returned to school.

"He has some nerve. Quitting school with Ramona—now that

he's killed her, he returns to finish his education," Phoebe whispers. I look around, hoping no one's heard, when Phoebe squeezes close to John.

"You killed her," she hisses. "Murderer."

Horrified, I look away.

Despite the fact that John may or may not have killed Ramona Romanovsky, he got an A from Dr. Zucker. Phoebe got a C −. Even though years later she became very heavy and went to bed with my future husband, Narcissa got an A. As I was on a diet, my grade rose from a C to a B +. I became so thin that, if Dr. Zucker hadn't bowed to a higher authority and died, the next year I'm sure I would have gotten an A.

The Orgy at Group Therapy

Lou entered the room at a run, skidding to the chrome and leatherette seat he'd occupied for the past three years. He had a fear of his seat being already occupied, but at the same time he sort of looked forward to it because he might then be forced to make a change. So far he had nothing to fear. All of the members of Miss Corporal's afternoon therapy group always took the same seats.

Lou slouched into the familiar chair in the usual way, his backside at the edge of the seat, his head resting on the thin edge of leatherette backrest spanning the top between two even bars of chrome. He could feel, despite the air-conditioning and its comforting hum, a trickle of sweat on each side of his head dripping down from under his bangs and a small heavy mustache of dew.

Wendy was seated demurely on the chrome and off-white upholstered couch opposite him, knitting. Her cool demeanor and false indifference aggravated him until his skin itched. Suddenly he found himself propelled out of his chair into the larger, real leather and chrome swivel highbacked seat of the therapist, Miss Corporal.

Wendy was shocked out of her usual catatonia for one eighth of a second, but not enough to say anything or even drop a stitch.

Bobby, splotched with eczema, sat on the cough at the opposite end from Wendy. One leg, crossed over the other, went up and down rapidly, as his tongue washed from one side of his lips to the other. Bobby's leg moving up and down reminded Lou of a water pump. He wanted to ask when the water was going to come out of Bobby's mouth but didn't have the nerve. An atmosphere of protectiveness surrounded Bobby. Everyone in the group was powerless to say anything nasty to him.

Suddenly the door opened and framed in the doorway, nearly touching the lintel, stood the statuesque and disdainful Miss Corporal. Throwing her long black hair back over her shoulder with an exotic movement of her head, she strode through the deep carpet like a panther, her high black patent-leather boots making not the least sound. Still, everyone's eyes were on her six-foot frame. Her long bare arms swung loosely from broad shoulders, the wide shiny metal bracelet on each wrist glinting sequentially.

Lou's eyes went to her breasts. He often tried to see whether or not she wore a bra. If she did, it was one of those soft natural kinds, because her breasts drooped slightly, although they were a beautiful size, neither too small nor too large. Lou willed himself to consider the droop an imperfection, but it remained, instead, intriguing as were her two wide, austere silver or steel bracelets, which emphasized the sinewy tendons and strength of her forearms and yet were so feminine. Lou pictured them as handcuffs or slave bracelets. He could almost see chains depending from them and could imagine her manacled to the wall by those wrists, hands flopping helplessly, long fingers describing powerless arcs, incomprehensible psychoanalytic sign language, white wrists facing outward emphasizing vulnerable elbows on a body which can only writhe like a snake.

This fantasy was in contrast to the real Miss Corporal, who, although incredibly beautiful and apparently powerful and self-sufficient, was cold and distant. Never once in all the years that Lou had to force himself to be vulnerable and exposed to her and the group had she reciprocated. Never once had she transgressed the barrier of therapist-patient, never once revealed a vulnerable, human Miss Corporal. Lou didn't even know her first name. This enraged him. He felt there was something wrong with this one-sided relationship, and the fact of her being a woman made it all the more difficult for him to be in a position of one-sided vulnerability to her. What's worse, she reminded him of Wonder Woman.

The only time the group showed any communal spirit was when Marty was there and did some detective work on Miss Corporal, but such was her immutable and unapproachable mystery that the information didn't serve the purpose of humanizing her. Though they passed it around secretly, with giggles, its veracity had to be doubted. She might have come from a different planet. Did she fuck? One had to doubt it. While Lou was a steady victim of sexual fantasies about Miss Corporal, picturing her with a real man was impossible. No one could fit the image.

"Lou," said Miss Corporal, stopping midway, but not awkwardly, "you've taken my seat." Her tone was patronizing and surprised, pleased, thought Lou, at the diversion from the usual routinization and habituation of the group. Miss Corporal, now engaged in resting her shapely ass on Lou's smaller chair, was completely unthreatened, certain of her own position as therapist.

"Do you want to play therapist today?"

"No," said Lou, breathlessly. "I just feel like taking a different chair."

"Oh," said Miss Corporal, smiling maddeningly. "Why are you panting like that, Lou? Is something making you anxious?"

"No, Miss Corporal," said Lou, panting. "It's because I had to rush so to get here. I realize that it's demeaning of me to put myself in a position where I have seven and one half minutes to rush here to the Village from my job on the Upper East Side, while all these other crazy, incompetent, unable-to-work welfare recipients sit here coolly. Especially you, Miss Corporal, wouldn't allow yourself to be in such a position," he continued as he observed her sitting in his chair, one neatly stockinged knee totally wrinkleless over the other trim knee, nylon gleaming gently in the perfect indirect lighting, the pressure of the nylon creating one white spot in a concavity of her magnificent kneecap, the only indication they were stockings, so well did they fit. The spike heel of her other boot was sunk incisively four inches into the white carpet. Suddenly he realized that he'd hoped that, sitting in his seat, she'd be transformed into him, slouching, sweating, despite his suit and tie, the only person in the group dressed that way. He'd also hoped that her swivel chair would transform him, which it did for a moment, but in his relationship with Miss Corporal he remained the same. Whether he was or not, he felt himself sweating and slouching even in her chair. How different from himself in his office, he thought.

"How do you feel about that, Lou?" asked Miss Corporal.

"I wonder why," he shouted, "I come here to this group of sickies. The reason all of you can come here in the middle of the afternoon is because all of you sickies freeload on welfare while I'm the only one who works."

Bobby's eczema was outlined carefully as his face flushed. "You're just jealous," he said.

"That's not fair," said Darby. "I'm not on welfare. I'm going back to school. And Bobby is a writer."

"You're going back to school because you hate working," said Lou. "You had a great job as a legal secretary. I don't like my job either, but I realize that I have to work. And how come you're so protective of Bobby? How come everyone protects Bobby?" whined Lou plaintively.

"Let's get off this nonsense. It's all avoidance. I want to tell what happened to me this weekend," said Bobby softly.

"He appears weak," said Lou, "but no one notices that he talks away every session. And he's boring, too. It's about time someone said so."

"You're more boring than Bobby, with your hostility, anger and narrow-mindedness," said Darby.

"Why not let Bobbsie defend himself?" asked Lou.

"Let me tell you what John Hawkes said about my work at the CCNY writer's conference this weekend," said Bobby.

Suddenly Lou became infuriated with Wendy, who said nothing

but just continued knitting, silently, imperturbably, week after week. No one had had the courage thus far to try to force her to speak. Lou, who'd never felt angry at her before, burst out, "What do you think this is, art therapy? If Wendy is catatonic maybe she should be committed to a hospital. Her knitting is getting longer and longer," he said, looking at the brown scarf that now twisted down her lap like a stream, reaching to the floor then winding about her legs which were heavy and short. Her lovely straight long hair entwined with the needles, which seemed to move automatically, eating up the wool hidden in a soft bag on the floor. It was impossible to imagine Wendy outside Miss Corporal's room leading a normal life.

"What's that dreck she's knitting anyway?" asked Lou, looking at Miss Corporal.

"Speak to Wendy, Lou," said Miss Corporal.

"What's that dreck you're knitting anyway, Wendy?" asked Lou. "It looks like shit's creek in varying degrees of wind," he said, referring to variations in the stiches, "and pretty soon we'll all be in it without a paddle." Nervous laughter from Bobby. Wendy arose and packed up her knitting bag as the group watched silently. Her short skirt bobbing around her heavy knees, she exited with determination, slamming the door, the sound echoing in the subsequent silence of the room.

"How do you feel about that?" asked Miss Corporal after five more minutes of embarrassed silence.

"I feel—" said Bobby.

"Good," said Lou. "Good for her. She never contributed anyway. She heard about us for years and never said a word. It's not fair."

"Lou, don't interrupt Bobby," said Darby and Miss Corporal in unison.

"Let him keep talking above my voice if he doesn't want to be interrupted," said Lou.

After giving Lou a funny look, Miss Corporal bestowed her glance on Bobby, who continued softly: "I feel embarrassed for

Wendy because she made a spectacle of herself and everyone was watching her. I feel that she herself must have been very embarrassed. But I don't really want to discuss Wendy. I want to talk about—"

"What about you, Darby?"

"I don't knowwww," drawled Darby slowly, stalling. "I guess I feel bad because Lou was so mean to her about her problem of not speaking and maybe she really can't talk. I mean maybe it terrifies her. That's why I was afraid to ask her. I always imagined how terrified I'd be if I were Wendy and someone made me try to talk."

Miss Corporal nodded thoughtfully, looking at Lou.

"Lou," she said, "do you think the anger you felt and directed toward Wendy was really meant for *me?*"

"I didn't know you were so vain, Miss Corporal," Lou attempted to joke. But he stopped to think about that. It threw him, so far-out did it seem. "No," he continued, as Miss Corporal persisted in staring unsmiling at him. "I felt it for Wendy. It was directed toward Wendy—what could it have to do with you, Miss Corporal?" asked Lou. "Actually," he said, before she could answer, "I envied the way Wendy was able to walk out on everyone and just slam the door. I wish I could do that. It could be weakness and avoidance on her part, but I see it as courageous. I'd love to be able to do that instead of being so polite."

"You're polite?" asked Darby.

"Lou," insisted Miss Corporal, "aren't you angry with me for the very thing you shouted at Wendy?"

"What did I shout at Wendy? I don't remember."

"Something about hearing us week after week and never contributing anything," said Bobby, fidgeting as if he were tattling on Lou.

"What? I don't recall saying that." Lou began to blush. "How about going out with me some night, Miss Corporal?" he asked.

"Why did you ask me out?" asked Miss Corporal.

"Why do you ask why to everything?" asked Lou. "I was simply overcome by an uncontrollable desire to ask you out. Why not go out with me, Miss Corporal? I like you. I think you're attractive."

"I'm sorry, Lou, I never go out with my patients."

"Because you think I'm crazy, but I'm not crazy, Miss Corporal, I'm not crazy. I only feel crazy when I'm in this room with all these other loonies and with you, Miss Corporal, and I can't imagine why."

"I think Lou is trying to take you out of the role of therapist so he doesn't have to continue therapy, which is difficult," said Darby.

"I agree. Now I want to talk about what John Gardner and John Barth both said to me at the CCNY writers' conference," Bobby said.

"I don't want to hear it," said Lou. "I agree with your wife that you should get a job."

"Bobby's a writer," said Darby. "Why should he destroy his chance to write by succumbing to his bourgeois wife's cheap moral work ethic?" She put her arm around the shrinking Bobby.

"Why did you put your arm around Bobby?" asked Miss Corporal.

"For the same reason I asked you out, Miss Corporal," said Lou. "She wants to fuck him. And I want to fuck you! I want you to go out with me, Miss Corporal, and I want to fuck you."

"Can you tell me what your fantasy is?" asked Miss Corporal.

Lou looked at Miss Corporal and shifted in his seat. He licked his lips. He was silent for a moment, beginning a movie in his mind. He stared at Miss Corporal but was absorbed in a fantasy when suddenly she appeared startled.

"I see your fantasies in your eyeglasses," said Miss Corporal.

Lou noticed behind her he could see, through the sliding glass doors to the terrace, someone rising, then deftly swinging over the terrace wall.

*

They all watched silently as if it were a dream, a feeling accentuated by the glass separating them along with its glacial distortion, until the terrace door was slid open with a bang. Framed in the doorway, even larger than Miss Corporal, was an enormous man, his outfit of tights and boots accentuating his muscularity, wearing a frightening ski mask over his face. The group was speechless with terror, yet there was an underriding feeling that Miss Corporal could protect them.

"That door is made of glass," Miss Corporal said to the intruder. Drawing herself up to her full height, she took a few steps toward him.

"How did you get up here?" she coolly demanded. "This is the thirty-third floor of a modern high-security building." Lou was tempted to laugh. He'd always thought her reliance on modernity and neat, straight lines a false security. Triumphantly and arrogantly, the intruder proceeded to remove his ski mask as if such disguise were superfluous when his superior physique was apparent. He threw it casually onto the chair Miss Corporal had vacated.

"Pick that up," she said. "I don't like my apartment cluttered. You didn't answer me. How did you get in here?" Silence. "Why don't you answer me?" Miss Corporal was adamant but cool.

"I'm not obliged to," said the man, who, Lou could see now, was an impostor in a Batman costume.

Boy is he together, thought Lou. He is the perfect, the dream partner for Miss Corporal, he thought with pleasure.

Miss Corporal did not appear imbued with similar emotion. She still persisted in expressing a cold hostility. The bogus Batman glanced out onto the terrace, and following his gaze, the group saw a heavy rope stuck into the flagstone with a pick, another head beginning to emerge over the ledge.

"About time," said "Batman." "You forgot to retrieve the rope. What if someone else also decided to climb up?"

"I sincerely doubt that anyone would," said Miss Corporal. "You project your own neurotic desires on everyone else, a classic symptom of paranoid schizophrenia." She hoped they'd leave the rope so that the security guard might see it.

"You told us you never diagnose mental illness in the group," said Bobby.

"Shut up," said "Batman."

"You climbed up so fast," complained his companion wearing

a Robin costume, "it was difficult to follow you. I just learned how to climb, and it's hard to get a foothold on these goddamn clean-line Bauhaus bricks."

"You and 'Robin' have a very sick relationship," said Miss Corporal. "I did a paper in graduate school called 'Batman and Robin: A Psychotic, Symbiotic, Suppressed Homosexual Relationship,' based on Karen Horney's ideas of masochistically dependent relationships, using you and Robin as examples of the sickness inherent in the following relationships: master and slave, professor and student, and sadist and masochist."

Lou was jealous. Never once before had Miss Corporal ever revealed that she had attended college, and here she was telling this "Batman" one moment after they met. Miss Corporal tried to get Lou's attention with a hypnotic glare. Once obtained, she attempted to indicate something with a special movement of her eyebrows. Lou wanted to understand what she wanted more than anything, but he couldn't figure out what it was. Each time she attempted, he had to shrug his shoulders. He was never good at charades and was becoming more and more nervous. Finally Darby, also watching, and good at charades, nodded. "Batman" looked at "Robin," who shrugged.

"What are you doing?" he asked. His voice was deep and pleasantly resonant.

"We're playing charades," answered Miss Corporal. Darby, while they were thus engaged, inconspicuously lifted the telephone receiver. Lou, sitting in Miss Corporal's seat near her desk, thought, oh, that's what she wanted and I couldn't do it.

"Let me do it, Darby," he whispered.

"'Robin,' would you please go over there and cut that telephone wire?"

"I can't bear that sick relationship," said Miss Corporal.

"Why? I said 'please,'" said "Batman," puzzled.

"Can't I just tell what John Updike and John Fowles said to me at the CCNY writers' conference very quickly?" asked Bobby.

"How come all those writers are named John?" asked Darby.

"I want everyone to undress," ordered "Batman."

"What?" shouted Miss Corporal. "Are you going to rape us?"

"No," said "Batman," "we're going to have an orgy. We're going to have a good time."

"When healthy people do something against their will, it's not called a good time, it's called rape."

"Well I don't want to quibble over semantics," said the would-be Batman. "To each his own. I call it an orgy, you call it rape."

Miss Corporal was beginning to fume. Lou was so interested in watching her interact that he was almost enjoying this intrusion. Everyone was waiting for Miss Corporal to save them.

"I refuse," she said. "You get out of here. We're not going to be your victims. There are more of us than you, so if you don't want to get hurt, leave right now!" Miss Corporal was angry but still fairly calm. "Batman" stood there, arms folded and smiling smugly.

"I know you wish me to become enraged and lose control, but I refuse to allow myself to be hooked," said Miss Corporal, who had regained a measure of calm. "Please, both of you leave immediately. 'Robin,' please," she pleaded, trying to see whether he was less immovable than "Batman."

"I'm sorry," he said in an effeminate voice, "I'm 'Batman's' partner."

"Are you sure you're not his slave?" asked Miss Corporal. "Why are you so passive? Why do you relinquish responsibility for your own actions?"

"What about this group?" asked "Robin." "How come they just sit there? You said you won't be victims, but they all look like victims to me."

"I hope they don't mind my answering for them, but they're all essentially passive," said Miss Corporal. "Why do you think they're all in therapy?"

"I don't know about an orgy with a majority of passive partners," mused "Batman," curling his lip in distaste.

"I think we should do this another time," said Miss Corporal, "when all the group members are present. Right now men outnumber women four to two."

"If you want to count Bobby as a man," said Lou.

"Everyone get undressed," "Batman" ordered again. Bruce and Lou looked at Miss Corporal to see what they should do. Darby, they noticed, was already undressed, gently moving her body, her hands under her large breasts as if presenting them.

"You know my problem resisting sexual advances," she explained.

"I said, get undressed," reiterated "Batman" calmly." Miss Corporal, noticing that "Robin" was pointing a gun at her, told the rest of the group to undress.

Lou was undressing and looking at the gun. He felt detached from what he was doing as if he were someone else or it were a movie he was watching.

Bobby attempted to pull off his shirt but began to shake and weep, dandruff flying out of his wispy hair. "I can't get undressed in front of everyone. I never could get undressed in front of people. Only my wife, and that took six years."

"Well, it's never too late to change," said "Batman." Darby, naked and voluptuous, went over to Bobby to comfort him and help him undress.

"Darby, why do you always protect Bobby?" asked Lou, already naked, squat and hairy.

"Lou," said Miss Corporal, "do you want Darby to help you get undressed?"

"Of course not," said Lou, "I am perfectly capable of undressing myself."

"Then don't get upset when Darby helps Bobby."

"I'm sure he's only pretending," said Lou.

"He's not," said Darby, pulling off Bobby's shirt as he held up his arms like a baby, his face red and wet with tears.

"I'm jealous that someone weak should get all the attention. Yes, I do want Darby to help me," said Lou. "I want you to help me too."

"Good," said Miss Corporal. "Isn't it better to ask for what you want instead of always putting people down?"

Miss Corporal, half undressed, went over to help Lou, then smiled. He was already undressed. "You do very well by yourself," she said to Lou, who hadn't realized he was already undressed.

"My shoes and socks, Miss Corporal."

"Do you want to try to take them off by yourself?"

"I can't," he whined, "I can't. It took me six years to learn how, and I can only do it in private."

Miss Corporal smiled wryly and patiently bent down. "Sit down," she said to Lou, who felt like an infant having his shoes and socks removed for him and had an uncontrollable urge to suck his thumb. He was embarrassed as his prick became hard and began to furrow on its own into Miss Corporal's black hair.

"Batman" was holding the gun so that "Robin" could undress.

"MAZASH," said "Robin," holding up his arms. Undressed, it was apparent that Robin was really a woman, small, childlike and lovely.

"Now it must be apparent that we are three and three," said "Batman."

"Who is that anyway?" asked Miss Corporal.

"A lady dressed as Mary Marvel," said "Batman." "Maybe now you won't think our relationship is so sick."

Miss Corporal seemed uneasy. "Is there really a 'Robin' or is 'Robin' always 'Mary Marvel' in disguise?"

"Truth, truth, what is the truth?" chanted "Batman." "Nothing is really the way we think it is. Truth is subjective."

"That's what I always said," said Bobby triumphantly, allowing Darby finally to open his fly. "That's why it's useless for us to be here."

"There's still a level of reality we can all communicate upon," said Miss Corporal with dignity.

Bobby was lying on the carpet trying to hold his pants on by keeping his legs crossed, but Darby, strong, was winning.

"Come on, Bobby, please," she pleaded. Bobby's whole body was blushing. Miss Corporal was finishing getting undressed as everyone watched, including Bobby, with his thin arms and triangle of hair on his chest like a goat's beard.

"Put the gun down," she said to "Batman" as she undressed,

coolly dignified, just as Lou would expect. She looked even larger naked—monumental. Her legs were long and shapely, her buttocks round. Her skin almost glowed, it was so white in contrast with her black hair. Lou felt that her nipples were very motherly.

"Very nice," said "Batman" appreciatively.

"Aren't you going to get undressed?" asked Darby.

"Of course," said "Batman," "I just wanted to be last so I can watch everyone else."

"A power trip," murmured Miss Corporal.

"For that you'll be punished," smiled the bogus Batman, pulling off his boots. "But truthfully, power is the greatest." Now everyone watched "Batman" undress. Lou unconsciously covered his own genitals as he watched "Batman's" enormous and muscular body emerge from his tight-fitting clothing easily, slowly, with poise. His prick, though not hard, was quite long and his scrotum hung well down between his legs.

"Tie them up," "Batman" ordered "Mary."

"You don't have to tie me up," said Darby. "I'll be good."

"Me too," said Lou.

"Tie me up first, please," pleaded Bobby. "I want to be tied up."

"She's right," said "Mary Marvel" to "Batman." "You pretend I'm your partner but you treat me like a slave."

"I'll discuss that with you later," hissed "Batman." "Let's have some music. What kinds of music do you have here?"

"I have all the Baroque composers, Vivaldi, Bach—"

"That tinkle, tinkle, tinkle?" said "Batman" grimacing. "Have you got any Rolling Stones?"

"No, I don't. If you don't like my taste bring your own records next time," said Miss Corporal.

"Boy, how hostile. Now, Mary, I want you to suck these two men off, while the shrink and I and the other woman watch," said "Batman," pointing to Lou and Bobby, both tied to their seats.

"I can do one while she does the other. It will be quicker," offered Darby.

"Good idea," said "Batman." "One, two, three, go."

"Who do you want to do?" asked Darby of "Mary Marvel," who was looking indecisively from Bobby to Lou.

"I'll take this one," she said, pointing to Bobby. "I think he'll come faster."

"Let me take him. I know him better. With you he may never get a hard-on."

"Boy, even now you're fighting over Bobby, when anyone can see how much more virile I am," said Lou.

"I don't see a thing," said Darby, looking from one to the other small, detumescent cock. "I'm tired of virile men," she said. "Besides, I'm not sucking off any redneck."

"Okay," said "Batman," "kneel down and—begin!" He shot off his gun toward the terrace.

The bullet smashed through the glass.

Bobby was startled and started trembling. The rope hurt his wrists. Darby's hands roved around his body comfortingly as her tongue flicked over his prick, which flopped to and fro, passively, like a giant maggot. He looked up and saw "Batman's" and Miss Corporal's eyes riveted on him and Lou. He wanted desperately to perform well but was failing dismally. Every once in a while, at Darby's skillful manipulations, he felt a flicker of pleasure which disappeared the moment he became aware of it. He tried to concentrate on Darby, who was kneeling, her long lovely hair flowing over her shoulders, full, moist lips surrounding his member and directly below, in easy-to-see perspective, her full, womanly breasts, triangle of light brown pubic hair, and thighs full and tight from the pressure of leaning against them, but he couldn't forget the piercing glances of "Batman" and Miss Corporal. He looked over to see how "Mary Marvel" and Lou were doing. Lou had an erection that went down even while Bobby watched, subsequently rising and falling like a bicycle tire with a slow leak. But the childlike, small-breasted and blond "Mary Marvel" turned Bobby on so that without even getting an erection he came into Darby's mouth.

"I came!" shouted Bobby proudly.

"Don't swallow that," "Batman" ordered. "You lie down," he

pointed to Miss Corporal, who did lie down after a small reminder about bullets.

Stretched out on the white rug, Miss Corporal's pale, colossal body appeared monumental as a landscape. There was complete silence as everyone inadvertently admired her aesthetic suitability to her surroundings, her innate physical superiority. Looking at her, Lou thought of the desert, of Monument Valley. When "Batman" told her to raise her arms over her head, Lou felt his prick go hard. Feeling an urge to touch it, but aware of being tied up, his hands constrained, prick pulsing outward, out of control, he was turned on more.

"It's hard, it's hard," he shouted.

"Bend down," "Batman" ordered Darby, "and spit out that guy's cum on her belly." He indicated Miss Corporal.

"Bobby's the name," said Bobby. "Maybe she'd better not." He was fearful of having his sperm on display. Perhaps it would be misjudged.

"Let me just tell you what John Cheever said at the CCNY writers' conference." Lou's prick went soft. Bobby couldn't keep his eyes off "Mary Marvel," who was wearing, he noticed, bobby socks, which turned him on tremendously. He thought of his wife Barbara and felt guilty. The realization that Barbara must have desires for other men like his for "Mary Marvel" disturbed him.

"I'm sorry I couldn't get hard before, 'Mary,'" shouted Lou. "It wasn't that I don't think you're attractive or that you don't suck good, I wanted to please you, it's just that I can never do anything when I'm required to. It's a sort of unconscious spite, even when I don't want it. I hope you're not hurt—"

"Jesus, I warned you about a therapist," said "Mary Marvel."

Darby was kneeling, holding one of her own large breasts and relinquishing a mouthful of sperm all over Miss Corporal's abdomen, then trailing it into her navel and down near her pubic hair.

"Wait, I've never seen Lou become so vulnerable. I've never heard Lou apologize before," said Miss Corporal, rising, "I want to make a note of it." "Batman" shot off his gun again into the glass.

Miss Corporal lay down again, hands raised. Darby didn't need orders but showed a terrific amount of initiative. "Batman's" prick was hard, so hard that despite its great length and girth it defied gravity, pulling up his balls.

"I realize now that I've always wanted to do this," said Darby, licking Miss Corporal's armpits, her palms, making Miss Corporal's fingers turn under, then sucking her breasts, her nipples, until they stuck out like fire hydrants, then tickling her waist with her tongue until Miss Corporal quietly twitched but never laughed. Miss Corporal, following "Batman's" orders, kept her hands above her head and her face absolutely expressionless, as Darby, voluptuous and turned on, slobbered around her skillfully, moaning and touching herself. She spread her own cunt wide. It was a peachy color and shone with moisture like a half-eaten persimmon. Her tongue foraged in Miss Corporal's perfect equilateral triangle of black pubic hair until droplets of dew were visible all over it, like a spiderweb in the rain.

"Spread her legs," ordered "Batman," who was commencing rubbing his own prick with one hand, gently manipulating his balls with his other. "Mary, set that one free." He pointed to Lou with his chin.

"Thank God," said Bobby. "I just want to watch so I can write a story about this for my next CCNY writers' conference." Lou, now free, rubbed the rope bruises on his wrists and, crawling along the floor, climbed over Darby, who had spread Miss Corporal's legs and was sucking her cunt, lifted Darby's ass, and inserted his prick. "Batman," ruddier and ruddier, was caressing his own prick with more involvement. He drew "Mary Marvel" to him with one hand and tongue-kissed her as she stood on the arch of his bare foot in order to be able to reach his lips. Bobby, observing her long neck curving upward and glimpses of her wet tongue, shiny as a pink slug, visible every now and then between her and "Batman's" lips, was both jealous and excited.

"Batman," noticing Bobby's priapism, said, "Would you like to fuck this woman, my sweet little sister?"

"Your sister?"

"Yes. I'm really 'Captain Marvel.'" Bobby's sparse eyebrows, mixed with eczema flakes, rose. Incest, he thought. These superheroes seemed to be interchangeable. They were all the same person in different costumes. Bobby had suspected that about reality all along. He looked over at the configuration on the carpet, but no one else was listening.

"Don't untie me," he said. "My wife would be upset. We don't have an open marriage."

"Okay," said "Batman." "'Mary,' carry his chair over here and turn it so he's on his knees." "Mary" placed Bobby with the chair still tied on his back so that he looked like a kneeling turtle. She straddled him, her ass propped on his thighs, legs sticking out beyond the chair behind him, bobby-sock-clad toes pointed, head back and curls swiping the carpet, but Bobby no longer had a hard-on. "Mary" rubbed the length of her cunt along his soft prick again and again crying, "Yip, yip, yip."

"I'm sorry," said Bobby. "I feel like a failure. But I can prove to you I'm not if you let me tell you about the CCNY writers' conference. In fact, I may win a $3,000 prize."

"Wonderful," praised Miss Corporal from the floor. Darby removed her mouth from Miss Corporal's cunt in order to praise Bobby.

Lou, panting, pushing his prick in and out of Darby's wriggling behind, said, "At least you could praise me. Do you like the way I'm fucking you? Tell me, tell me," he groaned. "Tell me how you like it."

"I like, I like it," moaned Darby. "It's so good, do it more, that's it, harder, oh, harder, deep—oh, it's so sweet, more, more, move it like that, I'm wiggling my hips, ohh, my cunt is so wet for you, do it, do it, do it—"

"Not so fast. I'm trying to remember this dialogue," said Bobby.

"Jabber, jabber, jabber," said "Mary Marvel."

"Ohhhhhhh," moaned Lou, "I'm going to come—"

"Oh, no," screamed Darby, "more, more, wait, please wait—" Miss Corporal was silent and relaxed as they both fell screaming between her legs.

"UHH, huhhhhh," could be heard, a deep rhythmic moan from deep within "Batman's" cavernous chest as he rubbed himself harder and faster, belly protruding, as with another coarse groan he shot his jism across half the room, all over Miss Corporal, the first jet landing on her pubic hair and partly on Darby's, the next on her abdomen, string-like, the next across her breasts and the last drops across her blood-red, sharply etched, bowed Wonderwoman-like lips. She licked it calmly with her tongue.

"Can we get up now?" she asked, her torso propped on her elbows.

"We're nowhere near finished," said "Batman."

"But you came," said Miss Corporal.

"I see you have no experience with Superheroes," said "Batman."

"I suppose that prize will encourage you to continue on welfare and not get a job," said Lou, standing over Bobby, who was still on his knees tied to the chair.

"Lou, could you please change the position of this chair?" asked Bobby.

"Since when do I pay taxes to subsidize the arts," murmured Lou angrily, placing Bobby on his back, the back of the chair underneath him, his knees up along the seat.

"That's fine," said Bobby, "thanks."

"I want Lou to fuck Miss Corporal," called "Batman."

"What do you want me to do?" asked Darby. "I'm capable of multiple orgasms," she said.

"Oh," said "Mary Marvel," "I'm not sure whether I can or not." Lou did not move.

"Come on, Lou," urged "Batman." "Isn't that what you've always wished?" Lou could not move.

"Turn the other direction," said "Batman" to Miss Corporal. "I'm tired of seeing you in the same position—north/south. Why don't you turn east/west now. Can you try to be more responsive?"

"Responsive to being raped?" asked Miss Corporal. "Batman" answered by shooting off his revolver into the couch. The foam rubber sizzled slightly around the brown-edged hole.

"C'mon—uhh—"

"Lou," said Lou.

"Lou, would you move my chair again please? I want to watch," said Bobby. "Batman" looked at Bobby and shot his gun again.

"Oh, not my Walter Gropius chair," cried Miss Corporal, showing emotion for the first time.

"Spread your legs," "Batman" ordered Miss Corporal. She reluctantly spread apart her long white thighs. Her legs were so long that her toes were foraging among the chairs and hassocks. Lou, holding his genitals, climbed in between them and sat there as if in a boat. He wished he had his blanket with him.

"Get hard," ordered "Batman." Lou looked at "Batman" incredulously.

"I can't get hard when you tell me."

"Batman" shot his gun again.

"Pretend you're not asking me for a few moments," said Lou, "then I think I can do it."

"Miss Corporal will help you," said "Batman." "Miss Corporal, if he doesn't get a hard-on I'm going to shoot him."

Miss Corporal sat up. She looked at Lou and lifted his chin until he looked at her. Softly, she said, holding out one breast to him, "I'm going to make you feel so good, Lou." She began to caress his prick, guiding his hand along her thigh and into the hair of her pussy. Lou could actually feel Miss Corporal's clitoris! She caressed his prick rhythmically now, and his lips wrapped themselves around one breast. It felt like a dream, but he could tell without looking that his prick wasn't hard yet. He hoped he wouldn't have an anxiety attack.

"Is he really Captain Marvel?" Bobby asked "Mary Marvel," who had obligingly moved his chair so that he could watch. She lay down next to him and began to touch his prick, then placed his hand on her cunt.

"Let's jerk each other off," she whispered. Bobby wondered whether that constituted infidelity.

Lou was lying on the floor. Miss Corporal tied his wrists together and ordered him not to move. She began to rub oil all over his body. Every time he moved uncontrollably, she gently and firmly held his hips. He was ecstatic, able to forget everyone in the room. Soon, soon, lushly, her fingers would be wrapped around his prick. He trembled in anticipation as her practiced fingers rubbed his buttocks until he could feel shivers in his chest. He could feel his prick like a flagpole, the sensation in it so strong, as if it were enormous, hot, and spreading out all over the room. He began to feel as if his whole body were a prick.

"I'm a prick, I'm a prick," he panted as Miss Corporal's oily finger edged into his anus. The ecstasy was so great he moaned. It felt as if her finger went straight up his ass and into his now enormous prick.

"Oh, Miss Corporal," he gasped, "this is like all my fantasies." He felt so close to her.

Bobby's and "Mary Marvel's" hands were moving faster and faster on each other, and both made grunting sounds. Darby was crawling around underneath "Batman's" huge, hard prick, which he had resumed fondling, waiting for a moment when she could get her lips around it.

"Please, please, I want to suck you," she moaned. "It's beautiful, beautiful. I never saw such a prick. It's so powerful and magnificent. It reminds me somehow of a Samurai. Please let me suck it, please let me suck it—"

"Anything to make you shut up," said "Batman." Just as Darby's luscious lips were about to encompass the enormous purple head of "Batman's" prick, he changed his mind.

"Never mind," he said, "help her." He pointed his black-haired head at Miss Corporal, who was deftly working around Lou, who, despite the fact that he was in ecstasy, was completely mistaken about his having an erection. His prick still flopped around, now between Miss Corporal's long red-nailed fingers. Looking, he couldn't believe it. He'd had the sensation of hardness as surely as an amputee feels a missing limb.

"If he doesn't get an erection soon, Miss Corporal, I'm going to shoot him," said "Batman."

"Why shoot him when it's my fault?"

"Who's to say whose fault?" mused "Batman." "Why kill a

criminal when his crime is the fault of society?"

Darby was squatted over Lou's face, and his tongue flicked in and out of her vagina while Miss Corporal sat over Lou's upper thighs, attempting to urge his penis into her vagina with her hand.

"I'm sorry," said Lou, "I could have told you, my prick has a mind of its own. No matter what you do, if it doesn't want to, it won't get hard. It has nothing to do with whether I want to or not. And I might as well tell you now, it's a spiteful prick!"

"Batman" was both turned on and disgusted. "Move away," he said, pushing Lou and Darby over. "Here." He handed the gun to "Mary Marvel."

"One minute," said "Mary," rubbing Bobby's prick as hard and fast as possible.

"Uhhhhh, uhhhhh, ooooooff—" said Bobby on the verge of orgasm. "OooooooooOOOOOFFFFFFF!" he exploded, his own hand limp and forgotten on "Mary's" cunt like a slice of lox over a bagel.

"Oh, my wrist," said "Mary," shaking it. She sat up.

"I'm sorry you didn't come," said Bobby, "I'm not good at concentrating on two things at once."

"Batman" threw his gun at her, and she lay down again, rubbing the muzzle slowly along her vagina. "Batman," flushed and priapic, all his muscular body glowing with perspiration, pushed Miss Corporal to the floor. He needed no gun now to overpower her resisting body. Her flailing hands and beating arms were soon wrapped around him, his long hard body extended over hers, his prick quivering at the mouth of her vagina.

"I want you to beg me," he said.

"No, no!" said Miss Corporal, "please, please, oh please." He put it in slowly while Miss Corporal moaned and moaned, moving her head to and fro, black hair sweeping back and forth along the carpet. Everyone was watching. Her hips rose up to gather more of his prick into her.

"Beg more," said "Batman." "Tell me you're my cunt."

"I'm your cunt, please, please put it in," said Miss Corporal, kneading his ass.

"UUhh," he groaned, pushing it into Miss Corporal to the hilt.

She screamed, saliva running out the side of her bow lips. "That's it, cunt, move it," groaned "Batman," as she swiveled her hips faster and wilder. "Batman" was moaning and deeply gasping, Miss Corporal whining long high whines.

Darby had untied Bobby and Lou and they were watching, passing back and forth a dish of smoked oysters she'd found in the kitchen.

"You really show initiative," said Bobby. "But now I'm thirsty."

"It's your turn," whispered Darby to Lou. "I don't want to miss any more."

Miss Corporal was moving faster than could be believed and moaning loudly, "Batman" becoming stiffer, more tense, moving less and less, gasping. Miss Corporal trembled and screamed, "OOHH GOD—OH NOO,NO,NO,NO,NO,N@##!!!" "Batman's" face was contorted, his eyes squinting. He took a deep breath. Miss Corporal relaxed under him.

"Did you come?" she asked.

"No, I held off," he said. "I'm going to make you come again and again."

Lou was looking in the refrigerator. Uncertain whether he should, but infected with the spirit of Dionysus, he extracted a six pack of beer and brought it into the living room. Now "Batman" was lying on his back and Miss Corporal was sucking his prick. She moved over so that her vagina was over his face.

"Do you want to feel my tongue?" he whispered.

"Uhhhhgggggghh, huuggggh," said Miss Corporal, "Batman's" enormous rod skillfully encompassed in her throat. Miss Corporal stopped and sat on his prick, moving up and down on it slowly, then round and round. "Batman" put his large hands on her waist and pressed her up and down on himself like a doll. They were both moaning incredibly as the group finished up the refreshments. "Batman" came finally with the sound of the Fontana di Trevi, which then evolved into a classic eruption of Mt. Etna, Miss Corporal screaming and nearly fainting over him. They both lay limp and intertwined, their bodies covered with perspiration, three drops of which ran slowly down Miss Corporal's torso, dripped along "Batman's" chest, paused and spilled onto the rug.

"We must go now," said "Batman." "Mary, get dressed." "Mary" said "Shazam," and was suddenly dressed like Robin again, except for his boots, which lay limp at his bare feet. "Oh, shit," he said, passing Bobby the bag of potato chips he was holding so he could put on his boots. Miss Corporal gazed at "Batman" as if she wanted very badly to say something and couldn't. He looked at her with a wry smile. Then he grinned winningly, winked, and followed "Robin" out onto the terrace. They all watched as both of them disappeared over the ledge.

"Everyone get dressed," said Miss Corporal to her group, which sat in mesmerized silence. "I hope none of you was too upset. We'll talk about it next week."

"Miss Corporal," said Lou, walking over to her, half dressed. Miss Corporal just lay there naked, her hands under her head, the silver of her bracelets glinting between strands of black disheveled hair, her ankles crossed.

"Lou," she said, looking at her clock, "time was up a long time ago. We'll continue next week." Darby and Bobby were already at the door, waving goodbye. Lou purposely took a long time tying his shoes and locating his tie. He felt a strong connection to Miss Corporal and didn't want to leave without expressing it.

"Lou," said Miss Corporal again, pointing to her clock.

Lou left. Waiting for the elevator, he had the strange feeling that perhaps nothing had happened, a detachment made stronger by the elevator causing his ears to clog. Passing the desk, he noticed the doorman and security guard both sitting there, relaxed, feet up on the desk. A weird sound emanated from the intercom. He soon realized that it was the sound of someone weeping and, strange as it sounded, that it must be Miss Corporal. She'd probably stuck something in the intercom button long ago to keep it open and alert the guard.

"Why didn't you come upstairs and save us from being raped?" Lou asked them angrily.

"Rape," said the doorman, "that wasn't rape. You guys were having the time of your lives."

"Some therapy group," said the guard. "I'd like to join that kind of therapy."

Lou listened, embarrassed, to Miss Corporal's long, dry animal-like sobs and left quickly, so he wouldn't hear them.

Letter to *Lifestyle*

Dear *Lifestyle* Magazine,

Arnold is squeezing my left breast, rhythmically as if he were softening an orange. He's attempting to press lips, from which the greasy and garlicky odor of green fettucine still emanates, to mine. I feel as if I will die if those lips ever press down on mine, I'll smother. First nausea, then death, where somewhere in the stratosphere above, the taste of green fettucine will combine with that of veal Marsala.

"How can anyone eat green fettucine?" I ask desperately, against my own better judgment, just before his lips can touch mine. I shrug his hand off my breast.

"Just because you don't like green fettucine, can't you be tolerant of other people's likes and dislikes?"

I know he's right, but I can't control myself. "All that pasta is no good for you," I continue, anger that I'm powerless to stop boiling up. I suspect it has little to do with the green fettucine. I wonder whether I could be jealous of him because he makes nine or ten times as much money as I do. He attempts to press his lips over mine again. He'd like to ignore my verbal indiscretion because he's horny and wants to fuck me. He's about to insert his slender, fastidious prick into me when I shout, "How could you buy a new house without bringing your children and letting them help you choose it?"

His body relaxes where it is and he becomes still for a moment. "I think you don't want to fuck me, Rhonda," he says with great dignity, in a low voice.

I remain silent. Perhaps we should get married immediately, I think, because it looks as if we're going to break up soon. But I can't imagine living in New Brunswick, New Jersey. And he'd mentioned getting rid of his housekeeper if he ever remarried. How could he imagine anyone would want to marry him and take care of his three children? But someone would. As soon as I leave, there will be a long line of lovely women with MAs and PhDs who would marry Arnold and take care of three kids. He's tentatively resumed inserting his prick, taking advantage of the silence. Did he consult me when he gave up his duplex on East 62nd Street and bought an ugly house in New Brunswick? My body is immobile under his frantic pumping. I'm frozen. This is the first time I haven't responded, and he hates defeat.

"Rhonda—" he moans. "I love you." After eight months of going out together, he says he loves me just as I begin to feel revulsion. That's why. But I feel embarrassed not to respond.

"That's it—that's it!" he shouts as I begin to move under him. "Good, good!, you're with me!!!" he screams in triumph.

All of a sudden I'm filled with the deepest regret that, in an access of abandon, I have allowed myself to get white paint on my favorite kelly green corduroy slacks helping Arnold paint his new parlor. I regret the same feeling that inspired me to buy him that beautiful expensive hanging planter for Christmas.

He is sitting on the toilet, head tilted in concentration. The sight of him sitting there, naked and vulnerable, is repulsive to me. At one time I felt good about the intimacy that allowed him to forget to shut the bathroom door when he was shitting, but now I feel it is sheer insensitivity. I can hear every sound. When he's finished, he walks over to the closet naked and extracts a box, which he hands me, an expectant and self-satisfied expression on his face as if he's sure I'll like it. I find myself worried that I won't. He watches me unwrap it. I hold up a stiff muslin Mexican tunic in an unusual style; it seems to have an apron attached to it.

"It's beautiful," I lie, unable to shatter his self-satisfied expression.

"I knew you'd like it," he says. "I was passing a store when I saw a fantastic dress in the window, covered with beautiful embroidery."

"This dress has no embroidery."

"I know. When the salesgirl was wrapping it, I saw this one. I asked her how much it was and it was even cheaper so I took it. I got a pretty dress and a bargain too!"

Arnold is elated, but I feel degraded by that story and thumb through some magazines on the night table to hide my tears. When the blurriness clears I can see the magazine is full of photos of naked women and letters from readers. I read:

Dear *Sexual Liberation* Magazine,

Sexual Liberation is for the people who want to freak out with subjects within their reach. I'm not saying there aren't any fantasies involved, but they are based on natural, fun-loving sex. One way of putting it is—if I could make it with Mother Nature, I guarantee you she would have this magazine in her snatch. Eddie M., Bronx, New York.

"What are these stupid magazines?" I ask. "I didn't know you read these."

"I don't read them. Those are some of the things we used in our Sexual Study Research Symposium at Rutgers. I sat in on this Intensive Sexuality course for doctors, who often have to give sexual advice to their patients and often know less than the patients do. I knew almost everything already," he says smugly. "One interesting thing I learned is that there are actually three nerves in the anus, about two inches in, which are sensitive to stimulation. I thought people only did it who have ass fetishes, but apparently anal intercourse for both sexes is probably really pleasurable, though I myself don't like it."

"Let's try it," I say, realizing we'd never done it together. In fact I didn't miss it, but I didn't like the idea that we didn't do it because he didn't like it. "You think my asshole is dirty," I whine.

"No I don't." He shakes his head sideways in that dogmatic way he has, which means that no further discussion could sway him from what he knows is right. "I just don't enjoy it."

"Dear *Sexual Liberation*," I say, "My lover doesn't like anal sex. No matter how much I beg him he still won't try it. He is not interested in sexual experimentation. Does that mean he is too rigid for me?"

He laughs genuinely, a mirthful giggle. "If you want to look at these magazines you can take them home," he offers.

*

Two nights later, when I was in bed, I remembered the magazines. I ferreted them from my unpacked overnight bag with relish, as I love to read junk at night before I go to sleep. I propped up the pillows, got comfortable and read:

Dear *Sexual Liberation*,

A few months ago my roommate brought home an issue of *Sexual Liberation* just to see what guys get off on. We read it cover to cover along with the next two issues. We'd like to make this contribution.

The other night my roommate was helping me with my chemistry. She often studies with no top on. Suddenly I could no longer resist those fantastic tits. It surprised her when I first began to manipulate her nipples with my tongue, but her reluctant uneasiness faded as she became extremely hot. Her nipples grew to twice their regularly large size. I was so turned on I could have fucked a doorknob. She came twice before I removed her soaking pants. By the end of the evening I had climaxed twice while Ilene experienced no less than five wild orgasms. Miss T. Clarke, Syracuse, NY

*

Another magazine, dear *Lifestyle,* was called *Lifestyle.* I couldn't stop reading them. At first I thought they were funny and perhaps written by the editors as a joke. Even the joyful and most sexual ones, even the ones seemingly written just to turn people on, seemed imbued with loneliness and insecurity, but I read them voraciously, slightly turned on, searching for ones that would be more and more satisfying, exciting or real. As intimate as the letters were, there was something missing, as in Anaïs Nin's diaries.

I put the magazine aside, closed my eyes and caressed my inner thighs. I was both exhausted and restless. I considered getting up to get something to eat, but was too tired. I lay there feeling some of the pubic hair which had escaped around the elastic edges of my silky underpants, tantalizing tendrils, conjuring the wilder mass restrained by the silk crotch, through the side of which I slipped my hand, flashes of portions of the letters popping into my mind in confusing profusion and I fell into a thick, unsatisfying sleep.

*

While reading manuscripts at work, tantalized by my own visibility as I watched salesmen, secretaries and editors walking around outside my glass cubicle, I suddenly had a desire to try to masturbate secretly, knowing I was completely visible to everyone in the corridor. My face hot and flushed, I continued working. Those letters are really getting to me, I thought, somehow frightened that I might be compelled to perform whatever came into my mind. In fact, I found myself thinking in the form of letters to *Lifestyle.*

"Have you ever seen these before?" asked Mr. Klugman.

He threw three *Lifestyle* magazines on my desk.

"Yes, of course, Mr. Klugman," I said.

"Take a look at the letters," he said. "We've just bought this magazine." His face attempted to portray a sort of humorous and tolerant disgust. "If you want to, you can edit all the letters for this magazine."

"Oh, Mr. Klugman! Thank you!" Despite the fact that this is a promotion from reading manuscripts to editing (of sorts), Mr. Klugman was surprised at my gratitude.

*

"Dear *Lifestyle*," I read, "I greatly enjoyed the recent letter of Miss T.Y. of Minneapolis on oral sex." That's interesting, I thought. People actually communicate indirectly through the magazine by responding to each other's letters. I poured my Spanish rice onto a paper plate and carried it back to the couch, eating and reading at the same time, peering over the dish, my eyeglasses all steamed up:

Dear *Lifestyle*,

I am a stewardess and recently worked an all-night flight between the coasts. While serving the meal, I noticed an attractive man seated at the back of the cabin near the restroom. By the time the lights went down I made up my mind. In the rest room I removed my pantyhose and panties, then proceeded to the empty seat beside the gentleman. Sitting down, I told him I noticed he was still awake and asked whether he'd like to talk. I put a blanket I'd brought along over me, commenting on how chilly it was. From that point on, while talking, it was quite simple to inch up my skirt, spread my legs slightly and gently begin to play with my cunt. Since he was but inches away, I was intrigued by the thought that he might join me readily if I told him what I was doing. But of course I didn't. It was more exciting this way. It was quite difficult to respond in our conversation and still keep my voice steady. In fact at one point he remarked that I seemed to be shivering. At that point I thought he might put his arm around me to help me warm up. The thought of me secretly rubbing off with his very arm around me made me ecstatic and I could scarcely conceal my fantastic climax. Ms. A.H., Los Angeles, Calif.

After reading a few more letters I became drowsy. I lay down on the couch, the open magazine across my midriff, and closed my eyes. A feeling of heat and comfort began emanating from the area of the magazine, spreading through my body almost as if a cup of hot tea or coffee were resting there.

*

After letting Arnold in, I sat down again and began reading the letters. I could sense Arnold standing near me with nothing to do, panting and breathing smoke, a horny dragon, his prick hard and breathing fire into his Bloomingdale's boxer shorts. I'm attempting to read and correct your letters, *Lifestyle,* for my job, but everything is obscured in all that hot smoke and my side is prodded with his stiff rod.

"Aren't you horny, Rhonda? I haven't seen you for a week. Are you seeing someone else?"

"Uh, uh," I said.

"Aren't you glad to see me? I didn't call you for a week to punish you for your behavior last time."

"That's nice," I said. "I thought you said that if we ever had problems that you were the kind of person who would try to work them out with me, not just split without a word. Remember? We were at El Faro's."

"I said if there were any problems I'd want to work them out, but I really don't think I should take any shit. If you make me feel bad I don't want to see you. If it's pleasant, I do. I'm not a masochist, I'm very healthy, you know."

"You should see a shrink."

"What for, when I'm so healthy?"

His head tilted, he shook it slightly from side to side. Despite his great health he didn't realize that that conversation was making him anxious.

"You need a shrink," I said, "because no one in good mental health can be so sure of him- or herself."

"Let's not discuss this now, let's go to the movies."

"I'd rather finish this work."

"But I didn't call you for a week! Wouldn't you rather go out with me than do that work? I think you're just trying to get even with me."

"Can't you believe that I'm more interested in my work than in going out?"

"I thought you hated your job. When you make enough money from your articles, you can quit forever."

I was suddenly enraged that he hadn't suggested equalizing our incomes in a Socialist way. "I love my job now," I said. "I'm editing these sex letters for our new magazine, *Lifestyle*."

Arnold looked down for the first time. "You're kidding," he said.

For an instant, dear *Lifestyle,* I sense that he's jealous of the letters, but rejects that as irrational.

"If anything," he says, "you should be more horny after reading these all day." He pushes me down on the rug.

"When I went to work with you one Sunday at Sloan-Kettering, while you were centrifuging those red blood cells to separate them from their membranes, did I push the test tube of blood cells in solution onto the floor, imploring that you fuck me instantly on the lab table?"

He's pulling off my clothing while I lie there on the rug making proof corrections on sheets and sheets of letters, which have spilled from their neat pile and are scattered everywhere. Arnold rips off his clothing. He is left only in his beard. Full and black, it reaches to the edge of his neck where it is shaven with a clean neat edge, like a suburban lawn, making him look more than naked, as if he'd peeled off an exoskeleton with his clothing.

"You imagine your vulnerability is well sheathed," I say, "but it's apparently invisible to you alone. I'm tired of being manipulated to protect you."

"What are you talking about?" he asks, nibbling my nipples.

His hot lips proceed downward along an invisible center line from my breasts past my ribs, abdomen and still further, slowed slightly by the fine cilia-like down. I picture him, well versed in anatomy, murmuring to himself, rib cage, lungs, heart, pulmonary artery, stomach, small intestine, kidney, large intestine and mons, where his beard mingles with mine.

"Let me read these to you while we do it," I say. "Let's read them together. I love being read to, ever since my mother did it when I used to be sick."

His nose ranges around my vagina like the neighbors' St. Bernard's. The tip of his glutinous tongue touches my clitoris with care so that I don't die of anguish from an immediate pleasure that would be too great to bear. I read aloud, Arnold's face buried in my muff:

Dear *Lifestyle*,

I have something of a problem. This girl I've been going with for six months keeps insisting that I insert something into her rear end while we make love. I used to use my finger, but now I lubricate a soft leather stick for this purpose. The problem is that half the time she refuses to have intercourse during a given session unless I stick it in. Personally I think she has got an obsession with this ramming in and out of her rear end, but I haven't told her.

"The problem is," I laugh, "they don't communicate."

Arnold raises his head from the depths of my cunt, but his body is still between my legs. There's a glow of moisture around his lips as if he's eaten a greasy dinner, but his eyes are puzzled and hurt. "The problem is," he says, "the girl is sick. She definitely has a fetish and the man should leave her."

"That remark completely reveals your attitude toward working things out with someone who has a problem or thinks differently from you."

Arnold tentatively tilts his head and pauses.

"Don't I excite you any more, Rhonda?"

"Of course you do," I say. "I just want to try something different, and with you. These magazines have opened up a new sense of possibility, experimentation. I want to share my involvement with my new job with you. We can't have a good sexual relationship unless we are willing to experiment and share, right? You know how I love to read— Please, Arnold." I press myself against his stiff, puzzled body. He is sitting with his legs curled in a pile, his torso rising out of the tangle like an Indian rope trick, not held up by the seductive conjuring of a flute, but by one arm, descending directly from shoulder socket to the floor.

"Well if we're going to do this, at least let's read something that isn't about anal sex. You know how I feel about anal sex."

"I know," I say, "you have a fetish against anal sex. Now you read."

He bends over, naked back now rounded, a freckle here and there on his white skin like raisins in rice pudding. He places the magazine in his lap gracelessly, yet the very gracelessness of it, his prick peering over the pages, is kind of exciting. He reads:

Dear *Lifestyle,*

I was fascinated by the February letter about the leg fetishist because my legs are adored too. I am tall and blond with small breasts and lovely legs. My husband likes them, but not as Diane does. She and her husband moved into this neighborhood six months ago, and since neither of us has children and we both work only in the mornings, it was natural that we became afternoon friends. My legs attracted her from our first meeting and I knew it. When she came up for coffee, I wore tiny, hip-hugger short shorts and paraded my bare legs before her, loving every compliment she paid me. One day, she reached over and, caressing my thighs, told me she couldn't resist any longer. I found myself pulling her head over and telling her to kiss them, and she did. When she started to caress them again, I said, "I want you on the floor," and she knelt before me. I extended my left leg and said, "Kiss all of it," and she did, right up to my crotch. I was on fire,

believe me, from the soft touch of her fingers and the warmth of her tongue. When she reached for the other leg, I said, "I want you nude," and with no embarrassment she stripped, knelt again and kissed my toes. This has become a ritual. Diane asks to worship my legs, and I send her into the den, following with a piece of soft rope. She is nude, on her knees, facing a big footstool with her hands behind her. I loosely bind her wrists and sit naked before her and move my legs here and there, letting her crawl on her knees to kiss them. I make her place her knees wide apart, and my foot, propped under her on its heel, sticks up and my toes rub her cunt. While she kisses my inner thighs, I reach under her, take her small nipples in the fingers of each hand and pinch and pull them. Finally I straddle her and she sucks me for hours on end. My husband benefits from this too. I'm still so hot when he comes home that sex before dinner is now common, and often by eight at night I'm crawling all over him.
Ms. R. H., Hartford, Conn.

While Arnold reads I watch his lips move to form the words, fluently and moistly, a glimpse of smooth tongue tantalizingly fleeting. His prick is hard, pressing against the edge of the magazine; he's flushed. I can practically see his chest vibrate with the beating of his heart. It's as if Arnold and the magazine are having some sort of liaison and I'm the voyeur. While Arnold is reading, I begin stroking him and touching myself at the same time. He looks at me in surprise as I've never masturbated in front of him before, but my feeling of abandon overcomes any embarrassment that Arnold's own constraint might communicate, abandon which is really liberation, dear *Lifestyle*. Having the sexy letter read to me while masturbating was far more exciting than when I read, or merely masturbated, as I was able to lose myself. I felt fantastic, even though Arnold kept looking at me surprised, his expression like that of an Australian kiwi, as if he couldn't deal with how I excited and disgusted him at the same time; he was horrified that even though he wasn't touching me, I was still so excited. Not able to stand it a moment longer, he pushes me over, lifts both my knees into the air with hitherto hidden strength and rams himself into me angrily. He grunts and I scream with pleasure at each forceful thrust.

"I'm going to come," I moan, breathlessly, an indrawn whisper.

"Yes, yes, come, baby, come," Arnold cries, tense, biting his lower lip. He's trying to hold back one more moment. . . .

"Read more," I scream, "read more."

His lips form a perfect circle within the blackness of his beard. He is perfectly stiff over me as if in the last throes of meningitis, yet I can feel him ejaculating, his body continuing by inertia, himself distracted from his own pleasure. He falls off me, silent.

"Arnold, are you angry?"

"I can't believe you don't understand," he says. "It's insulting that you become so excited by the magazines, more than you ever were with me—and when you're about to come, you shout, 'read more!'"

"You don't understand me either," I say. "That I'm hurt because when I'm the most excited you can't share and enjoy it and my excitement doesn't excite you, you just leave me feeling horrible, dirty and vulnerable because of your silly power trip that it has to be you exciting me. Can't you be more open and liberated? It's still you I'm making love with even though I may be turned on by some external stimulus. Philosophically, most people are turned on by something external, then express this turn-on with his or her partner. Besides, you were so passionate, your anger was so wonderful."

"Partner is such a dry twentieth-century word," says Arnold, "as is 'express,' 'liberated,' 'power trip,' 'external stimulus.' What about that old-fashioned word *love?*"

"Hug me, Arnold," I demand ingratiatingly.

"I can't. I don't love you any more."

"Why talk about that old-fashioned word then?"

Arnold is angry, and I lie there feeling bad. He begins silently to pull on his boxer shorts and slacks while I hope vaguely for some disaster to befall him, like his leg going into the fly of his shorts or both legs going into one leg-hole, just to dissipate the tension, change the mood to something livelier. Instead of saying goodbye, Arnold begins incomprehensibly to pile letters and magazines over my exposed, tense naked body as if burying me in sand.

Rather than feeling like cold magazines and stiff paper, it feels as if warm sand is covering all of me except for my head, the lulling repetitive rhythmic sibilance of sea in the background, sun seeping between the minute grains of sand and dripping comfortingly and warmly around me.

*

When I awoke, despite having fallen asleep on the floor, I felt more rested than I had in a long time. I sat up, magazines and papers sliding off me, but when I stood, I noticed one page was stuck to my upper thigh where there must have been some moisture or semen. After I ripped it off some backward letters remained on my skin, like a stamp or tattoo. Some perversity made me want it to remain, as if it were a souvenir of passion, a secret of possession, the mark of a lover, like a hickey, secret evidence of an intangible past pleasure that could have been a fantasy.

*

Arnold didn't call for a long time after, but I didn't miss him or anyone else. I felt really alive and creative, in fact, I began writing a long letter to you, *Lifestyle,* which I may someday make into a story. But something bothered me about the ambiguous ending of our relationship. I called him.

"Arnold, I don't care if I never see you again and I don't miss you, but I wonder why you chickened out of this relationship without even telling me you don't want to see me anymore. I think I deserve more respect than that."

"I'm not sure you deserve any respect," he says.

"How can you be so rigid, Arnold? It's as if you never had any feelings for me at all."

"I do want to break off with you, Rhonda, and I think it's better if we don't see each other again. I might desire you, but it would be useless."

"If you ever went to a shrink you'd know that it's better to end something and not just leave it hanging. Unfinished things tend to haunt."

"I did end it," he says, "in my own mind."

"Not really. If you don't communicate it, it proves that we never had a relationship at all, that all you needed was your own mind. You didn't even need me." In spite of myself that thought makes me cry. "End it my way," I cry, "or I'll end it first. I'll call you back and quickly tell you I never want to see you again before you can hang up."

*

As I leave to meet him at the Buffalo Roadhouse, I think that he could at least say, "Let's not see each other again," instead of "I don't want to see you any more." I'm sorry now that I ever called him because I don't want to see him so badly that I don't even care anymore how it's ended. I get there first and begin reading a magazine. I'm sitting right in front of the window, and decide to read a letter to *Lifestyle* and jerk off without using my hands at all, without anyone knowing. I can see Arnold arriving, through the corner of my eye, as my passion mounts. The moment he sits down next to me, my head falls back in ecstasy, eyes closing as if in a petit mal fit.

"I didn't realize you'd be that glad to see me," he says, pleased.

"The moment I saw you I had an orgasm."

"I'd better take you home and go up in the elevator with you," he says, still in the spirit of a lovely dinner, made even more comradely by the fact that we are no longer lovers and can afford to be at ease, generous and friendly. Arnold attempts to sit on my bed.

"Look, they're all over! Don't you ever clean? These magazines enrage me," he says, throwing them off. "These are what ruined our relationship. It's odd how you developed this fetish. It must have been latent while you were an English major."

"Don't be silly, I just like them. A fetish is something you can't do without," I say, walking over to my Random House dictionary. "Besides, this is my work, Arnold. Without me these letters would be a mess. Some of these people may have interesting sex lives, but they can barely write English. And I may write a book or a story about them sometime."

Arnold spots one of the letters I wrote about him for my story. "What's this? You can't write about me. I told you never to write about me."

"How do you know it's about you? I just used the name Arnold," I say.

"I know it's about me."

"Then I'll change the name," I say. "I don't mind. But don't tell me who or what to write about. I'm a writer. Do I tell you not to work with red blood cells?"

"But red blood cells can't hurt anyone. They're not your red blood cells. I don't want to be written about."

"After I write it," I explain, "it's mine. It's no longer about you, which you're too vain to understand. Whatever I write is an expression of my experience, which you're only a part of."

Arnold is more enraged than ever, but a falsely pleasant smile creeps over his face like an army of ants over an anthill. "Listen, forget about this magazine stuff." He holds his hands out supplicatingly, like the Virgin Mary. "Let's make love."

"Still," I say, "these letters are my work and I'm not giving it up." He holds me there on the edge of the bed sympathetically and begins to kiss me. It feels good to be held. I'd almost forgotten how nice. But even while I'm enjoying his warmth and kisses, a perverse idea occurs to me.

"Arnold," I whisper, "please hit me with one of the magazines."

Arnold looks at me as if I might be making a bad joke at the wrong time. "You're kidding," he says, his sweater still around his neck.

"Yes, I'm kidding," I say, "but do it anyway, please." I'm so excited by the idea I've lost all restraint. At that moment I realize I'm becoming more myself and losing my inhibition in spite of him.

Vulnerable, already naked, he looks at me, and desperate anger and disgust rapidly take each other's respective places on his face as if they won't fit there together. He begins to dress while I lie on the magazines. It seems we've done this scene before and I'm desperate for a change. Instead of leaving this time, he picks up a magazine and, teeth bared, whacks me across the abdomen with it. But he's too serious.

"I don't think you're having a good time," I whisper, a little frightened of his anger. Yet strangely, I'm becoming excited, the pain, fear and eroticism fusing into a kind of abandon. I try to masturbate as Arnold hits me again, really hatefully, as I've read in the magazine. This wasn't the greatest pleasure, but if I concentrated hard, perhaps I could get off.

I was about to climax when Arnold stopped hitting me. Looking into his face, I saw his hatred transformed into sorrow and revulsion. For a moment, I saw Arnold as a sad, hurt person whom perhaps I had sullied. I wanted to say I was sorry, but all I could do was watch him put on his shoes. He never looked up at me but tied his laces slowly and with the concentration of a nursery-school child, and left. Turning belly downward on the magazines, I wept, letting them rub against my tender skin—breasts, thighs—and spread my legs, so they could insinuate further into all my crevices as I squirmed and cried.

*

Dear *Lifestyle* Magazine, That was the last time I'll ever cry because of a man. I never realized until now that I'm really liberated, what a pain in the ass it was to have a lover. Life is so easy and so relaxed. I have all my energy for myself and I no longer have to be involved in someone else's personal anguishes and irresolvable neuroses. No more of that drain, drain, drain. Men just don't know how to relate and, come to think of it, neither do I. But is it worth trying? This morning, reading you, dear *Lifestyle,* I became excited. I pulled down my jeans as far as they'd go and touched my clit. Then I began to rub the smooth, glossy magazine around my vagina, feeling it rub between my labia, along my clitoris, slowly, with relish, gliding it smoothly along my well-lubricated orifice, attempting not to move my hips at all in order to prolong the slow voluptuousness of enforced passivity. No longer able to keep still, I began rotating my hips, up and down, slowly, then faster, round and round. I quickly opened the magazine to the letters page and pressed it to my swollen, wide-open cunt, against the full, spread lips, the hard clitoris, the gaping orifice, sliding it passionately, flatly against myself as if my vagina were reading paludaly, sensorially, absorbing the words blindly, cunt braille, hips writhing to meet the pressure building, until it burst cataclysmically, a lunatic jellyfish in an elliptically wavering surf."

*

"I hate the man my former wife is living with," says Brian. "He's so ugly."

"Is that your concern?" I ask Brian, who is balancing a glass of white wine on the ball of his knee, rolling it round and round.

"You're so clever," he says, "sometimes you pinpoint exactly the right spot for me. I should see you more often."

"At least once a month would have more continuity," I say.

"Why did you call me?" he asks, "if you're so bitter."

"I felt remorseful, as if I destroyed my relationship with my boyfriend Arnold. But I didn't want to call Arnold so I called you."

"Thanks," he says, dubiously.

"I wondered whether all the trouble I gave him was my fault, caused by a fear of relating to people, or if we just didn't get along, or if it really was his fault. Brian," I say, lecherously, "look at these letters."

Brian reclines his narrow body on the rug, his hand around his wineglass, protectively but gently, the magazine on the floor, my own hand holding it open for him, offering it to him. I wait a few moments for a reaction.

"Listen to this," he says. Wonder of wonders, Brian is reading them aloud automatically! "Dear *Lifestyle,*" he reads, "My husband and I very much enjoyed reading Annie Jones' erotic menus in *Lifestyle* recently. But what about the people who would find her dishes far too expensive? We can't afford asparagus spears in melted butter, Chartreuse, or select liqueur chocolates, but fortunately economy and eroticism can go hand in hand. My husband, who has a wonderfully inventive attitude toward sex, has often given me the marvelous pleasure of eating from my vagina. The sensation, as he draws a large, ripe banana through my labia, passing his tongue over my clitoris, is often sufficient to give me several orgasms of increasing intensity. Then I too can give him pleasure when I kiss and lick his penis, having prepared it with a delicious cold yogurt of the fruit variety, eating the dessert, sucking and swallowing while caressing his testicles and thighs."

"Let's try it!" shouts Brian, flushed, undressing rapidly.

His thin body is running for the kitchen with a speed unforeseen in my small apartment. How different from Arnold, I think. How willing and experimental. I'm drawing off my underpants when I hear screaming from the kitchen.

"What is it?" I ask, running in as well as I can with my underpants around my ankles. Brian is throwing my pots against the wall. "Brian, what are you doing?" I scream.

"You have no food here," he says. "I can't find a banana, or even a cucumber, not to mention any yogurt."

"Calm down, Brian, and we'll see what we can use."

"You're right again, Rhonda. I'm so impatient. How about cottage cheese?"

I picture eating cottage cheese off his prick, a bland diet breakfast, curds dripping past my lips on the up and down strokes onto my rug. "I'm not that fond of cottage cheese." My voice is muffled. Freezing, I'm practically inside the refrigerator searching the corners for remainders of food.

"All I see is mustard, ketchup and cocktail onions," says Brian. "It looks just like my own refrigerator. I though all women cooked."

"I hate to cook. I'm training for the greatest liberation of all, not needing to eat."

This is not that exciting, I think, watching Brian's flaccid prick swing to and fro in the forty-watt refrigerator light, myself shivering, my upper half refrigerated, underpants swinging from one ankle. This isn't as exciting as the letter. I feel as if we're in a Kafkaesque domestic scene where neither of us knows what we are meant to do. Finally I find some old sour cream left over from a party dip, so old that the liquid is on top and the cream on the bottom. As I attempt to stir it together, Brian finds a carrot that is soft and shriveled, one long hair growing from the tip.

"Wash it good, Brian. I don't want to be a victim of vegetable blight."

"Your superfastidiousness is detracting from our imminent delight," says Brian as we walk back to the rug, carrying our precious provender, aphrodisiacs, in our hands, my underpants dusting the floor for me.

"You'd better read more. I'm not excited any more."

Brian reads: "I have always loved having my breasts stimulated and often my husband will annoint them with his share of creamy yogurt and thrill me by pulling and sucking at my nipples." He stops to suck my nipples, then applies some cold sour cream to them with his fingers.

"I should have brought a spoon," he says.

"Who's superfastidious now?" I ask, breathing in sharply as the cold cream chills my whole body, shriveling my breasts. He places his lips around my nipple, snowy as Kilimanjaro, and spits out in disgust. "Phoo."

"Brian, my rug."

He begins to clean up and, seeing him naked on the floor like that on his hands and knees, I realize how we women look when we're cleaning. In order to make amends for seeing him like that, I begin to read: "My husband tells me that he gets great pleasure from imagining he is drawing a flavored milk from my breast, produced especially for him. This in turn leaves my nipples swollen and erect, begging for more." I'm unable to control my laughter as I picture begging breasts. "We can experience," I continue, "what we call oral orgasm, which we achieve by passing chocolate bars and sweets from one mouth to the other." "I wonder whether they're fat," I muse, placing some sour cream, scooped with my fingers, all over Brian's prick, as he stiff-leggedly lies on the rug, his upper torso propped by his elbows so he can observe the proceedings.

My application of the cold sour cream, after an initial inspiration at the chill, has aroused him so that his prick is standing up straight, but the cream, now heated, is becoming a disgusting liquid consistency, dripping rapidly. I rub the excess cream off my hand into his pubic hair. Brian, using one hand, lowers my head until my mouth encompasses his organ.

"Ohh," he moans, "It's sooo good."

But I'm about to throw up.

"Put the whole thing in your mouth and slowly move it up and down," he whispers.

"Brian," I say, raising my head as soon as he removes his hand, "I'm going to barf. I think the cream is spoiled."

"UUUuuugggggggghhhhhhhhhhhhhh," he says, running for the bathroom, gagging.

He's kneeling in front of the toilet bowl with his fingers down his throat. "Now," he cries, "we'll both die here of botulism and no one will ever notice until they smell our bodies."

"Brian, don't panic. I don't even think you ate any of the cream. The worst that can happen is we'll have a slight case of Salmonella."

We are lying on the rug, exhausted, Brian especially wiped out, white and moist from retching. I touch his hand tenderly.

"Well," I say, "that didn't work out, but it was funny. I admire your desire to experiment."

"Thanks," he said. "One of the things I liked most about that letter was its Socialist leanings. It appealed to the middle- or low-income audience and showed how poor people can partake of exotic forms of eroticism too— Why don't we just fuck?"

"Fuck?"

"You remember?" he asks. "Fuck?" He leans over to show me, inserting his prick.

Since I haven't actually made love with a man for quite a while I prepared myself for the shock of pleasure, but I felt nothing. Nothing at all. The idea of continuing when I felt nothing repulsed me. Maybe it was because my relationship with Brian lacked depth.

"Brian," I say, rising up, his prick still moving in and out, "Why don't you wrap a magazine around your prick and fuck me like that?"

Brian stops moving. "Aren't I big enough for you?" he asked. At that moment I realized I was no longer afraid of what he'd think or of hurting his vanity. I didn't care if he'd think I thought he was too small, too this, or too that, too passionate, too animalistic, too frigid, too feminine, not feminine enough or that I smell wrong. I was finally concerned with what I wanted.

"Of course you're big enough," I said, honestly. "These magazines just give me a lot of pleasure. They've changed my life. I'm stronger, freer sexually, a totally independent person seeking my own fulfillment. They are a true indication of the liberation of society today. Don't take it personally."

"But we're making love. How can I not take that personally?"

"We're not making love, Brian, we're fucking. You never minded seeing me whenever you wanted to get laid, telling me to hang loose, imagining I'd be ready to feel you whenever you were in the mood. Now you're getting what you want, only this time it was I who called you."

He downheartedly fiddled with himself for a few moments but couldn't produce an erection.

"Just use the magazine then," I said, rolling it up for him and applying lots of contraceptive jelly.

Wedding Night

The late afternoon sun, through the windshield of the car, looked like a small cold overcooked egg yolk, partially obscured by hard opaque clouds, a few streaks of pale, burst yolk yellow embellishing thick, white albumin, with gilded crisp, burnt-ochre edges. Ernst ducked his head and blinked at the sudden appearance of the above which had been hidden before, sunny-side over, and flipped both sun visors down with a practiced motion of one large slender hand, the other remaining on the wheel. Something about the ease with which the hand performed that simple action had the effect of arousing Maria sexually. At the same time, having glimpsed the hand, large knuckles protruding, hair growing like small islands in between each knuckle, she felt repulsed. She pushed her visor up.

"The sun hurts my eyes," said Ernst.

"I want to look at it," said Maria. "I want to remember what this sunset looks like now, to feel its essence."

"You want to remember always that today the sunset looked like various kinds of fried eggs?" He lowered the visor again. "Though I admit," he conceded, "this road is ugly, corrupted by modernity."

He had used his sharp chin to point outward at the atmosphere laden with excrescence, sulfurous yellow smoke and gaseous gray arising in various consistencies from the gasworks; a gray, bloated, gas tank skyline; the red, orange, pink and green neon of cheap diners, hamburger stands and grotesque billboards gleaming dimly in the late afternoon light.

"Actually," said Maria, "this landscape has a gross beauty of ugliness, an integrity of its own which suits our present day society. It's a vulgar new folk art."

There was nothing like Ernst's expressing an opinion to cause Maria to see and appreciate the other side of things with sudden clarity. "There's no need always to revere the landscape of the past," she said to Ernst's immobile and sulky profile as the car stopped for a traffic light. When the light changed and Ernst pressed the gas, the car didn't move.

"Goddamn motherfucking cocksucking prick of a car," cursed Ernst, uncontrollably, as Maria sank, cold and depressed, into the freezing plastic upholstery of the front seat.

She hated Ernst's cursing as if the car were the cause of all his problems. She couldn't shake the irrational feeling that it was all Ernst's fault that the car was stalled. "If you keep pressing the gas without waiting in between, you'll flood the carburetor," she said.

"Fuck the carburetor," said Ernst, fuming, his face alternatingly matching and contrasting with the stoplight as it changed from red to green and back again. He continued pressing the gas pedal frantically. A horrible odor of burned gas insinuated insidiously into the car, unnoticed at first because it went so well with the landscape that it appeared to originate outside.

"The carburetor is flooded," said Ernst, "Goddamn son of a bitching motherfucking cunt. Get out, Maria, we have to push it."

"You'll notice that most of those words you used denigrate women," said Maria, staring at him. Why get out? It was his car, wasn't it? "I'd like you better, Ernst, if you'd flag someone down to push us to the nearest gas station." The nearest gas station was only about forty yards away on either side of them, as there was one on each of the four corners of the intersection.

"Get out, Maria," said Ernst, "and when I say push, push."

Maria, behind the car, and Ernst, alongside, his door open, pushed in unison, and as soon as the car began to move, Ernst jumped inside and pressed the gas pedal. Miraculously, the motor turned; he drove into the nearest gas station, the one the wheels were turned toward, leaving Maria to run after the car in her long, off-white wedding dress and matching shot-silk high heels. She followed the "Just Married" on the back bumper, already dingy but glowing ominously, the phosphorescent paint reflecting all the lights, which, as it darkened out, became brighter.

"Lucky for modernity and ugliness," said Maria, "including four gas stations within two hundred feet." Tears ran down her cheeks, brown rivulets recalling the tiny beginnings of the mighty Mississippi, flowing over the mountains of her high, rouged cheekbones, as she stumbled, high heels bending under and back again on the oil-soaked gravel under the weight of her two large suitcases, which banged her thighs painfully as she and Ernst, similarly laden, made their way to the balconied chalet-style Holiday Inn next to the gas station.

Locked in the bathroom of their motel room, Maria sat on the edge of the sink looking at herself in the mirror, observing her eyelashes stuck together in large clumps, her eyes, edged in brown, dry river beds of brown winding down her cheeks evoking enormous amounts of self-pity, reminding her of this morning, her wedding morning.

*

As soon as Maria opened her eyes, she was apprised of Ernst's climbing through her bedroom window, poised on the sill a moment, the bright early sunlight silhouetting him with gold. His dark figure silently swung to the floor, his finger immediately moving toward his lips, silently entreating her to be silent.

"You aren't supposed to see me before the wedding, Ernst," she said as soon as her features regained their normal shape from the circular visage of her eyes and mouth upon his entrance.

"Boy, are you surprised," said Ernst, playfully. "Why aren't I supposed to see you? Who made that rule?" He lay down along the bottom of the bed.

"Get up," said Maria, "how can you act like this?"

"It's easy," he said, remaining there, his body settling somnolently and liquidly like a stretched slug. "I wanted to go shopping with you and your mother and you wouldn't let me," he pouted. "I'm just getting revenge."

"Ernst, surely you're kidding! What do you care what we women wear for the wedding? It's my dress and mother's, and it's only for one day."

"I do care," he said, "why shouldn't I? It's my wedding and my life as well as yours and I want to choose what's in it. I want it to be perfect."

"Who's to say what's perfect?" Maria said. "You choose your own clothes. It's my wedding day too, and I want it to be perfect," she rambled jocularly. "I don't want it wasted in arguing and sulking—"

Ernst didn't move or speak.

"Ernst? Ernst? please," she wheedled, caressing his hair where it curled sensuously against the edge of his strong jawbone, the rest of it soft and straight.

He pushed away her hand with a sharp movement of his head.

"Ernst," she pleaded, attempting to pull his face around toward hers manually by grasping his chin firmly but, with much effort on his part, he was able to retain his head in its straight-ahead position. "Ernst, sweetie, would you like a cup of tea to make you feel better, sweetie?" No answer. Maria picked up a *Bride's* Magazine from beside the bed and began to read, ignoring Ernst, who fidgeted. Finally he shrieked, "I'm not marrying you!"

"Why?" Maria asked, attempting to remain calm and keep her parents from hearing that he was in the house. "Because I didn't let you pick out my wedding dress and the bridesmaids' clothes, and my mother didn't let you pick out her dress?"

"Your mother's a cunt," he said.

"Ernst Roehm, I'm not marrying you," said Maria angrily, but her voice unnaturally high at the ridiculousness of it. She had a strange desire to laugh but repressed it.

"Now I'm mad at you for something else," he said.

"What?" Maria asked, now almost certain that this whole thing was a joke.

"Because you're the only one I depend on to comfort me and you failed miserably, by ignoring me."

"When did I ignore you? I offered you tea and everything."

"When you read the magazine and coldly ignored me."

"But Ernst, when I tried to comfort you, you didn't respond, so I gave up."

"You gave up! How do you think that makes me feel?"

"How do you think this whole thing makes me feel?" shrieked Maria.

Ernst put his hand over her mouth, a look of horror on his face. "I just wanted to come with you and you wouldn't let me," he whined, hiccoughing.

Maria held him, both of them lying on her bed. He wept on her chest, his eyes an incredibly deep blue when wet, almost violet, ringed with a pink that matched the tip of his nose. His face swollen, hot and wet, he seemed like an enormous baby. Maria felt quite contented comforting him.

They both heard someone on the stairs at the same time. Ernst, trembling and hiccoughing, suddenly ran behind the door. Maria's mother, breathless from the stairs, appeared in her long, rabbit trimmed nylon tricot robe and high-heeled gold slippers, her hairdo, done the day before, kerchiefed with a silk scarf so it wouldn't be ruined; most of the features in her fat, pallid face appeared to be missing because she had no makeup on, the rest having been removed through tweezing; her heavy arms were laden with foaming whiteness that partially slid over them as she reached the doorway, unrolling in one snowy cascade down Mrs. Strausshof's front, obscuring in its flow her rotund body, supported amazingly by her tiny gold pumps. She took one tentative step forward, trying not to step on the white dress she carried, now trailing on the floor, as if she were attempting to avoid stepping into a small stream.

In that instant Ernst grabbed her from behind, skillfully holding her arms, burden and all, with one hand, the other over her mouth, and pulled her toward the enormous carved-oak wardrobe. Her round, colorless eyes met Maria's for a moment before she was obscured in cascades and mists of tulle as Ernst, holding her in with one hand, shut the heavy door and turned the key.

"Ernst," Maria mumbled, "what did you do?"

"I put your mother in the wardrobe."

Ernst helped Maria, slightly numb, to the vanity table, switching on the makeup lights surrounding the mirror. "I didn't want her to know I was here," he whispered, scrutinizing Maria strangely. "Let me put on your makeup, please," he pleaded.

"Ernst, you're crazy. This is such an insane wedding day."

"Come on," pleaded Ernst, head tilted winningly, already wrapping a black silk scarf tightly over Maria's curled but uncombed hair, the edge riding evenly along her hairline to facilitate a clean application of makeup.

"I wasn't going to wear much makeup," she said.

"Come on, let me make you up the way I want, just for today."

Maria remained silent for a moment, annoyed. Her image of herself was a lovely, fresh, angelic beauty unaided by artifice—an image of herself at her own wedding that she had carried with her for many years as if it were already a wedding photograph; the muffled screeches of her mother in the wardrobe traced an edge of anxiety over every thought and feeling. Suddenly they deliquesced to minuscule sobs and hiccoughs.

"Do you think she's okay?"

"Of course she's fine. Let me do this makeup and then we can let her out quickly."

Maria's anxiety metamorphosed into mirth. She watched Ernst in her makeup mirror through the peripheral vision of her left eye as he sweated excitedly over the application of carmine to her lips with his delicate red sable brush. Her eyelids drooped involuntarily with

the delectable sensation of being touched gently, with concentration. When Ernst, gazing at Maria's lips before applying a
darker outliner and a paler rose, inside, a small shadow of mauve
inspirationally placed in the subtle cleft in the center of her full
lower lip, she felt as if her whole body were being subtly,
tormentingly tickled. Why complain about him, she thought,
when other, more conventional men have so far bored me? His
careful application of brown and pale mauve eyeshadow instead of
the usual blue or green was extremely innovative. Why shouldn't I
accept and enjoy Ernst's creative eccentricities? She heard her father
bark, "Klara, where are you?" and pictured him—pacing to and fro
downstairs on the thick Oriental carpet imported from Peking with
Marco Polo, obese, neat and stylishly ugly, thin gray hair smoothed
back flatly with Vitalis, plethoric cheeks emanating Old Spice,
biting the tip off a fat cigar and impatiently spitting the tip right
on the rug—as Ernst suddenly covered her whole head with the
black scarf, opened it and let it float over her parachute-like, then
somehow secured it skillfully under her chin.

"This is so that when I put your gown over your head it won't
ruin your curl and the makeup," he said, walking toward the
wardrobe. When the heavy door was opened by the future son-in-
law who had grabbed her violently and stuffed her into the dark
hold filled with wedding clothes, one off-white peau de soie
trimmed with Belgian Lace, and six rose, running into powder-blue
organdy tulle dresses, Klara suddenly saw, in a painful brightness,
her daughter on a chair, her head completely shrouded with black
silk, her features neatly and grotesquely made up vaguely visible
underneath, framed by a multitude of tiny light bulbs of the huge
mirror, her sweaty son-in-law to be—still delicately wielding his
tiny sable brushes, held somewhat like chopsticks, both in one
hand, one of them tipped in scarlet, the other covered with mauvish
goo—wearing Maria's silk scarlet and maroon robe, ostrich collar
surrounding his flushed face, belted at the waist, but exposing, as
he stepped toward her, his slacks underneath, due to the drag of its
sweeping train.

Terrified, Klara made no attempt to leave the closet; in fact, as

Ernst pulled out Maria's wedding dress from where it was semi-wrapped around Maria's mother, her hands, like disturbed pigeons fluttering the fabric, frantically assisted its passage out.

"Shit," said Ernst, holding up the dress. "What awful taste. The reason that guy can design like this is because he's a eunuch. All those designers are eunuchs," he continued, assisting the fabric over Maria's wrapped head, pulling her arms like a baby's through the tiny puffed sleeves, pulling it down. He removed the scarf, revealing Maria's face, red, hot and wet.

"You're crying!" he exclaimed, surprised, as her tears, liberated from the confines of the scarf, fell on the off-white fabric, a tiny puff forming where each drop fell, since the delicate cloth, embroidered with seed pearls, had been marked on a tag in the inside seam, "Dry Clean Only," a fact she repeated again and again in a low voice, in vain, while Ernst stood back and looked at her, head tilted, sharp nose pointed, hands out, his Adam's apple protruding, unaware of himself, he was so involved. He looks like a flamingo, thought Maria, panicking.

"You don't like my wedding dress," she whined. To herself she looked so pretty, so adorable, so ravishing in this white, virginal costume, this ancient symbol of purity. How many times had she pictured his reaction to her wearing a dress like this, walking slowly down the enormous staircase on her father's arm.

"This dress makes you look like Pat Nixon," he shouted "or Mamie Eisenhower, or—Mrs. Warren Harding!" There was a muffled gasp from the closet. "Why couldn't you choose something in a soft fabric that flows with the body, as if you had one instead of this thing—something with a life of its own, maybe a gentle crepe, something with a little sex appeal, like satin. Something more like they sell on Fourteenth Street."

"You want me to look like one of those cheap spics!" she shrieked in disbelief.

"Those spics know how to dress. They know what attracts men; they understand sexuality. You need a dress like something Mick Jagger would wear."

Maria felt terrified, as if she had to escape. She felt like the main character in a play in which everyone had his own script but she knew she didn't possess the courage to run, leaving the audience and other characters. She realized she needed Ernst to comfort her, even if he was the cause of her discomfort, and sat with him on the bed, now willing to conspire with him in resewing all the bridesmaids' dresses to Ernst's design, removing all the tulle, leaving only the tight satin sheaths underneath, cutting off sleeves, lowering necklines, creating large slits. The wedding party would resemble a bordello. Maria was having a good time, but she asked herself, Am I allowing Ernst to completely absorb me into his own insane reality?

*

"Maria, come out of the bathroom, the food's here," called Ernst.

"What food?" asked Maria. Her voice, still small and catching, almost moved her to tears again.

Ernst opened the bathroom door and saw Maria seated on the edge of the sink, fully clothed, her face still streaked, hair askew. "Oh, sweetheart," murmured Ernst, helping her off the sink, supporting her as he led her into the bedroom.

A teenage boy, arranging their food on a large portable standup tray in the middle of their large double bed, stared when he saw Maria, hiccoughing and brown-faced in her transformed wedding gown, which now had small tassles sewn to the breasts that jiggled as she moved, the long slits up the sides revealing almost her entire thigh; the end of the train way behind, still in the bathroom, leaving a small streak of slime as it unknowingly dragged a piece of wet soap underneath. He held his hand out automatically for a tip, his eyes never leaving Maria, as he dumbly backed out of the room.

"See how attractive everyone thinks my wife is?" asked Ernst, helping Maria sit comfortably on the bed without upsetting two bottles of soda, upright on the tray. "Why don't you take off this gown now?"

She docilely obeyed and sat on the bed in her underpants and bra. Ernst, fully clothed in his tuxedo pants and jacket except for the shirt, collar, and cummerbund already sitting on the bed, bit into the Colonel Sanders' fried chicken held carefully between his fingers, the hair of his chest showing along the long, black, carefully creased lapels of his jacket. Maria was hungry, but she couldn't control the tears that rolled down her cheeks despite the fact that she didn't seem to be crying and delved ravenously into the fried chicken and coleslaw, french fries and soda, disgustedly watching Ernst eat, wiping his greasy fingers on the thighs of his trousers before picking up his soda bottle, already opaque with fingerprints despite the earnest wiping on his clothing.

"You're getting grease on your tuxedo," said Maria.

"That's okay," said Ernst, "it's rented." He picked up a large piece of chicken and ripped into it with his teeth, flakes of breading flying everywhere on the bed, his mouth, chin and cheeks glossy with grease, reflecting the light of the flowered chintz-shaded lamps. The red flashing neon light right outside gave the grease a pinkish glow that appeared greenish when the sign flickered off.

After a while, Maria screeched, "I can't understand you; we are finally married, alone for one of the first times; I'm sitting here in my underwear, and you exhibit no desire for me; you just keep eating fried chicken! You don't desire me anymore," she cried.

"Don't be silly, baby," said Ernst. "The normal human response is to satisfy the drives of hunger and shelter first, then sex. I only want to have the strength to please you more."

"What you say may be true, but it can't camouflage the fact that you aren't overcome with desire."

"I don't want to get you greasy," he said, desperately.

"Those are just excuses," said Maria.

"Well, you don't show any great desire for me either," he said.

"There, you said 'either.' I'm afraid to approach you when I know you don't desire me," she said angrily. "Besides, you're supposed to ravish me tonight."

"Who says?" said Ernst.

"And then I wanted to go out and have a Wedding Dinner," she said, "with candles and roast beef, or steak, and wine."

"What the fuck is a 'Wedding Dinner'?" shouted Ernst. "This is a wedding dinner too."

"Fried chicken in a bucket and Dr Pepper?"

"It's a lovely dinner," Ernst said, trying to lower his voice. "Why do you have so many preconceived ideas? Let's try to enjoy the reality. Do you want this day ruined?"

"It is ruined," she said. "You didn't enjoy the reality when the car broke down. You cursed so horribly."

"I don't feel like going out any more tonight anyway," said Ernst. "I like it here." His glance roved around the fake-wood-veneered room, with matching wood-veneered night tables and marble-veneer head board. "Where could we go, anyway, in the middle of Route 22 in New Jersey?"

*

Maria looked at herself in the bathroom mirror again, now attired in her new white nylon nightgown, wondering whether or not Ernst would like the style, as it billowed around her loosely. She felt good again, having soaked her eyes with a cold, wet towel and applied more makeup than usual, as she knew would attract Ernst. She opened the door a crack but was unable to ambulate. She wished he'd come and get her like before, but there wasn't a sound from the bedroom. Becoming increasingly bored, Maria self-consciously emerged into the dimmer light of the bedroom, turning off the bathroom light as she went.

She saw suddenly that no one was watching her. In fact, it seemed as if no one were in the room, except for a suspicious lump under the thin brown counterpane. Ernst was hiding. Maria decided to sneak quietly over and pull the cover down quickly, to surprise him. She tiptoed and stood perfectly immobile over the bed for a moment, then turned back the thin cover with one quick stroke. As the neon flashed its grotesque reddish light, she saw Ernst, in fetal position, partially on his back, thumb in his mouth, skin bluish-white like skim milk, blue irises reddish in purplish eyes, his hair and eyelashes assuming a thick, frightening black that matched his distinct, thin, bowed lips, apparently lipsticked, his chest hair curling over the amylaceous, mucilaginous folds of nylon nightie flowing over his chest, spilling onto the yellow sheet (which appeared peach); one slender, hairy knee protectively close to his chest, the other, because he wasn't completely on his side, slightly raised, framed darkly tinted but light-haired balls, one slightly larger than the other; the small purple tip of his prick peered from underneath the borscht-pink, handwrought Belgian-lace panties, pubic hair emerging through lacy openings and curling around the threads like delicate insects caught in a web.

"What's wrong?" he asked throatily when Maria screamed, his lips moving as well as they could around the thumb, which, despite the shock of her scream, he hadn't removed from his mouth, the forefinger of the same hand wrapped around his nose, pulling the sharp feature down, somewhat obscuring his upper lip in shadow.

"Why don't you take my nightie off?" asked Maria, suddenly calm, climbing in beside him. She was revolted but determined now to create the kind of wedding night she thought she deserved.

He complied, strangely passive, then lay naked and still, his color combination alternating each time the neon outside changed. The moment Maria, gazing at him, attempted to establish an emotional reaction to one color combination, the deathlike, red-and-blackish, purplish-whitish Ernst was suddenly transformed to an Ernst with faint, delicate skin, flushed with heat and excitement, feverish, large-blue eyes framed with dark, shiny lashes, each one seeming to have a small blond brush at its tip; with his carmined lips and high, damp, white forehead against the pale underside of his raised arm traced with blue tributaries, he appeared so vulnerable, like a child. His vulnerability was repugnant and arousing to her at the same time.

Ernst looked deeply into Maria's eyes, removing his thumb from his mouth, the top joint gleaming wetly. He placed his hand on Maria's, took it and placed it around his not-quite-hard prick, held it clasped there a moment, then moved it up and down. She allowed her hand to move under his for a few moments until he began to writhe. More and more excited, he removed his own hand.

"Please, please, please make me come, make me come," he begged, gyrating helplessly.

Maria had a sudden suspicion that she was being used and that nothing was going to work out correctly. "You're ruining my whole honeymoon," she yelled, removing her hand right in the middle of one of his up-hip motions.

"It's our honeymoon," he corrected calmly, whispering breathlessly. "And don't scream."

"If you weren't sick you wouldn't care who heard me," said Maria. "You're sick, sick, sick. We're supposed to fuck. I bet you can't do it. I married a man who can't fuck," she whined, in wonder.

"No, no," he said rapidly, as if her words made something real that hadn't actually been formulated before. "I'm part of a study by Illinois University in which the Department of Health, Education and Welfare pays volunteers to take a drug, then monitors their physical reactions with a ring-like transducer for the National Institute of Drug Abuse to determine whether drugs enhance or inhibit physical reactions and/or fantasies. Besides, only tiny breasts turn me on," he whined, looking at Maria's round, full tits in terror.

He remained totally limp as Maria climbed on top of him and sat there, her knees cradling his hips, her large breasts almost obscuring her face from his view. He looked up at her, fearfully, wide-eyed, as she put her hand between them, searching for his prick, which she fished out. Rubbing the bottom up and down so it would remain hard enough, she managed to successfully stuff it in, not without some effort. She rubbed her body rhythmically up and down, frantically pressing her clitoris against his motionless groin until she obtained a small, silent orgasm.

Love

There seems to be no room for the air that enters my body when I breathe; my heartbeat is shallow and rapid, expressing a lack of certainty it will continue, drowning as it is with all my organs in a quicksand of fat like almonds dropped in butter cream. My breasts are tributary mountain ranges of my abdomen, high, rising toward the middle like an enormous overflowing cupcake, as I lie here comfortably in condoned catatonia, a semi-stupor of enforced immobility, on a special bed, or two or three pushed together, merely breathing.

"You've been close to death," says Dr. Stone. I attempt to nod, wondering whether he means recently or in a larger sense.

"Don't move," he admonishes my hypertrophied, amplitudinous self as he inserts an intravenous needle into a vein of each pendulous flabelliform arm lying alongside me, white vulnerable veiny sides up in supplication, accepting the needles calmly like white whales swimming in the sunshine, harpooned by surprise. It's a relief to be here, not to have to deal with anything, to feel rewarded for remaining alive ten more minutes, Dr. Stone praising me simply for being alive. I'm completely protected in here.

"You fatties," says Dr. Stone, "begin to destroy yourselves early."

"Don't generalize," I answer. "I'd been thin for thirty years until I left my husband, and since then I've eaten my way through twenty-five relationships."

"Don't talk," he says, "it's too much strain. You like to look like that." He wrinkles his nose in disgust, pressing his finger into my flesh as if he's not sure what it will turn out to be a pile of. I'm glad he finds me disgusting, though at the same time it embarrasses me to be so hideous, constantly seeking signs of others' revulsion, yet at least this way we can relate to each other as people.

"Dr. Stone, would you help me onto my bedpan?" I ask, relishing the unattractiveness of the situation.

"I'm sorry," he whispers, "it's not my job. Ring for the nurses."

Perversely, I who used to enjoy being thought of as pretty or sexy, am getting a kick out of Dr. Stone gagging as he watches me being hoisted by twelve nurses, six on each side, onto the bedpan, after my enormous, specially made hospital drawers are pulled down, which immediately disappears under my myoedematous girth as if suddenly absorbed.

"Do you get a castration complex watching that?" I scream at his running body, gone already, footfalls on the disinfected gray vinyl linoleum echoing through the corridor.

*

Holding a glass cup containing hot wine punch of sugar, oranges, red wine and cloves, and one waterlogged slice of lemon, its rind swollen, livid, I'm swirling the maroon mixture to make sure the lemon is really dead, heady vapors rising into the overheated air, rarified molecules sifting to make room for them. I'm watching Barbara's skirt rise on her legs tantalizingly, slowly, her hand hoisted holding the candle she's going to use to light her menorah, telling the story of Hannukah as she gesticulates with it, perlustrating her hem, the whiteness of her upper thighs, as every movement I measure with my eye the minute changes up or down, waiting until she raises her arm farther to light the candle, breathless, waiting for the flame to catch (another sight I love) my eyes preferring to remain riveted at her hem, now reaching the bottom of her hips. Is that her crotch or just a shadow? I'm pondering, my eyes chewing up the darkness to discover the visual truth when I feel a coercive pressure on my back. Due to the coagmentation of bodies in the proximity it is difficult to turn anything but my head, where, out of the corner of an eye, I can stare into a small overripe face on which oatmeal-cookie lips break into a granular grin and wispy hairs flow from one side of his head to the other like cirrus clouds faintly obscuring uninhabited land, forehead shining through the transparency like a headlight in a fog.

As if not in answer to any question I'm going to ask, he answers, "I'm a lawyer."

"I'm a person," I say, "and I wonder why you're pressing your body into mine."

"That's simple, because you're so lovely I couldn't resist. Just because I'm Jewish I should feel guilty?" He is holding a bowl of noodle kugel above my head so it can't be contaminated by my hair.

"Have some," he says, placing an overflowing, exuberantly profuse spoonful under my nose, so closely I can no longer see it, an incursion of cinnamon, like Lieutenant Calley's company, bombarding my olfactory neurons.

If I don't open my mouth immediately, the noodles will either fall on my new pink suede boots or my wine satin shirt, so I allow my mouth to fall open, a form of receptiveness I don't enjoy, and he shoves the spoon in firmly, observing me chewing intently as if this were part of his creative process, a work in progress, the excess dropping off the corners of my lips.

"Good?" he asks. I shake my head, unable to speak.

"You have a nice smile," he says. I wonder when he's seen it as my mouth is still writhing with kugel, a cement mixer spinning, mixing noodles, cottage cheese, salt, sugar, cinnamon with saliva. I know that he told me he's a lawyer immediately because he's insecure about being so small and ugly. He doesn't realize that I'm impervious to that type of status admiration.

*

Sitting in our living room, my lawyer husband in his study taking an important phone call, I'm ensconced on the white velvet couch, boots buried to the knee in the white fur rug, reading a Gothic novel by Mary Stewart. I'm aware the house is immured in heavy silence, the children upstairs in each of their large rooms, or downstairs in the soundproof playroom watching color TV, or making a film. I feel a comfortable malaise. I've just arrived home from a successful shopping excursion: for my daughter, I've bought two T-shirts, hand prints by Picasso, edition of 25—one of a devil, saying underneath, "Grandma's Little Angel," the other, in fancy lettering, "Me encantado Puerto Rico," and for myself a Gucci shirt, handsewn sequins all over the front in op art style, in one color except for the words LAWYER'S WIFE in sequins of another color, the two colors chosen for their vibratory similarity of wavelength, very exciting to look at, but dangerous, as epileptic seizures can be caused by the excitation of sensitive brain waves. It's lovely to be able to afford to live dangerously and still remain completely secure.

My husband emerges from his study relieved to see my cool beauty, dark sensuosity, the comforting presence he can now relate to. He approaches, a sweet smile forming, "Is dinner ready?"

*

Crossing one leg over the other as I sit on Barbara's couch, Barry quickly bends down to read the name embossed on the sole of my boot.

"Fred Braun. And a John Meyer blouse." His glance glows with frank admiration.

"How do you know what kind of blouse I'm wearing?" I ask.

"I read the label when I was standing behind you."

"But you were so close, how could you have seen it?"

"I'm shortsighted," he says in a low voice. "How could you, a woman on welfare with three children, afford these things?"

What's a welfare investigator doing at Barbara's Hannukah party, I think. Perhaps he's ready to report me for buying something. What have I told him so far? Is there a tape recorder concealed within his jacket?

"That's a nice jacket," I say, to throw him off the track in case he's suspicious about my penetrating perusal.

"Yes, I'm really pleased with my image now. Come over here," he says, pulling me into the bedroom to the bed dripping coats like hot fudge and nut sauce over a sundae. Letting go of my arm, he riffles through the Turkish Afghans, seals, goatskins, lambs, rabbits, eventually pulling out a worn version of a John Wayne cowboy hat minus indentations in the crown and tries it on for me, glaring seriously underneath the brim, straightening the modified Daniel Boone jacket for a moment, farinaceous fringes like lo mein. He grabs my arm.

"Under here," he says, pulling me under the bed. "Look, look," he passionately grips my arm, throwing shoes and dust out of the way, seeking something, pulling our wine and noodle kugel underneath with us.

"Look at these," he cries, finding one boot. "Wait a minute, look at these." Tiny dots of perspiration are all over his skin like canned peaches baking next to pork chops.

"Don't you like these boots?" he asks, breathing hard, shoving brown leather cowboy boots under my nose.

"Smell," he says stroking them. "Nice? Wait here." He pushes me farther under the bed and returns quickly, bearing stuffed potatoes with carrot sticks rising from them like the masts of ancient schooners and a dish of potato pancakes. Sliding under the bed while holding the dishes upright, he puts his hand up my skirt, force-feeding me with the other; potato pancake, mashed potato, kugel and wine leaking down my chin.

"I only do the grooviest cases," he pants, "you know, like draft dodging, getting out of the army, you know, groovy political issues." Throwing me down in the dust he looks at me tenderly. "Your hair looks so nice next to my boot—the two browns. Open," he says, spooning kugel into my mouth, then, throwing the spoon out of the way, buries his penis in cream cheese and onion-soup dip and then my mouth.

"Ah," he opens his mouth sympathetically, "Eat it baby, it's so good for you," he moans. "So good—" His voice trails off, ejaculate eddying down my cheek as he slowly relaxes, observing me tenderly as I wipe a spot of sperm and noodle kugel off my lips, my bloated abdomen pushing at the buttons of my blouse from inside.

*

Biting into a hamburger held upright on one half of the roll in an attempt to compensate for some recent overeating, I watch Roberta, dark brown hair flowing over Weight Watcher's body, opening her lips slightly, cautiously, to receive the golden french fry with its surface of nearly microscopic droplets of melted salt, clenching her eyes at the heat of it, her open mouth enclosing a faint puff of steam like a pale cloud, immobile for a moment within the crater of a volcano. I stare my own mouth open.

"I told Bernie to go out," she says, swallowing, "and I made dinner for Michael."

"How did Bernie feel about that?"

"He doesn't want me to have to limit my relationships to one person. He even took the children with him so Michael and I could be alone. We had chicken enchiladas. It was marvelous. Mix a can of enchilada sauce and tomato sauce, olive oil, chicken, pepper, onion, olives and grated cheddar. You can buy frozen tortillas. Then you dip the tortillas in hot oil to make them pliable, stuff them, and pour sauce all over them. Oh, it's marvelous. I just feel so close to Michael. It's weird, I can't understand anything he says, yet I understand more everything he says than everything he says. I feel, I know we're communicating on a high level. I also made guacamole and used taco chips, and, for dessert, spumoni. I was dying to make love with him, I just felt we were so together and I think that's what he wanted too, but I couldn't be sure and I think he felt he couldn't be sure about me too, even though I'm not sure. It could also be because I'm married and maybe he's not certain about initiating anything under those circumstances because it isn't clear what kind of marriage Bernie and I have. But he bent down to kiss me goodnight and it seemed there was all this love in it, it was the gentlest, most delicious kiss—and when his lips met mine, I tasted the oil, faintly, then the pepper and onion, the sauce and after, almost imperceptibly, a tiny bit of sweetness from dessert."

After Roberta's description of her relationship with Michael I can no longer resist the vestigial rancid coleslaw on my dish, contained in its miniature, upside down nurse's cap, to which I impart the flavor of imaginary chicken enchiladas, which might or might not nullify my abstention from half a hamburger roll in terms of saving calories, so I eat that too. Fearful of rejection, my arm slowly crawls over the table like a soldier in a minefield, and I gingerly take a french fry off Roberta's dish and eat it, intensifying our camaraderie.

"Another order of french," says Roberta to the waitress.

"I'll have one too," I say, my heart beating furiously.

"Sharon, did you notice the way Bernie looked at you when you called for me? Was it different than usual?"

"No. A little. He looked as if he wanted to devour me."

"He really likes you. Why don't you come to dinner on Friday night with the kids?"

"Okay," I say, washing down the french fries with cherry No-Cal.

"Where's Roberta?" Bernie's large form is immobile in the doorway; his bleu cheese eyes stare at me as the children squeeze past.

"Bernie, it's impolite to block the entrance of your apartment when I've been invited to dinner."

"I'm not trying to be impolite," he says, close into my face, "I just wanted to share with you the way I'm enjoying my new feelings about proximity."

"Is Roberta here?" I ask, searching for her beyond his fixed form.

"She went to play guitar for a sick neighbor. She'll be back soon."

"That's a beautiful salad."

"Roberta made it," he says proudly, allowing me inside. "It has more flavor because it's made with flavorful oil that mixes better with the vinegar instead of flopping heavily to the bottom of the bowl, leaving bitter vinegar spots and spots of oily oil without any flavor. Look." He rubs some on my arm. "See? It's absorbed instantaneously by the skin."

"It's also absorbed instantaneously by my blouse."

"I'll fix that in a minute," he says, blushing, eyes pressed to my chest.

"What's the matter with your eyes?" I ask.

"I can't see. I didn't want to wear my glasses tonight because I wanted you to like me. I chose between being beautiful and seeing. Don't worry about the stain; I can get it out in a second. It isn't everyone who could get out a grease stain like that, but you happen to be lucky enough to be at the house of the best carpet and upholstery cleaner around."

"It was you who got this stain on me," I say.

"Ball-breaker. Let's try some of this wine," he says, putting the label to his eyes. "When you do a job well people notice and I'm the best carpet cleaner around. And I don't charge much. Fair all the way," he says, the glass tipping over and spilling wine all over me as Bernie pours it in.

"I'm hungry," says Zach, as Bernie blindly blots my pants with a dishtowel.

"I'll fix this for you, too."

"You certainly are fixing them," I say as he looks at me evilly, nearsightedly.

"Castrating Bitch."

"I'm hungry," says Zach.

"Listen, remember before, when I said I wanted you to like me?"

"When?"

"I'm hungry," says Zach.

"Remember, about the eyeglasses? Well I didn't just mean that. I meant more."

"I'm hungry," says Zach.

"When's Roberta coming back?"

"Any minute," says Bernie, bringing out a large platter of fried chicken pieces.

"Look at these," he says, holding up a piece. "All meat and no bones. My mother taught me how to do it. Just pure chicken enwrapped in crusty bready goldeny browny oil. Look how the skin absorbs this oil," he says, rubbing it over his hairy arm. Then, removing his sweater, he exposes a beaver body, rubbing the piece of chicken around his abdomen, bits of crust remaining in his chest and belly hair like leaves caught behind rocks in a mountain stream.

"I expect you to eat all of this."

"It isn't fair for you to have expectations of me," I say.

"I just want you to eat it all because it's good for you. Besides, there's a love potion in it. I said a chicken incantation. Do you want me to teach you how to make it?"

"No, thanks, I hate to cook. Just give me the ingredients of the love potion."

"Listen, I know you want love. I can tell. That's part of my attraction for you. I want to give you all the love you need and more. Not just sex, though that too," he says, rising from his seat as I stuff my mouth nervously with a huge hunk of chicken breast.

"Come," he says, bending over me and taking a tiny bite out of my neck. "Sit on my lap while you eat, baby."

"No," I scream, as Timothy, carrying a large bottle of grape juice into the children's room, drops the whole bottle, the children coming out of the room to stare as the magnificent dark purple cascading defluxion disembogues to be sucked immediately into the carpet, where it glows wetly, woolily, noxiously purple.

"Oh," I say, "grape juice stains."

"Don't worry," says Bernie, "I'm not the world's greatest carpet cleaner for nothing," taking a large plastic container from the corner and pouring solution profluently over the rug.

"This is good stuff. I made it myself from a special formula." He takes a machine from where it's standing propped against the wall and starting the motor, runs it over the soap, which begins to spread. More and more purplish-gray suds erupt all over the rug, as the children and I watch hypnotized. Bernie stands suspended for a moment, vibrating with the machine, gazing at me earnestly.

"My greatest dream is for you to come and live with me and Roberta so that I can give both of you all the love I have for you," he says, staring at me while foam spreads out from under the machine, flowing all across the floor.

"Let me do the stains on your blouse," he pleads, coming closer with the machine. I stuff a chicken leg in my mouth and run for the door.

*

A filthy, featherless, emaciated chicken ceases scratching itself under its wing with its beak, runs over to slip a fortune in the slot slide, then poignantly runs to a cup holding a few grains of corn to take its own reward. My fortune is, *Those who crave too much sometimes get more than they expected.*

"It's not your fortune," says Timothy, "it's mine. I put the dime in."

"It's my dime, so it's my fortune," says Thomas.

"I can tell it's my fortune, but anyone who wants it can have it, though it suits me best," I say, realizing that that's the passive manifestation of my personality. The children feed in dime after dime, not realizing how shabby the whole scene is and how the chicken is being exploited. The children ask Thomas for more and more dimes, and even when there's no reward of corn left in the cup, the chicken continues to send down fortunes, touching its beak to an empty reward cup anyway, in a passive, useless indictment of us all. It should refuse to do it.

"You don't have to keep giving them dimes just because they

ask," I tell Thomas, who still dispenses them.

"I spent these forty dollars in dimes because I like you so much."

*

All the Chinese restaurants on the street still have long lines extending outward, flaccid tongues protruding from watering mouths.

"Where shall we eat?" Thomas asks.

"I'm hungry," says Alex.

"I'd like to eat wherever the line is shortest," I say.

"You certainly are discriminating," says Thomas scornfully.

"Food isn't that important to me."

"How many?" asks the waiter. "Seven?"

"Isn't it marvelous," Thomas says, his eyes moving over our mob, "we're just like a family." I look at the children, who are dripping saliva all over the plastic-coated menus, except for Zachary, who's mixing a soy sauce and sugar aperitif, while Thomas studies the side of the menu that's written in Chinese, attempting unsuccessfully to penetrate the symbols.

"I just know they have different prices for Chinese people but I can't prove it. Do you trust me to serve your children or do you want to?"

"You can do it," I say, watching the large spoon scrape around the bowl, creating eddies in which large, unpigmented wonton cave creatures swim, attempting to buck the waves, as Thomas, trying to be fair, counts out each string of pork and wonton, each whale and tadpole equally.

"I hope you can see how much I like your children," says Thomas as two waiters place platters of food on the table, every spot becoming filled with succulent, sumpy dishes.

"God, I can't eat another thing. It's just come to me. The reason you're not in love with me is that I'm fat," Thomas pouts.

"Well," I say, stuffing rice with lobster sauce into my mouth, "it's partly true, but it's a good excuse for not having the problem of having anyone love you. Keep eating."

"I will, and you know why? Because you're so insensitive, glib and impertinent."

I put mustard on some of my fried rice, covering the rest in black bean sauce, ceasing for one moment to slip one hand under the table surreptitiously to open the pants button at my waist, feeling enormous relief as the two edges burst apart.

"You're on my mind night and day. If my wife Joan weren't such a good listener to all the words I poured out about you, I'd have really been fucked up."

"Good old Joan," I say, seeking the egg in the lobster sauce with the spoon as if dragging a lake, picking shrimp and snow peas from another dish with my fingers.

"You have to love me," says Thomas, sucking a piece of lobster out of a claw with long suction-filled kisses, "love me; it isn't just sex, though it's that too; I'm mad about you, and if you don't love me soon—I just can't bear the agony I've been going through. Do you want some of this lobster before I finish it?" he says, reaching over, his knit shirt sliding up his side exposing his flesh, pale, sequaceous, like roast chicken with its skin pulled off, unsuccessfully groping for the shrimp in black bean sauce.

"You have to make love with me."

"I can't make love with you or love you just because you want me to."

"But. But," he says, puzzled, eyes following his hand across the table, encompassing in his gesture our huge repast.

*

"Then, Dr. Stone," I say, as he disgustedly pokes my flesh with his finger, his fastidious, circumspect pressure answered with an argilaceous ripple that echoes over the hills of my body like a rock thrown into a mountain pool.

"You're doing very well."

Proud, I answer, "It's not a problem to do well here. I never see food and don't desire it at all."

"I think at this point you may survive. I caught you just at the right moment," he mumbles, adjusting the ends of his stethoscope necklace into his ears, touching it to my chest gingerly as if it were an extension of his body, not wishing to contaminate its round tip by repulsiveness.

Good, I think, good, in spiteful glee.

"Then," I continue, after he finishes, "I noticed that my clothes were becoming tighter, and I didn't like the way I looked so I decided to diet, and since I couldn't decide between high protein and Weight Watchers, I bought a Dr. Atkins book and a calorie counting book and the Scarsdale Diet book and did them all. I also decided not to go out for a while."

*

"Carl? Is Marsha there?"

"Marsha went to Florida with her mother for a week. It was an immediate decision. Because of the cold she's had all winter and the free hotel room with her mother, and probably the free food, she decided she needed the rest. But she decided without me," he whines. "I needed a rest too, and she left me with everything— work, thesis, the housework and the kids!"

"I'm sure you'll be able to handle it, and when Marsha comes home she'll be healthier and more productive."

"I hope so. Guess what?" he says excitedly. "I finally passed my French exam for my doctorate. I practically have it now. Why don't you come up and visit?"

"I'm too busy to visit, but I'm calling to find out whether the food's arrived from the co-op so I can pick it up."

"It's here. If you stay and visit a while, I'll save you time by driving you downtown witn it."

In their large pantry, having waded past sixteen overflowing bags of everyone's co-op food, I'm standing in front of Marsha's refrigerator removing my meat, which is leaking meat-blood everywhere and, as I lift it up, falls out the bottom of the bag onto the floor next to the cat litter.

"We have good stuff this week," says Carl, inspecting the meat on the floor. "Leg of lamb, two chickens, chopmeat and chicken livers. I didn't look in our bag. I'm leaving it for Marsha."

"Do you have anything I can put this in?" I ask.

"I can lend you this plastic bag, but you'll have to return it because Marsha and I got matching ones and we want to keep them. I'll lend you hers. It has a large *M*. The only reason I'm helping you so much is because I like you; you've been a good friend for a long time now." Picking up most of the meat with my hands, covered in chopmeat and blood, I look like the victim of an accident on the production line of General Motors. I shove it into the plastic shopping bag with the *M* that Carl is holding open for me, as if offering Marsha herself. Reaching with bloodied hands into the profusion of the engorged, plethoric, redundant refrigerator, I feel myself grabbed from behind, like undersea prey, tentacles reaching around my waist and over my shoulder. Two of the eggs I've gently taken out, lying in my bloodied hands like breech foetuses turned and removed, drop to the floor where they lie next to the chopmeat, the golden yolks settling into their gelatinous amniotic beds, still trembling; Marsha's eyes cracked open with awareness coming to haunt me.

"I couldn't help it," says Carl, "I've always wanted you and since you've split up with Roger you're more attractive than ever." He points to the floor. "Look, the ingredients for steak tartare."

"You can get diseases from steak tartare," I say, attempting to lift the bag into the shopping cart, the leg of lamb falling out as Carl whispers urgently into my ear when I bend down to pick it up.

"Please stay a while. Let's go to the movies. Or we can stay right here. I want to get to know you better." He looks at me holding the leg of lamb like a club; "That blood all over your hands excites me."

"Let me wash," I say, suddenly exhausted and hot. I pick up a peach and sit down on the floor for a moment, right outside the pantry next to some of the other people's bags, biting into the peach, nurturing the cool, tart, pungent succulence, feeling, as I delicately dispose of it, my perspiration drying. Directly after eating the last fragment, without even giving me a second to wipe my mouth, Carl's lips are pressed to mine like a bloodsucker, squeezing the tart peach juice from my lips back into my mouth. Unprepared and unbalanced for the sudden pressure, I fall over onto my elbow, Carl on top, spilling the bags all over the floor.

"Say you'll stay, say you'll stay," he litanes into my mouth, muffled by the beard and moustache, which now surrounds both our orifices as we fall farther, breaking some of the bags, peaches, grapes, scallions, lemons, cauliflower, nectarines and lettuce crushed beneath us, or rolling out of the way.

"Look at this peach," says Carl, pinning me down with one arm, stopping the peach with the other as it rolls by. He wraps his lips around half of it leaving the other half sticking out of his mouth like a breast; when he pulls it out, one half completely gone as if digested suddenly by powerful enzymes.

"Yum," he says, masticating the words; "taste this." He shoves the half between my teeth; my lips skid on peach fuzz; his other hand closes over my breast, which seems like yet another peach half. As I twist my shoulder ineffectually, still unable to reach the peach with my hand, Carl pulls my shirt aside, exposing my breast as I mumble, takes a bite of it, his moustache nibbling about it like a school of pike picking at seaweed. When he releases me, I remove the peach from my mouth.

"Whose peach is this you've taken? The food's getting all mixed up."

"Fuck the food. We'll fix it later. I've wanted you, I've wanted you," he says, removing my blouse and holding one breast in each hand.

"Let's eat these now."

"No," I say, pulling away.

"I mean these nectarines. They're crushed and if we wait any longer they'll be totally inedible. It doesn't feel right to waste food."

*

I picture Carl at the gray wood-grained Formica table with his mother, her hair pinned back neatly but with the same waviness that Carl's will have later, though now his hair is light brown and straighter, his face rounder, hairless, his gray-green eyes displaying his mother's tendency to hyperthyroid as they bulge toward the food on his plate.

"I don't want any more."

"But you didn't clean your dish," whines his mother; "The children in Europe are starving."

"Why don't we mail it to them?"

Carl rises, pulls off his pants and rushes to the sink with nectarines held lovingly in his hand, inspecting their rescuable properties affectionately, his erect penis bobbing as he walks briskly, pointing on the upswing to his gently cupped hands as if their contents were the object of his great passion, while his thin hurrying legs covered with dark fur seem unaware of any sexuality in the rest of his body. Biting the rinsed fruit with nurturing voracity, he puts some to my lips, crushing me to the floor, quickly relishing me like another piece of crushed fruit, surrounded in waves of smashed summer fruit ambrosia.

"Come, please, come, come, come."

"I don't want to; I can't."

"Please, please."

"No, get off me. It's useless to make it with a married man. They're so involved in *that* relationship."

"Nonsense, nonsense—you're wrong—" Limp, surrounded by fruit and vegetables, like two turtles dazed by the sun in a dirty tank, his head is above mine, immobile, eyes novocained. I ask, "What are you thinking?"

"Well you know, I'm in love with someone. I married the right woman for the wrong reasons."

I lie there pale, dehydrated, the moisture—sweat, and now tears—pressed from my body by his senseless superincumbent ponderousness.

Replacing the food into bags, Carl shakes his head in joyful disbelief. "I can't believe it. I passed my French exam and made it with you all in the same day."

Weeping and eating as I divide the food, I wonder whether anyone would ascertain vestiges of perspiration or pubic hairs on their fruits.

*

"I'd like to take you for a romantic dinner in the country to a special place I know."

"I can't get a baby-sitter on such short notice."

"Well, bring the children. I like children. It'll be fun for them too. Being with kids is such an ethereal, almost religious experience. They're so pure."

"Okay, I'll bring them," I say with misgiving, knowing Bruce.

I picture us coming to visit him, me walking regally up the brownstone steps in my gray boots, velvet knickers and cape, looking like one of the Three Musketeers, while the real musketeers disguised as angels run around me, and through my legs, in their hurry to see Bruce and his dog, which is dressed up in an apron for the occasion and barking jealously as we approach.

"Don't mind Sarah," calls Bruce from the threshold, "she's jealous of women."

"Well, she has no reason to be jealous of me," I demur, flattered.

"What are these toys?" asks Zachary, running his hand along the small white sculptural constructions placed all along the white seating platform, knocking them all over.

"Pick them all up, Zach."

"Oh, no, let him leave them," says Bruce, "I had them in a special order anyway, a combination aesthetic, astral, horoscopal and numerological arrangement that took me endless years with a ruler, compass and charts. I'll have to fix it myself."

"What's this?" asks Timothy, suspending a large black construction over the glass coffee table.

"Careful!" shouts Bruce, jumping out of the white seat like an explosion of nerve gas from its storage tank in Utah, while Timothy, startled, drops the black construction, which falls to the floor, not without first going right through the coffee table.

"I just wanted to know what it was," wails Timothy, "and he

scared me jumping up just like the ghost of Watkins Glen in my comic book."

"I told you horror comics are no good for you."

"It was a construction," says Bruce hoarsely, through a constricted throat. "But don't feel too bad about the table; it was specially made extra-thin glass, made to order so that it would appear as if it were nothing. I'm very interested in things that are but appear like nothing."

"I'm hungry," says Alex.

In the kitchen there is food on the table in a lovely design. Sarah is already helping by carrying things from the refrigerator in her teeth. Hand-blown goblets surround two bottles of wine, one red and one white, and in the center a large platter filled with golden moussaka, surrounded in turn by cut glass dishes of black olives, green olives and large strips of pimiento, limp, one atop the other like bodies in a mass grave, sardines in a similar condition, Italian lox and Spanish carp.

"Some wine?" Bruce asks the children.

"Do you have any juice? We hate wine."

"No, I don't," says Bruce.

"Do you have any peanut butter and jelly?" asks Zach. While Bruce makes them peanut butter and jelly sandwiches I sample some of the moussaka in its white bowl.

I wonder where the children are. Looking into the living room I could tell they'd been there by the jelly prints along the white couch, white chair and white walls, where Sarah in her apron was attempting to lick them off, when I see them finally behaving, sitting quietly on the floor in Bruce's white dressing alcove.

"I know how this was made," says Timothy without looking up, sensing my eyes on him like the blind fish on the dark bottoms of the oceans.

"Smart fellow," says Bruce. Then, looking more closely, I watch the color drain out of his blue eyes until they become almost as white as all his furniture and his jacket. Wow, I think, he's really getting everything to match, when I see next to Timothy and Zachary on the floor all the different triangular shapes and shades of wood veneer they've peeled off Bruce's antique, hand-constructed chest from Pompeii; they've repeated the pattern like a puzzle on the white floor. Bruce is weeping aloud, Sarah running around and barking, desirous of comforting him.

"We'd better go."

"It's okay, I love children. I'm just a little tired."

I look at Bruce questioningly as he weeps and herds the children downstairs with a screwed-up face.

"I'm sorry." I begin.

"Oh, Sarah, I love you so much," I hear him weep as I run down to the children.

*

We pile into Bruce's blue bus. Looking straight ahead in concentration, Bruce turns the ignition key and presses his foot on the gas.

"Are we there yet?" asks Zach.

"Zachary has a very special sense of humor," says Bruce.

"I'm hungry," says Timothy.

"Me too," says Zach.

"We're going to a wonderful restaurant in the country."

"I'm hungry now," says Alex.

"But you just ate," I cry, "you just had sixteen bananas, grilled cheese sandwiches, cereal with raisins, and oranges and nuts. You couldn't possibly be hungry."

"Well, we are," says Zach, getting up from his seat in the back so he can stand directly behind Bruce, real close, whispering confidentially, his sweet, moist mouth now and then brushing the blond hair at the back of Bruce's neck, gently and intimately, with a secret softly whispered: "We eat a lot."

"Hey, there's a toy back here. Can we play with it?"

"Uh, uh. Don't touch it, it belongs to someone else," answers Bruce, his white skin turning red, causing the lighter blond hairs along the edge of his hairline to glow silvery like the outline of foam along an edge of a wave where it meets the sand, rolling flatly up, etching circles at sunset, his eyes purposefully fixed outside along route nine.

"Move over." Timothy pushes Alex's head off his lap.

"Don't push," says Alex. "I just wanted to rest a minute because I'm carsick and I might throw up." She gives a sharp kick to Timothy who jumps back, startled, pushing over Zach who begins kicking wildly and angrily.

I turn as much as I can in the front seat, flailing my arms, hoping to hit one of them or all as they continue fighting, but I keep missing, my aimless strokes whipping in the air like a beater mixing heavy cream.

"It's difficult to drive like this," says Bruce.

All of a sudden it's quiet in the gentle dusk, musky earthy moisture heavy with the hissing of rushing water.

"This is it." Bruce slides open the doors and helps us out of the van, tiptoeing, his whole aspect worshipful. "The beautiful spot," he whispers, "I wanted to show you. Do you like it?" he asks me, grabbing my hand.

"It's incredibly beautiful."

"Do you like it?" he asks Alex.

"It's okay. Can we go eat now?"

"I thought you were carsick."

"I am, but I'm hungry too."

"Mommy, I'm bored," says Zach, staring at the stream. "And I'm hungry."

"The restaurant I want to take you to is on this road—I'm sure," says Bruce, becoming more and more nervous, moving the car slowly forward. "I'm sure it was up this road, but all I see is grass and trees and hills, unless—it isn't here anymore."

"Hurry," says Timothy, panting, "I can't wait anymore, let's eat any place." Bruce is driving around in a panic now, moving the car senselessly back and forth, unable to decide which way to go.

Bruce is about to sit down next to me in the stuffed leatherette booth of the diner we finally find when all the children move in and begin fighting to sit next to me as he half sits, half stands, waiting for the verdict and trying to keep his balance while being pushed this way and that.

"Why don't you children sit at a separate table, all to yourselves," I say in a seductive wheedling tone, as the children settle around me, one on each side and one on my lap, Bruce banished to the other bench opposite us.

"Read me the menu," says Alex, looking complacently at her hands, preparing to listen as if I were reading her a story.

"You read it yourself."

"I can't," she says, beginning to cry, then shrieking, "I can't, read it to me, read it to me, you have to."

"Menu," I read: "Spaghetti, succotash, hash brown potatoes, french fries, yams in syrup, baked potato, black-eyed peas, navy beans, hot dog rolls, bread, buns, stuffing, salami on buttered white, soupe du jour—chicken noddle soup with chicken fat, and dessert—ice cream and chocolate pudding pie, rice pudding and bread pudding."

"I think I'll have some ice cream and some chicken noodle soup with fat," says Zach.

"There's an awful lot of starch on the menu," I observe, having just begun my protein diet that day, as Timothy spills his water all over the table where it slowly eddies around all the silver and is instantly sucked into the napkins.

"Wipe it up quickly."

"Wait," says Timothy, "doesn't it look like an overheated rhinocerous drooling," referring to the moisture dripping on Bruce's pants.

"It's okay, this ice water dripping on my newly cleaned and pressed white slacks feels good on my overheated legs," explains Bruce as the waitress places his spaghetti with white bread and canned peas in front of him.

"Can I taste your peas?" asks Zack, taking a handful in his small filthy fist, the dirt on his hands suddenly dissolving in profluent pale pea juice, dripping a trail of dirt drops as he cautiously eats them out of his fist, alternating the top and the bottom as if eating cream from a cannoli, the juice squeezing out and dripping onto the yellow islands of chicken fat in the soup under his hand, where gray, they remain contained, a bloated noodle showing out here and there like the Loch Ness monster. While Bruce observes this horrified, Alex pulls a large string of spaghetti from his dish, slips the tip into her mouth and sucks it in; the sauce is pushed along the spaghetti and collects at her lips where the last of it is sucked in with a pop, sauce exploding all over her cheeks and Bruce's white shirt.

"More peas," orders Zach, then, deciding better of it, he crawls under the table in order to approach the waitress more closely and orders, "More peas, please."

"That's the first time he's ever said *please*," I say proudly.

"Sarah loves you," says Bruce, as Sarah, no longer jealous of me, is jumping affectionately all over my wide crepe palazzo pants, which don't button anymore in the back, the open button of which I enclose under a sleeveless silk shirt over my sensuous blouse in order to suppress and dissemble the bulge at my waist; the loose, swinging, decumbent flow of veil-like pants also dissembling the new thickness of thigh. Is it because I'm fat that, though Sarah is sitting on my lap, Bruce is sitting at the other end of the table picking at the grapes I've piled onto a platter with cheese and crackers in varying shades of yellow-gold, ochre, cadmium, lemon, and cream, like van Gogh's sunflowers? Bruce hands me a round box containing a flat Italian nougat cake composed of liquored fruits, buried in confectioner's sugar like the Magic Mountain during the blizzard.

"Why are you waking up the children?" asks Bruce in sudden panic as I climb Zach's loft bed with the cake balanced in my hands so perhaps they will awaken and be convinced to help decimate this new volatile viand before I can solitarily incorporate it.

"I hate this cake," says Zach, annoyed at being disturbed.

I cut a slice of the cake, my knife barely able to move through the hard, moist, sugar-inundated cherries, citrons and raisins and currants, compressed for more weight, more richness, more moistness, trapping the knife; I try to trap Bruce's eyes, blue, cool, clear as cucumber pulp.

"Sarah's not jealous of you anymore. She loves you," he says, attempting to squeeze a last piece of cheese between his lips as mine move closer and closer, beginning to encroach on space reserved for his culinary articulations, chasing his eyes with mine round and round as they glibly escape my heavy, pervasive ones.

"I don't like to kiss. It's too frustrating. It seems so pointless."

"Then take off your clothes," I say nervously, stuffing more of the cloying dulcitudinous confection into my mouth, imagining I'm succumbing to a strange manipulative seduction as I hand him my written guarantee that, if we kiss, he'll not leave frustrated or in pain, as I've never had the temerity to be the cause of the dreaded blue balls.

"If I stay, Sarah will have to stay, too."

"That's okay. She seems to like it here and she doesn't bark at me anymore."

As I lie on the loft bed with Sarah, the dish of cheese, grapes, and Italian cakes is placed next to me as Bruce clambers up—thin face first, then his hirsute slender chest, his heavier middle and his long thick legs—beginning immediately to press short kisses onto my body. Sarah watches carefully, her mouth open a tiny bit, tongue contained inside, thin black lips a little drawn, as Bruce kisses my lips, short fast kisses like Morse code, so fast I can't read it, removing them the moment I begin to feel them, losing communication, touching my clitoris fast; as soon as I begin to feel that, he inserts his penis, and with three loud moans, two long and one short, just as I might begin to feel the voluptuousness inside me spreading like an African lake heavy with hippopotamuses in the late afternoon sun, he's come. He looks at me, his eyes flashing the message Did you come? mine answering with emptiness. He lies on his side munching on grapes and cheese, his arms around Sarah, who's sucking the crumbs that fall into the heavy hair on his chest like a vacuum cleaner on a flokati while I lie alone, finishing the remainder of the confection, my bloated body like a damaged Campbell's soup can containing botulin.

"Tell me," asks Bruce, turning his head from Sarah, who's licking his lips, "do you have another lover?"

I pause a moment, wondering whether he's jealous and wants to make sure I have none or whether he wants me to have one.

"No," I say, deciding to tell the truth as Bruce, seemingly agitated, is pulling bits of Sarah's fur off in quick movements like his kisses, pieces of her fur flying all around, gray in the dim light, reminding me that my allergy doctor told me not to have animals on my bed.

As I ponder my self-destructiveness, I'm aware of the heavy coating of fur on Bruce and wonder what sort of animals Dr. Gonad meant.

"Yes, I'm sure," I say slowly, trying to recall whether I've forgotten one of my lovers.

"Well I have," Bruce says, still picking Sarah's fur, "and the usual is happening. I'm becoming more involved with one of you and it's her. She's very young, only twenty-one, and has only one child who looks just like me, with light hair and blue eyes, not like your dark gypsy children." I picture us both in a lineup in bathing suits, our bios underneath. She's slender, with soft wrinkleless skin, wearing a one-piece white lace wedding/bathing suit, virginal, veiled, waiting—flushed with anticipation—to learn the wonders and joys of living, while I stand there next to her, trying to be sexy in a black bikini, flesh popping out from under the elastic edges of the suit which cut deeply into my white, flabby, scarred, damaged flesh, weather veined, weighty legs like dying tree trunks choked by parasitic mosses and varicose vines; her smile is thin, sure, very much like Sarah's, while my eyes, large and vulnerable, tremble like a light bulb at the onset of a power failure. I wipe some confectioner's sugar from my chest with a damp finger and look at Sarah who, tongue rolling out in a yawn, looks back at me contented.

*

Without raising my head, which is so bloated I can't lift it anyway, I can see over my abdomen a nurse's cap, gliding, disembodied, and then Dr. Stone's hair, his head, floating closer, sitting on top of my mammoth belly like the head of St. John the Baptist on a serving platter, but floating across and over to my side, it achieves a body clad in white, one button open at the collar, which flaps over, brown tendrils of hair tenderly caressing his neck as they wind gently into the collar.

"I saw *The Iceman Cometh* last night," he says, sitting beside my bed, "and the play lasted almost four hours. It's not that I'm prejudiced, but I don't think a black person—James Earl Jones—is right in the role of Hickey." He's staring sleepily at my fingers as he speaks, which are spread on the coverlet, immobile, miniature sausages, joints demarcated by rings of tight flesh.

"I read the play and can't see anything in it that would imply that a black person couldn't play the part," I say, my eyes on my fingers trying to determine whether he's mesmerized by them with horror, interest, or absentness.

"Don't talk. You're not allowed to exert yourself yet," he says, beginning to touch my fingers gently with his own slender fingertip, absently tracing around them, his finger behaving as if it has disembodiedly discovered a sensory delight, until he gets up abruptly, and stethoscopes me hurriedly but no longer gingerly.

*

The sun is bleeding into the sky, like a stabbed sunny-side-up, still, pink-purple clouds, puffy and sharply defined, seemingly thrown there unmoving like used Johnson & Johnson cotton balls. Rushing uptown, I watch the colors deepening as I walk in the direction of Riverside Park, the hot decadent mature smell of summer mingling with a cool crispness not quite manifest, and wait impatiently at the top of the brownstone stairs for Marvin to open the six locks on his door. Carefully stepping over the hidden wire for the burglar alarm, we embrace, Marvin holding me against his apron with one arm, the other hand holding the cooking spoon, dripping gravy. Luckily he doesn't notice how fat I'm becoming because when he looks at me the cones and rods of his inner eyes form specially projected images of women from *Playboy* magazine.

"Quick, let's go outside to the park. If we hurry we can watch a fantastic garrulous sunset."

"Well—I'm cooking now," he says slowly, wasting minutes, head tilting earnestly, brushing the freshly washed dark hair out of his eyes with the wrist of the hand holding the wooden spoon. "Can't we wait till I'm finished?"

"Sunsets don't wait." I turn to the window, to point a bit of it out to him, to tempt him, like the smell and color of something delicious, a taste to make him want more, seeking frantically a scrap of sky beyond the air conditioner, unsuccessfully, and rush into the bedroom where, there too blocking the window, is an air conditioner. Frustrated I glance up at the skylight, a gesture only as I know there's no sunset visible up there, and I notice that it's covered completely in plastic.

"How could you close yourself in this way?" I ask in desperation. "You can't see, hear or smell anything outside."

"You know I can't stand the heat," he says in a long whine, "and in the winter there's never enough heat." He carries his forefinger to the shelf under the skylight, turns it over and runs it along the shelf, turning it upright again like a tray of hors d'oeuvres, triumphantly displaying spots of soot.

I'm buried in the five hundred Sunday *New York Times*es on the floor while Marvin is crucially inspecting the progress of each portion of our dinner. The phone rings and rings. I look up at Marvin, who's bringing a spoon to his lips carefully.

"Aren't you going to answer it?"

"No."

"Why not?"

"Because the only person who ever calls on Saturday night is my mother, and I don't want to talk to her now because I'm with you," he says, stuffing a dried banana into my mouth. "Try this. I got it at the new Indian store that opened on Broadway." Then he opens a jar, fills a spoon with semigelatinous marmaladinous substance (which, while hanging over the edge, manages to maintain its molecules in one lump), and while I'm still masticating the banana, shoves the spoon into my mouth.

"What is it? Ginger?"

"Mango chutney."

"I'm allergic to mangoes." I spit it out onto the counter.

With a disgusted look on his face Marvin picks up one of his oval sponges after deliberating which one to use and wipes the counter carefully.

"I find this very symbolic of our relationship," I say. "I think you're too fastidious for me."

"Nonsense."

My statement passes through his consciousness like roughage through a digestive system, emerging completely, having made no impression. "Will you be okay?" he asks.

"If I don't turn red and swollen and stop breathing within the next half hour I'll be fine."

"Let's make love before you become swollen," he says, putting his lips to mine, hands at his sides, sucking the chutney flavor out of my mouth with his in a snakebite rescue kiss. "Umm, good. Come to think of it, we can't. The dinner will be spoiled. It's just about ready."

It's good to see Marvin so passionate, I think, as, sitting at the round table, he spoons out some of the prune and raisin gravy. His eyes roll into his upper lids; his body shudders in seismic delight, tongue sliding over his lips amorously.

"Did you come?" I ask as his mouth opens for a spoonful of rice. His lips curl in self-doubt.

"I'm afraid the rice is a bit overdone. Do you want me to make it over again?"

"Of course not. Food doesn't mean that much to me."

"Well—" he says doubtfully, smacking his lips over the rice, stabbing it with his fork to see whether the grains are stuck together.

"Don't be silly, we already missed the sunset, I don't care that much about rice to spend the whole evening indoors cooking."

Suddenly, watching him moving his lips in various ways, smacking them with varying sucking sounds—a fugue of mouth music—I realize that although he appears completely different physically, even the exact opposite—dark where David was blond, brown eyed where David's eyes were blue, thin and medium height where David was tall and heavy—that he's a reincarnation of my first husband. I recall David at his mother's house at dinnertime; even after we were married she still wanted to cook for him. His father sits at one end of the enormous table which took up the length of three rooms with large doorways, his mother at the other, David, his brother and I somewhere in the middle. His brother, three years younger, but already way over six foot four, the baby, has a giant glass of milk always beside his elbow, which he always spills. Edna, plump, in bedroom scuffs, screams at him while he wipes it up, confused, as she pulls the sponge out of his hand, and wipes it herself, on her hands and knees. Unable to eat we watch her sacred labors. Meticulously manipulating the sponge so that it sucks up the whole spill, she rises, disheveled.

"Look at these cracks in my knees from you," she says, looking at Eugene, who's nervously fingering a glass.

"Don't touch that." She pulls it away from him as his fingers move to finger the pitcher. "Don't touch that. Hymie, how's the potatoes."

"A little cool," says Hymie from his throne.

"Shall I heat them a little bit?"

"Okay," Hymie says.

She rises, her own dinner untouched, and runs into the kitchen softly on her scuffs.

"Don't touch that," she says, running in just in time to rescue the cranberry sauce spoon from Eugene, who's fussing with it. "How's the pot roast?"

"It's very good. A little cool," says Hymie, considering.

"Give it to me, I'll heat it up a little. Eat, David," says Edna uneasily, gobbling her food so she can run back and forth into the kitchen, as David has stopped eating for a moment, absorbed in observing me eat, his eyes glazed over. Edna is more and more uneasy at the seductive expression on his face; she watches him rise and pull me downstairs into their basement carrying my dish of food.

We sit on the couch next to his paintings of naked women and basketball players.

"Eat, oh, eat," he says, pulling off his clothes, already erect, absorbed in observing every facet of my mastication. Suddenly, he pulls my head down over his penis, saying, "Eat me, eat me baby, put it all the way in, move your tongue around it, now out a little, now eat just the top, the mushroom head, baby, chew it, suck it, harder." He squeezes the bottom of his organ and a rush of ejaculate pours into my mouth in squirts as if squeezed from the bottom of a plastic mustard bottle.

"Make love with me now," I say.

"I can't yet, and we have no time to wait; my mother might come down. Let me do it with this carrot," he pleads. "Or one of these bananas."

"David," his mother calls from the top of the stairs, "dessert."

*

"Let's find out what time the movie starts, Marvin."

"In a minute," he says, obstinately sucking chicken bones, breaking them with his teeth, forcing them to bend, his teeth bared.

"Can I call?"

"Wait a minute. Finish eating."

"I am finished. I can't eat another thing."

"Let's wait till it goes down and then eat some more. We haven't finished everything."

"Let me call the movie. I don't want to eat any more."

"Well, wait till I'm finished," he says biting into a tiny button mushroom removed from beside the demolished fowl on the dish.

"Okay, now I'll call."

I sit on my seat, stuffed, in a stupor. Tears stream down my face when Marvin tells me that we missed the first fifteen minutes of the last show.

After turning on the air conditioner, he presses me into the newspapers, floating on top of me, head held up to avoid drowning, ignoring the ringing of the phone. His eyes close immediately after he comes, his body on top of me becomes heavier and heavier, his penis slowly slips out of me, just resting between my labia like sweet Italian sausage in spaghetti sauce; his snores slowly evolving above the hoarse hum of the air conditioner.

*

Outside, it's drizzling. I walk fast, anxious to be back inside. The cold rain making nothing of my shirt, I might as well be in a cold shower, raindrops like pigeons settle on my eyeglasses, obscuring my vision.

"One minute," says Marvin loudly, pausing on the street, "you're leading me. Is there any reason why you're walking so fast?" he says, walking especially slowly, like the giant in Jack and the beanstalk after a heavy lunch of thirty-three sheep, before, still hungry, he smells an Englishman. He purposely pauses, peering into a window full of fruit and cheese. He hears me sniffling and looks over.

"Why are you crying?" he asks, surprised and annoyed.

"I don't know," I weep. "I feel as if I'm married and need a divorce."

Marvin's removing my wet clothes, peeling them off like banana skins, avocado skins, orange skins, and stuffing pieces of Cakemasters breads into my mouth.

"Is it good? How's this one, do you like it, good baby?"

"Go answer it," I say as the doorbell rings.

Marvin, on his knees on the bed, is hurt and insulted.

"It might be about my children. Maybe something happened to one of them. You didn't answer the phone last night. It makes me feel creepy to be cut off from every outside contact just because I'm here with you."

Still insulted that I don't want to eliminate outside reality when

I'm with him, he slips his medical lab coat over his naked body, holding it closed at the waist, his erect penis pulling it out at the bottom like a crinoline-lined ballgown, pulling it up enough so that, under the ballgown, bald, bony knees are apparent, deliberately taking his time. Just as it appears that whoever it was at the door has departed, the bell rings again, insistently. Exasperated, Marvin goes to the door and opens it. His mother sweeps in in fur coat and fur hat, father following.

"I kept calling," his mother said, handing him her coat to hang up. Marvin carries his coat into the bedroom using it as a chance to warn me.

"Don't come out."

"Why not? Surely they know you must see women?"

"No," he whispers.

"What about Judy, who you went with for three years and were going to marry? Didn't they ever meet Judy?"

"No, my mother wouldn't like anyone I was going to marry and no one I was going to marry would have anything in common with my family, so there'd be no reason for them to meet."

"Marvin," his mother calls, "I was calling to say that Daddy had a convention and we wanted to have lunch with you but now it's too late to go out, so why don't we just eat something here?"

Peeking out of the bedroom I can see that Marvin's father has already removed his coat and hat, his mother has Marvin's apron on; it holds her around the waist, tightly caressing her heavy hips. Marvin has both of his refrigerators open, computing the contents and making mental meals.

"It's time you should defrost," says his mother.

"Hi," I say, emerging naked from the bedroom.

Marvin's father looks up from his *New York Times.* "Marvin, you didn't introduce us."

Marvin spins around speedily, his lab coat, suddenly free of surveillance due to the sudden shock, swings open. As his eyes run crazed along my nude body, I can see his traumatized testicles shriveling. His mother rising from her perusal of the contents of the refrigerators, holding some tinfoil-wrapped items in her arm, smooths her stiff coiffure with her other hand. "Marvin, your manners."

"Mom, Dad, this is a friend of mine, Sharon. Sharon, this is Mom and Dad," Marvin says monotonously, his lab coat still wide open, genitals shrunk into his body.

"You should comb your hair more neatly," says Marvin's mother as I sit down at the table, legs crossed, picking at some cheese lying there. "You shouldn't pick like that. We should all begin eating together—and with your fingers! You should know better. Didn't you learn any manners? Marvin knows his manners. Well, since you seem to know this apartment better than I do, why don't I relax while you prepare the luncheon?"

"I don't cook," I said, "ever. I only use frozen food and paper plates. I'm committed to not cooking or doing dishes anymore. But I especially don't cook when my three children are with my husband.

"Are you married?" she asks.

"Yes, but we don't live together."

"Marvin," she says, sitting on his lap, pulling the hair on his chest, "You shouldn't be hanging around with a thirty-five-year-old divorcée with three children, you should be with someone nice, young, a college graduate, someone you can marry, a virgin. Someone who at least combs her hair."

*

"Dr. Stone," I call, waking up startled from a dream of being raped, "I see you there, behind my belly, hiding."

"I'm not hiding. That's very paranoid of you. I'm giving you a gynecological examination," he says, turning his fingers, already in my vagina.

"I'm studying the effects of obesity on the size, shape, and color of the vaginal lining." He's looking into the darkness, seemingly absorbed in whatever it is his finger is feeling, mumbling and nodding to himself like an old Jewish man saying prayers.

"What did you discover?" I ask, after he's shut off the flashlight he used to peer into the cavity of my body, explorer of my dark caves, surreptitious spelunker of hidden caverns, his pale rubber glove hanging half off his hand like a failed condom.

"It's too complicated to tell you." he says.

I see him coming toward me after sunrise, a line of colleagues behind him like a guided museum tour. "You wouldn't believe it. When I brought her here she was on the verge of death, a bloated blimp whose vital organs had almost ceased functioning, pale and disgusting, barely resembling a human being but rather like a bleached and beached whale. When I first saw her, I told the nurses what to do, then left the room immediately, having lost complete control over my vomit reflex. Later I could hardly examine her without gagging—her skin bilious from a malfunctioning liver; her eyes, inhuman, two dark dots, raisins in risen dough, uggchh; and her breasts, hanging over each side of her gargantuan body like Tibetan mammoths who've lost their footing, clinging hopelessly to the sides of the mountain. And now, with my special treatment, and no food, none at all, only water, straight through the vein, so she doesn't have to use her mouth, which might condition her to desire to eat, she's doing fine."

"Aren't you desirous of food at all?" one of them asks as they mill around timidly, proving conclusively that I don't look all that great yet. "Don't you ever think about it?"

"No," I say, "I'm relieved never to have mealtimes, never to see food, never to have to cook it."

"Don't people try to smuggle things in for you? Sweets?"

"She's not allowed any visitors," says Dr. Stone.

"It's been a pleasure," I say.

*

"I'll take care of you," says my editor, stirring his drink, the heavy brocade curtains of the South Tibetan Taste Restaurant moving like chain mail constructed of pure gold. "I really love your work, it's something special."

"Do you think it will make money?"

"I'm sure. Are you going to write a novel?"

"Yes," I answer, lifting up a shrimp scampi in hot sauce by the tail with my fingers, rubbing its brownish, broiled, buttered surface into the burnished sauce on the dish, rubbing it into the rice and biting it, leaving the tail alongside a row of other tails on my dish. "I'm working on a novel about an American revolution that fails because a member of the C.I.A. is among their group disguised as a washing machine."

"Have some of this Tibetan lo mein with bean curd and jellied chantarelles," he offers, waving for the waiter dressed in special Tibetan folk uniform executed in solid gold. "How much do you need to live on?"

"Oh, I could manage on ten thousand, the three kids and I have lived on much less, especially in the tenement, but now that we moved we need a bit more. I'd like to keep on writing. I have another book of short stories almost completed now."

"I'd love you to keep writing; you have to, it's very important."

"Do you think I could get an advance on my next book so I can finish it, since I've already sold one book to Whore House?"

"I'm sorry, not on a book of short stories. You know no one reads short stories."

"What about my novel? If I give you fifty pages and an outline can you get me an advance?"

"I'm sorry, I can't get you anything, I can only take you to lunch, but you can take these leftovers home in doggie bags. If you're frugal they should last a few months."

*

Arm in arm with Raphael, we're waiting on line to get into the movies.

"I admire the way you take care of your daughter and give money to your former wife and pay her rent and take her out to eat and help her out and the bank account you set aside for a new apartment for her when she wants to move. I'm even a little jealous because my former husband does nothing to help me and wouldn't even if we were starving to death. Some men are selfish and resentful, but when they have children they should help," I say, reaching the ticket-taker.

As I pass my three dollars under the glass, Raphael whispers, "Can I borrow some money for the movie? Otherwise I can't go. I have money, but it's in the bank, and I didn't get a chance to take any out."

"You could have told me before. Besides, you knew we were going to the movies. What if I didn't bring enough? Then we wouldn't have been able to go," I say, my ticket in my hand, wishing I could refuse him and let him wander off into the night, while I, liberated, entered alone. I pause a moment, aware of all the others behind us, staring at his dark face, his lowered head, his trembling lips, a bit of drool about to descend from his heavy lower lip where it's pooled.

"Okay."

"Good," says Raphael, softly, "can I borrow five instead of three so I'll have enough to last me until tomorrow when I go to the bank? I'll give it back tomorrow, in fact, since you work near my bank, why don't you take this withdrawal slip and get the money for me?" Sticking the five-dollar bill under the glass, he says, "One child's please."

"How old are you?" asks the tickettaker.

"I'm sorry, I made a mistake, one two-dollar golden age ticket please."

Seated in the dark, I smell chili. Raphael takes my hand and places it on his long, lank penis, coated in corduroy, and as my eyes begin to adjust to the dark I can see on his lap a dish of rice and kidney beans with chili powder.

"I didn't have time to eat all day. Want some?" he asks, handing me a spoon.

*

Outside the movie there's a man selling silver bracelets.

"I'd like dessert. Let's go to Sutter's. How much are these?" asks Raphael of the jeweler, picking up a pair of bangle bracelets, as he picks my pocket from behind, counting the bills.

"Five dollars is too much, I only have a dollar fifty here," says Raphael, riffling his change conspicuously, large eyes ascending into his lids as his head descends in dejection.

"Okay, I'll take it," says the bracelet man, as Raphael significantly surrounds my wrist with one of the bracelets, adorning his own hairy wrist with the other one.

"I just want coffee," I say.

"There's a dollar minimum so let's order something for you anyway and if you really don't want it, I'll have it after I finish mine. Once I had a girlfriend, who I really liked, but every time I was with her she'd talk about an old boyfriend of hers named Tommy, and when we made love she'd cry 'Tommy, Tommy!'"

"How could you stand it?" I ask, sipping nothing but a spartan capuccino, cinnamon rising into my nostrils, sweet spice on top of foam. "What kind of a game was she playing with you?"

"It was very painful and after a while I couldn't stand it, so I had to split." Raphael's eating the cherry cheese à la mode surrounded by fruit tarts he's ordered, when a loudspeaker pages, "Raphael Gonzalez, Raphael Gonzalez, your child Jesusa has a fever. She's with your former wife Susan at her aunt's house and Susan wants you to come there immediately to help carry Jesusa down the stairs, take them home and carry Jesusa up the stairs to your house to keep her there till she gets well, and to run to the drugstore and get whatever medicines she needs."

"I have to go," says Raphael, rising. "I'll pay the tip and you pay the bill."

"I'll pay the tip and you pay the bill," I answer, stuffing my mouth with my uneaten apple turnover.

"Okay, we'll each pay our own. Goodbye," he calls, running out, as, still standing, I finish everything on his dish too.

*

Raphael, standing in my doorway with an enormous parcel in his arms, stares at me from above it, his eyes resting on top of the bag, ready to fall in, asks tremulously, "How is our relationship today?" as he empties the bag onto my butcher block table: a thirty-pound container of heavy cream, a ten-pound bag of sugar and eighteen crates of strawberries.

"You're so intense," I say, looking at all the stuff.

"I thought I'd make some whipped cream and strawberries for you and the children."

"The children aren't home."

"Do you have a large bowl?" he asks, pouring cream into all my bowls and dishes, seeking one large enough, finally pouring all the cream and sugar into the bathtub. Leaving a trail of dirty bowls, he takes the hand mixer and whips the cream.

"I don't want any."

Fearing my rejection of his cream, Raphael, his eyes protruding, insecure, ready to jump into the tub, pulls me toward him gently and kisses a hot question mark into my lips, as I undress and quickly jump into the tub, stuffing cream into my mouth, light and cool on my skin as I slowly sink in, having it fold gently about me, chewing the sweet-acidic strawberries Raphael is throwing into the tub, which leave behind small pink valentines on the whipped cream.

"Raphael," I say, whipped cream inside and out, environment simulating the uterus enough to make me feel secure, "I've been doing an equation lately. It's me–you = you–Susan = Susan–her boyfriend Phil."

"You are no good at math," says Raphael.

"Raphael, I need you more. I need more of you. She doesn't want you."

I'm confident that he'll respond to me; our relationship's been extraordinarily intense. Haven't we been together all summer, almost every day and night, eating at The Front Porch, Mother Courage, Hong Fat, Greenberg's, The Lion's Head, The Riviera,

The Inca, Buffalo Road House, Mama Leone's, The Cauldron, El Faro, La Bilbaina, The Bistro, Jai-Alai, O'John's, The Bus Stop, Sutter's, Sandolinos, Szechuan Taste of Seventh Avenue? And haven't we, in perfect communion, camaraderie, each paid for our own dinners? He looks at me, uncertain, hesitant, dips his hairy forefinger in the whipped cream, and dabs it on my nipple.

"I'm sorry," he says, running out.

*

I'm sitting naked on the couch, surrounded by leftover spaghetti and meatballs, cold chicken, peanut-butter-and-jelly-and-chocolate donuts, when the phone rings.

"John, I can't come to dinner with you and Peter and Beatrice. I'm not hungry because I'm eating." I hang up and tie a special wraparound dress on my tremendously bloated body, seduced by the logic of his response, which is, "Since you're eating anyway, why not eat with us?" I float out to meet them, assisted by them all into Peter's station wagon downtown into the midst of the San Gennaro Festival to an Italian restaurant with long communal tables. We order sheep's heads, shrimp marinara, macaroncelli with mushroom sauce, veal alla marsala, and calamari, zuppa de pesce and twelve bottles of Chianti Classico, and while an Italian band files into the restaurant, amidst the bombilation and pandemonium of band music, I'm lifted onto the long table by Peter and Beatrice.

"You look so nice tonight, so large," murmurs Beatrice, "so open, so receptive, so capable of giving, so loving—"

"So sexy," says Peter, slowly opening my wraparound dress, manipulating my comfort by moving some of the platters, decadent with desecrated remains: Peter and Beatrice are stroking my bloated abdomen and removing their own clothing. Despite the length of the table, it is narrow; my body, taking up most of the width, rolling from side to side, is framed in demolished dishes, rococo, my hair resting in old clam shells.

"Waiter, can we have another table here?" asks Peter.

"Not on Saturday night," says the waiter, slipping out of his pants while balancing a platter in each hand.

"We've been so close, I feel so close now," says Beatrice, insinuating her head between my enormous thighs. While Peter pours spaghetti sauce all over me, Beatrice intently removes it with her tongue all around my inner thighs, moving her tongue slowly, a jellyfish swimming, voluptuously closer to my clitoris, a drowning clam in clam sauce, soaked and swelling. She sucks it, mumbling, bubbles rising, "Don't you feel so warm and loving, let's enjoy our closeness, don't you feel so full of abandon," she murmurs, muffled in marinara, still sucking my clitoris as I feel, from above, Peter's parmigiana cock, pistonlike, sliding up and down my impaled tongue, as the waiter, lying on Beatrice's back, slides his penis into her, his hand in my vagina, his other hand holding Beatrice's breast, as she moans and moans into my marinated cunt. John, still seated alongside the table, holds my hand and watches.

"John, come on," says Peter. "Where are you?"

"I can't," says John to my chocolate-chip eyes, "I liked you when you were thin, but now you're not attractive to me anymore, you're so ugly, I just can't get it up."

For a moment he's gone, but returns with an enormous statue of San Gennaro in his arms, dollar bills pinned all over it. He rubs it rhythmically, moaning like Popeye with a corncob, cries, and dollar bills fall all over me, as I lie among balled-up napkins, dead zeppole.

*

I see a head—floating toward me in the silent penumbra, a shadow, tenebrious. My arms pinned to the bed with IV needles move inadvertently, ineffectually twitching as I attempt in vain to raise my own heavy head. I'm relieved to see it's only Dr. Stone, now semiluminous in the moonlight, floating slowly, arms outstretched, holding toward me a package, wrapped in the words, "Since you're doing so well."

"Let me open it for you." He holds up a small basket of painted fruit.

"How clever," I say, considering the nature of my infirmity, "to give me effigies of fruit!"

"It's marzipan," his blush glimmers in the murk. "I thought it might be okay. I wanted to show you how much I like you," he whispers, pulling the blanket off me, leaving me exposed, trembling and chill.

"No baby, don't move," he implores, removing my pants; then, pulling down his white slacks, pale penis phosphorescing, he fondles my fantastic breast, stuffing marzipan into my mouth where it's flooded by saliva, odor of almond escaping into the room, aphrodisiac, as Dr. Stone climbs my body, holding onto my hair as the prince held Rapunzel's, stuffing more marzipan in my mouth, his penis in my vagina.

"No, no. You're killing me!" I cry, needles chafing as I try to move my arms. "You're killing me," I moan, muffled in marzipan.

"I like you, I like you."

Can This Marriage Be Saved?

by Dr. Raphael Robinson, PhD,
founder of *The American Institute of
Family Relations*

March 18. The American Institute of Family Relations
had its first appointment with Mrs. Snow White Bergman.
Dr. Paul Popper was the counselor.

Snow White, an attractive woman in her early thirties, arrived for
her appointment desperate and in tears. She was tall, long black
hair contrasting with her white white skin and riveting red lips.
Despite the fact that her face was bruised near one temple, her neck

had a bandage on it, her hair was messy, her fair face swollen with weeping, and her clothing somewhat unusual, Mrs. Bergman was beautiful. Dr. Popper was surprised to see her wheeling with one hand a large stroller, with difficulty, toward his desk, holding an infant in her other arm. Enormous limbs were visible over the raised stroller hood. Dr. Popper thought that perhaps having such a grotesque child might be the cause of the Bergmans' marital problems, when one of the carriage wheels, which had been violently listing with every revolution, rolled right off. A small child ran out from behind Snow White, who balanced the stroller while the child replaced the wheel, adjusting the pin which was supposed to hold it on, then silently wrapped her tiny hand around the chrome carriage handle just above an area as thick as stucco with encrusted strained foods and pretzel droppings.

Apprised of the fact that Mrs. Bergman had seven stepchildren from her husband's previous marriage and two of her own, Dr. Popper arose from his desk and inquisitively peered around the stroller hood. Curled inside was what appeared to be an American eagle, absolved of its feathers, the nostrils of his enormous nose moving in and out with every breath as his beady eyes bored into Dr. Popper with suspicion. Snow White, with one hand, pressed the levers that released the hood, which descended like an enormous bellows. Suddenly exposed, Prince Bergman, who by now Dr. Popper had ascertained it was, pressed farther inward until his head was folded under himself.

"Good body tone for an adult," remarked Dr. Popper.

Snow White pulled and prodded until Prince Bergman reluctantly rose, unfurling himself, stepped out of the carriage, and stood there on thin legs, shoulders slightly hunched. Despite his grotesque birdlike appearance he was quite handsome, in good proportion and swarthy. His pinkies moved rhythmically toward his wrists with every expansion of his nostrils. His vulnerability was endearing.

"Your punctuality is proof of your willingness to work with us. What do you think, Prince?" Dr. Popper had to look down at their folder to check Prince Bergman's given name. The Prince remained still except for an almost imperceptible simultaneous raising of one eyebrow and the upper lip on the opposite side of his face.

"Don't you have anything to say?" encouraged Dr. Popper.

"I think this is all a bunch of horseshit," said Prince Bergman.

"He didn't want to come at all. He doesn't believe in therapy," said Snow White, apologetically.

"You needn't protect me by explaining your husband for him," said Dr. Popper. "I'm perfectly capable of taking care of myself. By the way," he said coldly to Snow White, "this was supposed to be your private session."

"I know," said Snow White, "but the Prince didn't want to stay home alone."

Dr. Popper stared at the Prince, with contracted eyelids, attempting to appear authoritative.

"Prince, would you mind waiting outside in the play area?" he said firmly.

The Prince only smiled, his thin lips spreading, sharp corners cutting through the cheeks, until a long mouthful of tiny teeth were visible. He didn't move. The little child released the stroller handle, looked up at her father and nervously reached up to his arm.

"Daddy, you don't believe in him anyway." She turned him slowly and led him out of the room.

*

Snow White Speaks

The moment the door closed behind them, Snow White collapsed into a chair and began weeping, tears falling all over the baby she held in her arms, its long white christening dress wending its way across, then streaming down the side of Snow White's crimson dress like a path, until the baby began to cry, waving tiny spotted arms.

"Why are you crying?" asked Dr. Popper, focusing on her black and blue cheek.

"I don't know," cried Snow White. "I think it's because after fourteen years I just can't take anymore. I'm so ashamed to come here like this." She fingered the bandage on her neck.

"Tell me about it, Snow White," encouraged Dr. Popper, settling comfortably in his swivel chair, sipping the coffee previously brought him by his secretary, which is now cool and bitter.

"I keep thinking I should get a divorce, but I'm not sure. When the Prince beats me up, I think I will, but as soon as I'm feeling calmer, I'm not sure again. I'm not sure I should be treated this way. I can't tell whether I'm unhappy or not. I'm not sure what exactly is expected of me as a wife. I tried filling these out, but sometimes the result is positive, sometimes negative. They're no help at all!" She rummaged in her purse, peering over the baby, craned her swanlike neck and threw a pile of questionnaires torn from magazines on the desk. The top one read, *Divorce Dilemma— Do you really want that divorce?*

"Even our Lüscher color test shows we aren't right for each other. His favorite color is black, which means he is in love with death and is a possible psychotic, while mine is magenta, proving that, while I am still too childishly dependent on fantasy, I'm mostly a cheerful, strong person."

"Start from the beginning," said Dr. Popper, biting the tip off a cigar, removing it from his mouth and rolling it between his forefinger and thumb, "and tell me as much as possible about your parents and their marriage, and your siblings."

*

Although I was a wanted child [began Snow White], my very existence seemed to be a harbinger of trouble from the beginning. One day, my mother, probably already pregnant, was sitting next to the window, sewing. Moved by the scene and the heavy silence, she pricked her finger and three drops of blood fell to the snow below. Entranced by the snowscape, completely white except for some sharply etched black crisscrosses of the undersides of branches, and those three drops of scarlet forming an isosceles triangle, she looked up at the heavens, squinting from the snowflakes, and said "I wish for a daughter as white as snow, as black as ebony and as red as blood." She'd wanted a child anyway, to help define her time, since my father wouldn't allow her to work; but, having one girl already, my father wanted a boy, so by wishing for a girl my mother was defying him.

When I was born, my father, finding out I was a girl, began screaming at mother for her ineptitude. She merely wept. There was always a large puddle of blood under her bed. She never recovered from her fear of thinking she had power over events.

For a while, Daddy got a nursemaid for me. I think they were lovers because I have a strange memory of his large, craggy, heavy-haired head at her other breast while I was nursing. Mother languished weakly for a few more years. During my visits to her room, we could hear father producing mystifying moans with mother's nurse behind the thin partition of her adjoining quarter. I was curious about these noises which seemed to diminish mother, as a grater wears away an onion. I witnessed many unresolved arguments, all of them exactly the same. Mother would say that Daddy's behavior kept her ill and weak with pain and Daddy said that mother's weakness and pain was what drove him to his behavior. Only once was the argument different.

"Why do you have Snow White dressed in boy's clothing?" asked Mother.

"I don't want my property to go to any old asshole she marries just because she's a woman."

"Property, property, all you think of is property."

"You are mistaken," he said, his dignity wounded. "I also think of sex." Soon after, my mother died.

My older sister Rose was born seven years before me. One day mother was strolling in the garden looking at the roses. "I wish to have," she said, "a girl with cheeks as pink as a rose, hair as yellow as a rose, and lips as magenta as a rose." My sister's nickname is Rose Red. She always hated me, was jealous of me, and blamed me for mother's illness and death. During that time, Rose often had to care for me. She made many unsuccessful attempts to rid herself permanently of the burden, but when Father was around she pretended to care for me as if I were her own child. She'd take her thumb and index finger and press them like tongs into my cheeks until my jaws involuntarily separated, and into that smooth, salivating cavity would shove spoonsful of various strained substances. I have repeated memories of Rose settled comfortably in Father's lap as I foraged the floor for minuscule goodies, to the rhythmic squeak of my plastic panties.

When Father informed us both that he was about to remarry, Rose had a fit.

"Why do you need anyone else?" she pleaded, "don't I take care of you well?" As she supplicated, she ripped off her clothes until she was quite naked, pulling on him and entwining herself around his legs like a vine, rendering him immobile, her long tea-rose hair wildly awry and streaming to well below her knees.

Father got married anyway, to the most beautiful and unscrupulous woman in the kingdom, and was very proud of his new wife, the sister of Cinderella's stepmother. She had a daughter from a previous marriage. Father and his new wife had many arguments about who favored whose children, but finally this very strong woman succeeded in disposing of Rose Red. She made Rose perform many of the servant's duties and forced her to care for me full time. Rose told Father, and when he spoke to his beloved bride about it, she threatened to leave.

"After all, they aren't all my kids," she said, "how can I be expected to take care of them without help?"

"Well," said Father, "your former husband doesn't pay any child support, so who do you think has to support your kid?" He was very cocky, but after a week and a half of enforced sexual abstinence, he told Rose Red to listen to her new stepmother and do whatever she said.

Soon after, on Rose's tenth birthday, Father betrothed her to our neighbor, an ugly toad, in order to increase his land and fortune. He began attending church in penance for having yelled at his first wife for having only girl children. He began to realize that females were not the liability he'd thought.

"How can you force me to marry that ugly toad?" screamed Rose Red, never a pliant child. She was disgusted, frightened and enraged. "I hate being manipulated," she wept.

"Maybe he'll turn out to be a prince," said Father calmly. "You have to rid yourself of romanticism and realize it's money and being taken care of that are the important things."

Rose Red ran away with the goatherd.

The Queen was happy because she wanted to marry her own daughter to the toad and her daughter was only eight. She left me alone now but acted strangely. I began to think she was insane. One day I heard her talking to herself.

"I'm so bored," she said. She took a small mirror from under her skirt and looked into it, moving it around as it was too small for her to see her whole face at once.

"Mirror, mirror in my hand, who's the fairest in the land?" She answered herself, "Snow White."

A sinister look of hatred germinated and flourished on her face as if the words *Snow White* were magic fertilizer. I became chilled with fear, shivering and perspiring at the same time. Very soon a letter arrived from Rose Red telling Father that he was right—money and being taken care of were everything. I wondered whether I should try to escape or wait for Rose Red to save me.

One day in the garden, while I was deciding what to do, something was thrown over my head, I was pushed to the ground and, as I struggled in vain, my hands were tied. I was lifted and packed loosely over someone's strong shoulders, head hanging over one side and legs the other, completely prostrate, mouth bitter with fear. The only thing that saved me from fainting was an underlying excitement at the prospect of change.

The length of time and gentle manner with which I was being transported, led me to believe that perhaps I was really being saved, when suddenly I was thrown to the ground. As I attempted to inhale, in order to replace some of the breath I'd involuntarily expired when my back so quickly and unexpectedly met the ground, whatever was covering over my head was roughly removed.

"Thanks for saving me, Ugly Woodcutter," I gasped gratefully, as soon as I saw who it was.

"Save your verbal thanks and lift up your skirt," he said, unbuttoning his fly, protruding gray eyes engorged.

"I thought you were saving me." I whined, holding my skirt tightly about my knees.

"I already saved you," he said, taking out an enormous prick, which, not fully hard, hung outside his fully dressed body like some ornament or half-filled purse. "I was supposed to kill you, and I haven't. That's saving you. Now I want to get rewarded."

"Let me pick the reward," I moaned.

"My job is so ill paid," he muttered softly, his hand wrapped around his penis, moving up and down, "I'm merely taking one of the fringe benefits." He dropped to his knees, still kneading his prick, which by then protruded like a unicorn horn. He roughly pulled up my skirt and stared at my pantaloons, drooling onto my knee. I tried to crawl backward, then to rise and run, but he was still holding my skirt, which he pulled hard, throwing me prostrate at his feet; holding both my wrists in one powerful, sinewy hand, he ripped down my pantaloons with the other. Leaning over me directly and leering fearsomely, he held both my shoulders now with his hands and pinioned my pelvis. Removing one hand from a shoulder, he used it as a lever, raising one knee from underneath, then pressing that leg, folded up. Now he thought access was guaranteed. While my struggles rendered him ravenous, he wasn't prepared for the further resistance of my virginity.

"God damn it, God damn it, God damn it," he repeated rhythmically, ramming into my obdurate opening as I remained limp and passive now, thinking fear a fine anesthetic, until suddenly it really hurt!

"Ouch," I shrieked.

The woodcutter's ugly head reared back, his teeth exposed, as if he were in pain too then, just as suddenly, he relaxed.

When he lifted his body off mine, I saw blood on his damp, limp penis, caked in his pubic hair. I lay there on the grass terrified of the blood and otherwise completely shattered. How could it be worth all that trouble, I thought. Glad to be left alone, I paid no mind to the machinations of the woodcutter. Tempted to ask why he was slitting the throat of a screaming wild boar he'd just captured, I refrained, thinking, better it than me.

I watched as the woodcutter roughly removed the boar's heart in the total silence of the cool forest, framed in the last, harsh, metallic light refracted through the lower branches of the trees, which appeared ominously black, as did the blood now splashed everywhere. The woodcutter held up the heart triumphantly, then rubbed the gelatinous muscle up and down his prick, which was still exposed.

"I should have used this," he murmured, "it's less trouble and feels just as good."

*

"That was my very first sexual experience," said Snow White, hiccoughing.

Dr. Popper nodded sympathetically, retaining the exact balance of empathy and detachment of a good therapist, his own erection well hidden by the heavy desk. He nodded for her to continue.

*

"The woodcutter ran with the heart when he heard the sound of a chorus singing, 'heigh ho, heigh ho.' It turned out to be the seven dwarves, workers in Daddy's mine and roommates.

"Please let me stay with you for a while," I pleaded. "If I return to the castle now I'll be killed."

They looked at each other, delight brightening their dusky countenances.

"It will be a good treat to have white master's white daughter as a servant," said one of them. "You can stay with us as long as you like," he told me, "and in return you only have to take care of all our household needs." Naturally, I agreed. "And clean up the grass first," they ordered.

I often thought of running away as I performed my tedious and monotonous duties, but knew not where I could go or how I'd be

able to keep myself. In the meantime, I began to have dreams of
marriage. I daydreamed day in and day out about someone falling
in love with me and taking me away. One day, while the dwarves
were at the mine, I was visited by an average apple seller, who was
suddenly superlatively endowed, transformed due to my desire to
escape. I immediately fell in love with him.

"Take me away with you," I pleaded. "I love you."

"I love you too," he said, kissing me, "that's why you should
give yourself to me now so that we can have the satisfaction of
consummating our passion even if something goes wrong." He
convinced me to go to bed with him and also to buy one of his
apples.

"I'm not really an apple salesman," he told me as we lay together.

"Thank God," I said. "That's such a lowly occupation."

"I'm really the Queen's messenger," he confessed.

"That's even worse," I said.

"If you fuck me again, I'll tell you which side of the apple the
Queen gave me to kill you with is the poisoned side. Let me think,"
he mulled, "the red poisoned, green not— green poisoned, red
not—" Suddenly he was silent and remained so.

"What are you thinking?" I asked.

"I'm trying to decide which way I want to exploit you. In any
case, I've got what I wanted already."

I was deeply hurt as you can imagine, and I realized I'd been
taken. At my wits' end, I decided to eat the apple meant for me but
couldn't recall which was the poisoned side. Desperate, I bit into it
anyway, and before the whole piece was swallowed, was already in a
state of catalepsy. I was conscious of what occurred around me,
though my body was completely paralyzed, approximating in every
detail death or coma.

The dwarves debated for over a week whether to hook me to a
machine for my vital needs or not. During this time, they devised a
way to make their fortune by enclosing me in a Plexiglas case and
exhibiting me as a dead person who never decays. Later on they told

people I was the Virgin Mary, found in a cave in the woods.

After seven long years of tourists filing past, Prince Bergman came along. The moment he leaned over the Plexiglas I fell in love with his long row of tiny teeth. Finally, I thought, someone has really fallen in love with me, because Prince Bergman began negotiating for my purchase, not an easy task, as I provided a fine income for the dwarves.

Finally, having agreed to sign a document called the Emancipation Proclamation, and having given the dwarves a lifetime annuity, he carried the entire plastic case to a magnificent castle where, in an upstairs room, I was witness to a silent, passionate argument between the Prince and a woman who I later discovered was his mother and who was pretty upset at her son's choice of a bride. Nevertheless, the Rabbi went through the ceremony, with Prince Bergman standing next to me, enclosed in my glossy case, on which hundreds of festive candle flames were reflected, his mother still screaming angrily at his other side. Later, mollified and tear-streaked, she prepared his favorite dinner, linguine à la Marsala, and finally left the room.

No sooner were we alone than Prince Bergman, with superhuman strength, pried the top off my case and attempted to pull me out. Impressed by his desire and his active will to make me come to life, I felt a sudden real love and real desire to live. As he dragged me, my legs hanging limp, I felt myself choking, dislodging the bit of apple, which I coughed up.

"Be careful where you spit that, will you?" asked the Prince, surprised.

I soon felt my arms could move, and I held him, waves of passion searing through me like electric currents conducted by the liquid with which I seemed to be filled.

"Oh, kiss me," I said.

He seemed embarrassed by my aggressiveness. I realized that we were married and could do as we pleased. I felt so open to him. He broke away and began to crawl into the Plexiglas showcase. I attempted to pull him out but he resisted, so I climbed in, lay down next to him, and as best I could attempted to undress.

"No, no, just take off your socks," he pleaded.

All he said in the morning was, "I knew I couldn't trust a woman."

"So what if I'm not a virgin?" I asked. "I thought that was outmoded."

"Maybe even now you have a lover, who knows how many?"

I could hardly believe it, but he was seriously distraught.

"I knew I'd end up marrying someone just like my mother," he persisted. "She had secret lovers and I'm sure you will. Which of those black dwarves fucked you?" he asked, grabbing my neck.

*·

"Now, Dr. Popper," continued Snow White, "even after all this time he's still paranoid. He just beat me yesterday."

She touched her cheek where the blueish mark was beginning to turn brownish like a bruised peach.

"He even thinks the children aren't his. And, although I spent seven years knitting seven shirts to throw on his seven children by his former wife, who had a spell put on them—now I take care of all seven kids, plus our two—he imagines I'm out all day just fucking around! Besides, he does nothing around the house all day except lie in that showcase he first saw me in! Finally I insisted we come for marriage counseling."

Snow White was no longer weeping. She seemed relieved simply to unburden herself, though her face and eyes were still swollen. She sighed lengthily and hiccuped. Dr. Popper, stirred, helped her wheel the stroller to the door, where he surprised himself by sticking out his tongue until it reached Snow White's bruise, which he licked.

*

Prince Bergman Speaks

Despite not having finished the tower he was building out of blocks, Prince Bergman, escorted in by his child, sat down on a small, uncomfortable stool meant for Dr. Popper's arthritic feet.

"Don't think I don't know what you and my wife were doing in here," he said, smiling inappropriately. The child was attempting to become invisible by lying flat on a spot on the carpet that was the same color as her clothing.

"Would you please play outside?" Dr. Popper asked the child gently, assisting her ascension by gripping her suspenders.

"Don't hurt Daddy's feelings," she requested amiably.

"I won't," reassured Dr. Popper, "I just want to speak to your daddy alone."

"I'm not her father," said the Prince.

"What do you mean?" asked Dr. Popper. "Mrs. Bergman told me that you have two children."

"I'm not sure that those two are my children. They could be anyone's."

"Do you believe the seven children you had with Cinderella are yours?"

"Yes. Cinderella was a virgin when we married and not that kind of woman at all. Cinderella and I had other problems. Snow White is like my mother, the Queen."

"What did happen with Cinderella and yourself?" Dr. Popper asked.

"She ran away with someone. She insisted she was too young, desperate and naive to realize at first that I was never in love with her but had a foot fetish. I should really leave Snow White the way Cinderella left me but I can never decide to do it. Snow White thinks I'm still in love with Cinderella but I'm not. I love Snow White, but I hate her. I throw the I Ching to help me make decisions but usually the result can be interpreted either way."

A fairly lengthy silence followed during which a variety of expressions filtered across the Prince's expressive face.

"Can you tell me a bit about your family life when you were a child?" asked Dr. Popper, noting that, despite the Prince's hostility there was an underlying desire to please. The Prince's face flushed darkly.

"I hate my mother," he said. "She's a selfish woman who cares nothing for her children or her husband or anything except having lovers and obtaining material goods. My father is weak. I hate and feel sorry for him at the same time. He also cares for no one as long as he can avoid arguments and my mother's tantrums. One example of his docility is that when Mother was pregnant with Rapunzel she developed a craving for salad greens in the garden below, which belonged to someone else, so, not even thinking about restraining her momentary selfish desires, she actually traded her baby to-be for a few moments of gustatory joy. And guess who picked the eens for her!

Subsequently, Mom spent all her time seducing men and attempting to hide her lovers from my father, but unfortunately, I saw them. Every time I opened a closet there was one. They were under the bed, behind curtains. I wanted to tell Father, but I didn't dare because I felt he knew but wanted to hide it from himself so that he wouldn't have to do anything, and that telling him would hurt him.

My mother looks like a whore and has bleached blond hair. She's so selfish that she keeps trying to convince me I have too many kids and should get rid of some by losing them in the forest. My father would most likely accede to that base wish, but I'm not like him. Despite how my mother disgusted me, I used to sleep with her because I was afraid to sleep alone. Come to think of it, most of my experience with women has been bad: the evil witch who owned the Victory garden and now has Rapunzel; my selfish and lying mother; the bad fairy who changed my seven children into swans for seven years; the bad fairy who came to the baby's christening and said that when she's fifteen she'll prick her finger and sleep for a hundred years; Cinderella, who deserted me and the kids; and now Snow White, who's not that bad except that I'm sure she cheats on me. She's sexually aggressive. Even on our wedding night she practically raped me. I didn't want to rush, I just wanted her to touch my prick with her feet. Come to think of it, Snow White doesn't like me to have a good time. She resents it. I love to spend lots of time in the showcase where I first saw Snow, but she just can't stand for me to be in there. I can sense her disapproval as I lie there. If she leans over the Plexiglas to look in at me and I see her distorted face, I pretend she's a witch.

She has a Puritan ethic of work, work, work, but she doesn't understand the spiritual growth that I attain while lying in the case deciding what to do. It appears as if I'm idle. As a matter of fact, my mother hates my lying in there too, but she blames it on Snow White for not being more demanding of me. I really hate my mother and I never would see her again but I don't want to hurt her. I don't want to hurt Snow White either, but she drives me to it. The other night I nearly strangled her. I couldn't control it. But I love her and don't want to hurt her."

There was silence again. The Prince slouched on his seat in a relaxed posture belying his anger and upset, which was only revealed in the purple flush pervading his face and the rapid revolving of his ankle, sending the foot of the leg he has crossed over one knee around in small circles.

Dr. Popper, calmly observing the Prince, drew in on his pipe as he held his tilted lighter in a hairy hand above the small briar bowl newly filled with perfumed tobacco.

"What do you think?" asked the Prince.

"What do *you* think?" asked Dr. Popper, between long inhales, during which he kept his eyes on the long orange flame of his lighter as it was sucked into the pipe bowl.

"I think this is a bunch of horseshit," said the Prince, rising, nostrils flaring. At the door, he paused for a moment.

"Do you want to interview my mother?"

A child's voice called from the corridor, querulously, "Daddy, daddy, are you okay?"

*

The Counselor's Analysis
Despite the Prince's stated hatred of his mother for her selfishness,

unfaithfulness and temper tantrums, he actually resembled her quite a bit. After a while, Prince Bergman was able to see how some of his actions resembled those traits in his mother. When this was pointed out to him, it quite depressed him and he took a turn for the worse, not moving for days, showing how he'd also incorporated his father's passivity, which he also hated.

Though he genuinely liked his father, he felt sorry for him and angry with him at the same time, creating confusion in his feeling of identification with the male member of the household, who he felt was a prick. His negative experiences with women in general and a mother who lied to him when he was young failed to build up the necessary trust created by loving parents; he especially didn't trust women and their love of him.

After a while, the Prince began to see how he was unable to conceive of a woman really loving him. But he couldn't seem to realize that he'd have to stop blaming his mother and begin to work out his own problems responsibly. He began to stay out of the Plexiglas case for longer periods. The Prince was devoted solely to the state of his own feelings. Day in and day out, he carefully measured his depressions, migraines, fantasies and decisions, and speculated not at all on the possible feelings of his wife, who herself came from a terribly flawed household and childhood. He also realized that he'd manipulated his little daughter into the role of his parent. We finally convinced him that she was too young to take care of him, and that actually he should be taking care of her. Also, that if he helped out more with the care and support of his nine children, or hired a housekeeper, his mother would never again suggest taking some of them into the forest. She was, in an indirect way, say, telling him he was cheap.

*

After a while, Snow White realized that marriage is not an escape, that she'd have to work hard to make something out of it. She also began to realize that the husband she thought was so powerful, because she allowed him to boss her around and because he was prone to violence, was actually very passive, much resembling her own father, whom she discovered she hated and resented for not standing up to her stepmother and protecting herself and Rose Red. She had also blamed him for remarrying and allowing Rose to leave, but I explained that Rose Red could not fill the role of wife for her father, or of mother for her, and should not. It came as a surprise to her that she was also harboring a resentment toward her mother for dying. She had the firm conviction that people pretended to save her from someone cruel or something evil, only to ill use her themselves.

*

Snow White discovered as time went on that she wanted to work out this marriage less than she thought, only she didn't have enough courage to leave. Her conflict actually became worse as the Prince showed small signs of improvement. He no longer had to be wheeled to our sessions and, while not nearly as verbal as his wife, he responded fairly well and nonhostilely, although retaining his nervous habit of curling his pinkies back to his wrists rhythmically as he breathed. Unfortunately, as her marriage showed signs of improvement, Snow White became more and more panicky, realizing, as she saw more and more possibility of their staying together, how much she really hated the Prince.

*

I had little hope for this marriage despite some changes for the better. One day the Prince was so moved he began to weep. Snow White, surprisingly, sat impassive, looking at me and the Prince.

"Your husband," I said, "is actually crying. He's made himself vulnerable. Don't you feel like going close and comforting him?"

"Uh, uh, I don't believe it," she said coolly. "He'll cry now, but nothing ever changes, so what's the use of getting all emotionally invested again and again, when a few moments later everything is the same? Am I supposed to believe that crying is an end in itself?

In fact, after he's returned to his normal state he's meaner and more distrustful because he hates himself for having been so vulnerable for a few moments and doesn't want anyone to think they're getting away with anything."

Prince Bergman gazed up at her, his widely set eyes large and glazed, eyebrows at the bridge of his nose raised touchingly, the skin below shining wetly, forehead corrugated miserably, long mouth trembling. Then suddenly his face, already maroon, metamorphosed from misery to rage. In less than a second he had his hands around Snow White's neck.

"That's not true." His words exited with difficulty from between clenched teeth.

*

Coming from different cultures only added another dimension to their problem. While they shared a similar financial class, they had different ideas about how to spend money. But those problems could have been alleviated if they had learned to communicate. The Prince finally did admit that he had a foot fetish, which, although it wasn't as pronounced as it was with his first wife, would never completely be defeated. Snow White was willing to go along with most of his ideas of pleasure. She had been very traumatized by her first rape and subsequent sexual experiences and, despite a liberated appearance and flirtatious manner, she began to understand that she was afraid both of men and sexuality.

*

It was fairly obvious that Snow White was most unlikely to become a top housekeeper. Fortunately the Prince was a slob and didn't demand anything approaching perfection as long as his wife didn't spend any money. She did take a few lessons here at the Institute, on various methods to lighten the dullness of domestic chores, and this eased the burden.

*

Finally, Prince Bergman was able to admit that it wasn't that he fell in love with Snow White but that he wanted to *be* Snow White. He envied her femininity, passivity and beauty, and the fact that she could lie in her showcase day after day with nothing more expected of her. When she awoke, she posed a real threat. Within this relationship, his psychological problems and neuroses flourished like a mold in moisture. His own attempts to take Snow White's place and remain in the case were not met with the best reception. Nevertheless, at our last session I was encouraged enough to ask the Prince once again how he felt about the counseling.

"A bunch of horseshit," he said.

*

One day Snow White arrived alone except for her baby, late for the first time for a session both she and Prince Bergman were scheduled to have together. Minute dots of perspiration lay on the surface of her skin like cool dew on ripe orchard fruit just before dawn; her black hair hung uncombed down her back like ropy vines.

"Is anything wrong?" asked Dr. Popper.

"I can't find Prince Bergman. I hoped he'd be here."

"Why are you so worried? Maybe he'll be a little late."

"No, I knew he wouldn't be here," she said. "Yesterday, when he opened the door to the hall closet, sitting in the corner, wearing the Queen's clothes, was a young man."

"Why are you wearing my mother's clothes?" asked the Prince.

"She lets me wear them all the time. She's very sweet to me. Why do you ask?"

My husband became enraged and locked the man in. When the

King arrived at the castle, Prince led him to the closet and opened the door. The man stood, trembling, nearly prostrate with fear and lack of air, still in Mrs. Bergman's clothes, in which he looked like those dolls dressed in long gowns that don't have real hair, only a scant coloring painted on with a few apt strokes.

The King, tears streaming into his wrinkles like a rainstorm where there's been a drought, said, "Where? What are you showing me?"

The Prince looked at his father disgustedly, then began to run back and forth along the hallway as if his rage, which couldn't be contained, blew him back and forth like air rushing out of a balloon. Trying to calm him, I suggested that his father had his own reasons for condoning that behavior and he had no right to force the King to react the way he would.

The Prince, far from calm, ran down into the cellar, where the Queen, who likes to work, has a beauty shop. He threw her hair dyes and shampoos from the shelves, and began ripping the hair dryers apart in front of the Queen's customers, calling her a pig and a whore. The customers, terrified, all ran upstairs at once, creating a congestion at the moat. I slumped into one of the heavy hairdryer seats, broken helmet askew like a drunken astronaut's, to nurse the baby, who was screaming so hard her red mouth, like smashed fruit, refused to close over the nipple stuffed into it.

The Queen sat under another dryer weeping and shouting, "What did I do to deserve this?" The Prince, some of the dryer wiring still between his teeth, stood meekly in front of me watching the baby, who after six or seven false starts was finally sucking, only its flushed face, cap of perspiration, and long shuddering sighs indicating its former excitation.

"I know I really love you," he said. It was the first time he'd ever told me that straight out, without any ambiguity and, despite the scene that preceded it, I felt so happy. Then he said, "Are you a part of the conspiracy?"

"What conspiracy?" I asked, my skin instantly goosefleshing.

"The conspiracy to kill me," he whispered. "But surely you

know about it. Is it true you're really not part of it? But of course you're part of it."

"What are you talking about? Is it political?"

"Possibly it could be considered political, partially political, but more holy, religious. It's a punishment conspiracy to kill me for being so rotten."

"I'm glad you finally realize how rotten you've been, but I'm sure no one is planning on killing you," I told him.

"Oh, then you're not part of the conspiracy," he said, relieved. "Then I have a chance to make it up to you if I live. But you must be part of it. Are you sure you're not?

He kept me awake all night describing who of our friends, relatives and servants were in on it, secret hints he'd noticed, messages, half smiles, half frowns, secret codes, specially colored clothing, and so on. This morning I must have dozed for a few moments and, when I woke, even before I opened my eyes, I just knew he was gone! During the day I received six or seven phone calls from him where he said he was at the top of the Empire State Building, The World Trade Center, The Statue of Liberty, The CBS Building and the Triboro Bridge. He absolutely refused to come home nor would he wait where he was. Fearing for his safety, I made him promise he'd either meet me here or come here with me.

*

"He must be hospitalized immediately," said Dr. Popper. "Try calling the castle." The tiny rubber feet on the underside of the phone squeaked on the glass desk top as Dr. Popper pushed it closer to Snow White. Against the black her hand appeared startlingly white, her nails like scalloped potatoes, which Dr. Popper felt like eating. He wanted to lick the perspiration off her face. He could practically feel the salt running onto his tongue. He was aware of the sound of their breathing and the faint ringing of the castle phone. Finally someone answered.

"Can I speak to the Prince?" asked Snow White.

"Sorry lady, this is the fire department. Can't talk now."

"Oh, God. I know something horrible has happened," murmured Snow White, throwing her cape over her shoulders and the baby with one hand.

"Wait," said Dr. Popper, "I'll come too. I may be able to help." For a second Snow White thought Dr. Popper could save her, she was so desperate and he so sympathetic.

*

In Dr. Popper's air-conditioned Buick, he was aware of her leg pressed against his, the tips of her long ebony hair tickling his polyestered thigh. Oblivious, Snow White Bergman pulled back her cape and began unbuttoning her dress. Before Dr. Popper, with his impaired peripheral vision, could see anything, the baby's head was plastered in front of her, swaying rhythmically back and forth, accompanied by gurgling gulps. Above the baby's head her white breast swelled hard and phosphorescent in the dusk, so white along the edge of her red cape he could almost see a vivid wavering green line there.

As the car rounded a sharp curve in the road, the castle was suddenly visible on top of a hill, its edges black, backlit by an ominous orange glow which bled into the greenish sky. They drove right into an enormous dark cloud of smoke, in which it rained cinders. Dr. Popper could see that Snow White had become rigid. The baby, sensing the tension, let go of the breast and began to shriek. Snow's whole breast was now visible. Her tension manifested in him a wave of excitement so great he thought he'd have to stop the car and go to the bathroom. He didn't dare look directly at her breast, but he saw the blurred whiteness wavering in his weakened peripheral vision.

"Oh my God," she said, closing her buttons like a blind person, still staring straight ahead.

Dr. Popper involuntarily stepped on the gas. He screeched to a stop near the moat. The drawbridge was already down and they stormed across, creating a terrible clatter in the unnatural quiet. They found the Queen crying in the vestibule.

"What happened?" asked Snow White. "Is the Prince here?"

The Queen didn't answer. "Oh where did I go wrong?" she moaned, her body swaying back and forth like a Jewish man praying.

"What happened?" asked Dr. Popper.

"He set the castle on fire. It's all her fault." For the first time she looked up, acknowledging Snow White in order to bestow a malevolent glance on her.

Snow White shoved the baby at her mother-in-law and began running into the corridor.

"Take this back," screamed the Queen, holding the baby in the air. "Because you decide to have a baby does that mean it's my destiny too?" she called after her.

"He's locked in the dungeon. The doctor's with him," she told Dr. Popper.

"This is not the most cheerful environment," he said, after he'd caught up with Snow White, as they attempted to find their way downstairs with only one candle.

The entire castle was drenched in a horrible, pervasive, acrid, odor which hurt the throat despite the fact that there was no longer any actual smoke. Amazingly, it invaded even that multilayered cellar. Approaching the heavily barred hold where the Prince was being detained, they saw him between the bars, leaning back on a hard chair, the doctor sitting beside him on a low stool, the Prince's arm lying across his lap inside up as the doctor sewed, bathed in the orange glow of a gasoline lantern.

Still, the heavy smell of smoke could not disguise, as they neared that cell, the moldy ancient must of seeping sea-absorbed urine, which caused Dr. Popper to draw in a breath he couldn't complete. He was thinking that if he thought about it he might actually retch, while Snow White, reaching the cage first, unsuccessfully attempted to pull open the huge heavy gate, then rattled it back and forth. The doctor neither moved nor looked up, but sat calmly sewing with a long black thread.

"One minute, hold your horses." A heavyset guard slowly sauntered toward them, still masticating some of the enormous pastrami sandwich half wrapped in wax paper that he held.

"Great Katz's pastrami," he told them wonderingly, his words puncutated with exclamation points of meat. "Do you people have a pass?"

"I'm Mrs. Bergman, said Snow White, "and this is our marriage counselor."

"Good luck," he said. "It's never too late. He looked at Dr. Popper suspiciously, but shot the bolt and pushed the heavy gate outward, looking Snow White over lecherously as she entered.

"Ten minutes," he said. Then, to the Prince, "Try to work it out. Who'd want to lose a piece of ass like that, with such ebony hair, blood-red lips, and skin as white as snow?"

"What happened?" asked Snow White, sinking down beside the Prince's chair, looking at the irregular gashes on his inner arm being neatly stitched by the doctor.

"He tried to kill himself," said the doctor.

"You don't cut there if you want to kill yourself," said Snow White, exposing her own bluish inner elbow, indicating it with a forefinger. "One sharp cut here would do it."

"See? I can't even kill myself correctly," said Prince Bergman. "That just proves I'm so inept I should die. And my father is so inept he doesn't even have sharp razor blades."

"Still blaming your parents for your own failures." Dr. Popper shook his head. "Slitting the inner elbow isn't necessary," he said. "A clean cut on each wrist right above the hand will do it."

Prince Bergman looked around suspiciously. "I know you're part of the conspiracy. You're trying to kill me or you've been sent here to teach me how to do it by all those who think I'm too horrible to live."

"Don't be silly," Snow White reassured him.

"Tell me you think I'm too horrible to live," he pleaded.

Snow White was silent, recalling how he beat her up. Yet somehow she felt he understood for the first time how wrong he'd been and she felt she might now be able to reach him.

"For the first time I feel one with the universe. . . . I understand what love means." The Prince looked into Snow White's eyes. "I'm sorry I hit you." His eyes filled with tears.

Snow White was delighted. Her husband seemed a new person whom she could love. "Why is he in this horrible place?" she asked the doctor. "You could have sewn him upstairs."

"He's crazy," said the doctor. "Besides, he's being held for arson. He almost burned the castle down trying to kill himself. He really should be in a hospital, but he's been arrested."

"Did my mother-in-law press charges?"

"No, the State did. Property is more important than human life in this society, you know."

"Ha, ha," laughed Prince Bergman, reminiscing, "I burned mother's whole room down. I turned her jewelry box upside down and threw all her precious jewelry and shit all over. 'Here's fifty years of your life,' I cried. 'What does it mean?' She just ran out of the room. Then I surrounded myself with all her finest towels— Vera, St. Laurent—but I forgot the matches, so I climbed out and back again. I tried to light the towels, but they just burned a bit and petered out, so I went into my father's bathroom and began to cut myself with his shitty blades. When mother came in I smiled and held out my bleeding arms to her, finally feeling affection and forgiveness despite the fact that she's the one who made me crazy, but she just stood there staring. Then she ran. I looked through the window and could see her running with her short little legs down the hill. By the time she returned with help the castle was on fire."

"We must get you out of here. Let him out, he's not guilty," cried Snow White, running over to the guard.

"The Court has to decide that," said the guard, looking at her breast.

Dr. Popper was impressed by Snow White's loyalty and passion. Her face was flushed, eyes burning with intensity. He had an erection.

"I want to take him home," she pleaded. "It's the first time he's ever seemed normal."

"No, I'd rather stay here," whined the Prince, cowering. "They're still trying to kill me. But then, if I stay here, I know you'll have a lover. But I deserve it. I've been so rotten to you and the kids. So what if they're not mine. But maybe they are. But even so. Do it. Have a lover, please. I want you to be happy. I deserve to die. I hope they find me and do it soon, but they want to punish me by making me wait—" He looked at Dr. Popper. "Are you part of the conspiracy? But why should I imagine you'd tell me?"

The Prince, speaking in a low intense voice appeared handsome and loving. Snow White felt like making love with him.

"He can't go with you," said the doctor, preparing to leave, "but jail is not the place for him either. He needs help."

"No, I deserve to be in jail. Please," pleaded the Prince, dropping onto his knees, clasping arms together, all the little black stitches making jagged rows. "It's safer too."

Snow White's concern communicated itself to Dr. Popper. He felt her concern all over as if he were being tickled with it, a half-inch from the surface of his skin. He recalled her hard, white breast. His prick jumped like a divining rod yet felt too heavy to defy gravity. He surprised them by ripping off his clothing and breathing deeply, as if his clothes were strangling him and his enormous prick.

"Time's up," said the guard.

"It's of the utmost importance that we have just a little more time," said Dr. Popper, opening his attaché case. "Look, I really think I can help your marriage."

"How?" asked the Prince, suspicious.

"Listen carefully before you reject this idea," said Dr. Popper breathlessly, "I'll play the part of a lover to your wife. Then, when you see exactly what you were afraid of, up front, before your very eyes, so to speak, without losing your wife's love, or feeling that she's cheating behind your back, you may be cured. It's called psychodrama, and can sometimes cure a troubled relationship." ·

"Yes, if you want to cure it by ending it." Snow White looked at him and his erection suspiciously. "I just don't believe it. I don't believe in sharing sex, and that's not our problem," she said slowly.

Prince Bergman, strangely, said nothing against the idea, seeming slightly seduced by the element of fear and self-destruction.

"Besides," said Snow White, "How do you know I want to fuck you? You ask him as if I'm his property. Is that the concept of me my marriage counselor has?" She was feeling desperate. "We need a lawyer more than a marriage counselor."

"Wait," said Prince Bergman, "maybe it would help." He was breathing hard and moving his pinkie rapidly. He stood up from sheer excess of energy.

"But I don't want to. I know it won't work out. We'll all hate each other. We'll never want to see each other again. Our therapy will be ruined."

"Maybe not," said the Prince.

Dr. Popper slowly descended on Snow White and hovered over her in a paternal way.

"Is it because you find me repulsive?" His sudden vulnerability and transformation from the strong therapist frightened Snow White. Dr. Popper was trembling with desire. Snow White didn't want to but found it flattering. She wondered whether he'd save her, he was so fatherly.

"Trust me," he said softly, lifting her face with his trembling fist and gently, slowly placed his lips on hers.

Prince Bergman stood watching, hyperventilating and snorting like a horse. Snow White returned Dr. Popper's kiss diffidently, looking at her husband, who stood immobile, the veins in his forehead crawling like snakes as he ground his jaw.

"Now I know. This was all planned. You both planned this scene so you could fuck each other and not feel guilty. Maybe this isn't the first time. God only knows how long you've been lovers. Well go ahead," he said to Dr. Popper, "You can take care of her and support the kids too."

Dr. Popper's prick was still hard as a rock. He moved his hands toward Snow White and began slowly to unbutton her blouse.

She pushed his hand away, looking at the Prince. "I don't want to. I'm afraid."

"He won't do anything," pleaded Dr. Popper. "He's essentially passive. Come on," the doctor said to Prince Bergman, fiddling again with Snow White's buttons, "How do you feel? Verbalize, verbalize." He encouraged the Prince with a come-hither motion of one hand, the other diving into Snow White's bodice.

The Prince smiled inappropriately, one vein in his temple moving in rhythm with his jaw, which clenched and unclenched in time with his pinkies. He slowly raised his right hand, pointed his forefinger at Dr. Popper, and cocked his thumb.

"Bam, Bam, Ala-ka-zam," he said, aiming at Dr. Popper, who instantly began to enlarge and become hairy. "I told you," he said, relieved.

Snow White just watched, horrified, her blood-red lips ajar, as Dr. Popper slowly and unawarely metamorphosed into a giant grizzly bear.

He moved toward her lumberingly, as she began to back away, his words now barely decipherable. "I told you I'd help you," he growled. He wrapped his arms around Snow White and squeezed lovingly until her body hung helplessly limp.

Another Great Love
That Could Not Be

"Words are tricky bastards."
H. W. Blattner, *Sound of a Drunken Drummer*

D_{ear me,}
Of course this is a letter to you, but since we've decided the most
effective way to end our relationship would be to cut off contact
with each other, most likely you'll never see this letter. Of course it
wasn't really my idea to break off, nor was it my feeling that not
having any contact was the most effective way to do it, but with
your feeling that way so strongly, is there anything else I could do?

*

I do what I have to do. I try to do what's best for me now, but all the time I feel like a quadruple paraplegic in orbit. So of course I'm up here. Little did I know when I applied that I'd be needing a rest home, not an artist's colony. If I weren't brought up to be obedient, I'd have killed myself for sure. Well, I'm here. No one knows that I'm not well. They can't know how hard it is for me to live without you, how I don't want to, but have to.

No one knows that, for me, this is a rest home. When my taxi arrives, the nurse comes to the door to show me around. She shows me my room in the enormous wooden main building. It's lovely, with antique furniture, but the bed is somehow hospital-like—the sheets are white and absolutely smooth and the bedspread is a hospital spread.

"When you're ready I'll show you your studio."

"Do I get a studio too? I'll see it right now," I say. My eyes do not see details yet. She drives me along a road what seems an enormous distance. My studio is a small one-room house, German Gothic or Elizabethan English, with a screened porch, fireplace and an enormous window looking straight into the woods. Am I really capable of getting myself there every day? Will I really be able to work there.

Elizabeth has just arrived with my typewriter. I was watching for her car from my window. I can hardly recognize it, as I hadn't taken a close look at it before. My body is so tense that nothing informatory or sensory can penetrate now. My eyes skim things nervously and retain only vague memories. I long for the richness and intensity of the time before I became sick with this longing for you.

A man climbs out of Elizabeth's car and waits while she goes into the office. I watch him stretch. Someone calls me. I'm happy to have something to do, like retrieving my typewriter, because as soon as the secretary (nurse) left me alone I began to weep, hands pressing on the top of the antique dresser; I saw my mouth widen in the mirror, my face turn red, forehead wrinkle, tears come. I stopped immediately and rapidly unpacked. I didn't come here to weep. I can't blame you. It hurts me to imagine you aren't weeping also. Then the pain becomes worse. I want so much to be indispensable to you. I detest mulling on your uniqueness and my loss, knowing you are filled with hope for your future with someone new and better for you. You can and are already involved in the search, enjoying dating, being admired, while I feel so sick, abandoned and disillusioned.

You have your whole life ahead of you, but I didn't realize until two weeks after you moved out that I really wanted to spend the rest of my life knowing that it would be you meeting me at every plane and bus, you, sharing your body with me so imaginatively, so diligently. I love your diligence. I respect someone who works hard until they achieve excellent results. You are so much fun to play with, so attentive.

When I realized that your reading at mealtimes was simply a habit I stopped feeling rejected, didn't mind it. I could sense your panic on entering a restaurant without having a newspaper, anything, to read. You could always choose either Chinese or regular news. No one has read me so many articles and stories since I was a small child. I'll never forget the porno stories you read me, or the exposés about Eric Clapton, The Beatles, Brian Wilson, Jim Morrison, Patti Smith, Mick Jagger, Elvis Presley, Mink de Ville, Roxy Music, The Sex Pistols. And all the Chinese stories, the ones about Jews. And all the tragic Chinese love stories about Great Loves That Could Not Be.

The nurse is going to show Elizabeth to her room and studio, and we are following in Elizabeth's car. Suddenly the nurse has disappeared.

"Where did she go?" asks Elizabeth laughing. None of us has seen. There are three roads in front of us.

"There she is," says Stan. She's noticed that no one was following her and has backed up. Elizabeth has a room on the top floor of the men's lodge, close to the room of a painter, Diane, with whom she shares a bathroom. I'm relieved to have a private room and bath, fearful that someone will catch me in some extreme expression of sorrow. Then, suddenly, I feel panic at being alone and think that Elizabeth is fortunate to have someone's room nearby and an intimate sense of men in rooms below.

"Which way is Lauren's studio?" Elizabeth asks the nurse so she can take my typewriter there; it's in her car already. I, of course, can't recall which way we'd gone.

"Just point us in the right direction," I say. Jane the nurse seems good-humoredly annoyed. She can't believe I don't remember, but of course she doesn't realize how sick I am. Perhaps I should just tell everyone—better still, make a general announcement: "My husband, whom I'm very much in love with, just left me. I'm all alone, I miss him terribly and I'm not used to it. Moreover, I'm afraid I'll feel like this all my life." Then, if I faint or suddenly begin crying or throw up, it won't seem so odd. Perhaps I can even get the kind of sympathy I need.

Elizabeth invites me to have dinner in town with Stan and her. I'm tempted to accept, terrified at certain moments to be alone, afraid of the pain when it comes.

"No thanks," I say, putting my trembling hands awkwardly into the loosening waistband of my slacks, "I'd rather brave the dining room immediately and get it over with." She and Stan are figuring out where would be best to sleep. We laugh because there's a choice of a single bed in her room and a single bed in her studio.

"You can sleep on your sides," I tell them. I know we could have done it. We've done it many times.

I picture you up here with me. I know it's no good, you wouldn't like it, perhaps just to be obstinate. I'd have to entertain you, ignore everyone else. You'd tell me often how much you hate everything. But I wish I could imagine that you'd be home when I got back. For me, the end of the month is simply the end of the month. Maybe by that time you'll be in love with someone else.

It's raining hard now and my studio has become quite dark. It's beautiful, but in my state my first reaction to everything is panic, fear of that most exquisite pain. Perhaps instead of telling everyone

here that you and I have separated, I should say that my husband
has died and I'm trying to recover from that "feeling of loss." If you
were really dead, it might be easier to bear. It would be pure; no
analyses, no recriminations, no incomprehensibilities, no hopes that
you still love me. It would be fate and not your choice. It could in
no way be construed by me as my fault.

The horrible part of this is that no one can comfort me as you can
for your loss. It therefore becomes imperative to see you again and
again. If only we could have been such a comfort, so supportive to
each other before. No one understands either of us as well as we do.

At the same time, it's so painful. We ask each other, "What
have you been doing? What did you do last night? The night
before?" hearts pounding, attempting to be subtle, even obscure,
unrestful until we've pieced together the entire calendar of each
other's events in our absence, cataloging the suspicious and painful
areas for future probing, vague fears burgeoning at odd unexpected
moments from those tiny implantations. We know it shouldn't
matter now, anyway.

*

Of course I know that last Tuesday you went to the library because I
met you by accident. You saw me first. You were wearing a clean
white T-shirt, which stood out so brightly against your golden-tan
skin and black, black hair. I recall a bit of scarlet, which must have
been your bag. I always pictured you as black and scarlet, intense,
encroaching, bright. Your conversation sharp and bright, also black
and scarlet, purple and gold. You looked so happy. I was glad to see
you, but I'd been feeling bad.

"How come you look so happy?" I asked.

"I'm happy to see you," you said. I thought you were lying and
most likely had a date. I was on my way to dinner with Carole and
Jane, who arrived at that moment, too soon, before I wanted to
leave you, but we said goodbye. I walked off with my friends,
leaving you standing on the street alone. Later I suddenly felt
miserable.

"What's the matter?" asked Carole. She looked so concerned I had to make an enormous effort not to cry.

"I feel so helpless seeing you so vulnerable," she said. I never thought of myself as vulnerable and I can't get used to a me that is. I just wished I was with you. I kept imagining I should have asked you to come over later, even though I didn't know whether you would have said you would.

*

I know I'm not well, that this is not healthy. I'm living nothing but fantasies and regrets and memories. I know I must push them away. I know my fantasies, regrets and memories aren't real. I can't recall the realities; I'm not even sure I ever understood them. We both struggled to make each other see the realities we saw. But what I remember now is not even what I thought before or remembered before, nor is it what you remember. Why do I remember only things that make me feel bad? This artist's colony may suffice as a lovely rest home, but there's no shrink here; we're left to our own devices, mostly work therapy. Perhaps I should have seen a shrink while we were together, even though you wouldn't, because you didn't believe in them, the way a person doesn't believe in the existence of God. Perhaps then I could have learned how to be cool when I was upset, instead of causing all those arguments, the ones we had about every three days and which you can now recall better than I, as you noted them in your journal. Not that they were all my fault, but I feel now there were better ways I could have dealt with them. When I learned, it was already too late. You didn't want any more. I'm not sure what it was you didn't want any more of. You may recall that problem as being one of the lesser ones.

My reality may not be the true one; it's the sad one. It's hard for me to remember the things you did that hurt me, that were selfish, that repressed me, the things to recall that would make me feel better about our being apart. But when I spoke to you I realized you did.

"I wish you weren't Chinese. Then maybe we could be together now," I said to you.

I didn't like it when you said, "But I couldn't take the pain," reminding me that in your reality it wasn't our cultural differences that were the difficulty, but that I caused you so much pain.

*

"Is Hsueh-tung going with you?" my mother asked on the phone.

I never told her you moved out because she'd think, my third marriage ending this way, that I was some kind of idiot. She'd also worry because I'm alone. A man gives her a false sense of security. When I asked my sister whether she'd told our parents, and she said no, I said, laughing, "Maybe I should pretend we're still living together the way Hsueh-tung pretended to his parents for the last three years that he wasn't living with me."

Only when you were sure you were leaving, when we were crying at three o'clock in the morning and I begged you to tell your parents, thinking it would make it easier for you to make a commitment to me, did you call your parents in Hong Kong and tell them. For that matter, you spoke in Chinese and I don't even know what you told them.

"No, mother," I said, "Hsueh-tung has to work." I'm angry because her incredulous query implies that we can't be apart. "Husbands or, for that matter, wives are not allowed. It's not a resort, it's a place to work without interference."

She doesn't understand married people parting, even for a month, for work, especially when it's the woman's work. I'm very angry at her and at the part of me that also finds that kind of separation difficult, almost untenable.

Why didn't I just say, "Please don't move out"? But I did, I gave it one last try. I said, "Let's just live from year to year with a contract that makes us both happy. We can go over it every year."

"No," you said. "You're right, it's no good. I can't make a commitment and I have to move out."

Strangely, I didn't realize how serious it was. Part of me wanted you to move out. I never believed we should separate. I valued our relationship enough to feel that we should continue enormous efforts to work out our problems. But if you were going to move out, I was interested to see how it would feel. Even though I couldn't decide to separate, perhaps I'd feel much better without you and all our problems.

Now I recall what made me feel so bad that last Tuesday when I met you on the street (unless it was just too much Sangria, which caused Carole to caress me concernedly, her brown eyes slightly squinting in powerless puzzlement while I wanted no one to look at me). It was when you asked me, smiling, how I was, and I said I still didn't feel well and almost started crying, you took two white calling cards from your pocket. I was too upset to see them well or notice any name, but at the top was a line drawing of a pair of slushy sneakers, one horizontal, one vertical.

"Remember those sneaker beds?" you asked. "Well, the woman who designed them came to our office for some information.

"About what?" I asked. I jokingly tried to rip up the cards but you grabbed them as if they were very precious to you.

She wasn't the first woman you took out who came to the office for information. I pictured you intercepting lots of young attractive career women who have stopped by your office for information. "Let's discuss it over dinner," you say to them, or, "Would you like to have lunch? I was just going out." You take them to Chinatown and order in Chinese. They are impressed with your exoticism. You don't read the newspaper at lunch or dinner with them, as you didn't with me for quite some time. You even pay the check.

"She's interested in subway entrances," you said.

I want to say, "Let's not discuss this, it hurts too much," but if I don't play that game I lose the information, the sense of your life,

what you're doing, all control. The details feed my proliferating
imagination and appease it for awhile.

"We discussed our favorite spaces."

"What are her favorite spaces?" I asked.

"She likes all the most beautifully designed architectural spaces."

"And you?"

"I told her I liked subway ruins." I imagined her instantly falling
in love with you.

"It sounds like you wouldn't get along," I said.

You seemed so proud and happy to tell me, as if I weren't the
woman you'd left and who was so unhappy, but as if I'd hurt you
greatly and you wanted to get back at me by showing me how
desirable you are, how many available women there are.

Then Jane arrived. She looked puzzled to see you there with me,
as if I had betrayed her—after eliciting all her sympathy for my
misery, my bereftness—there we were, together.

"We just met accidentally," I say. "He's on his way to the
library."

Later that night, desiring to go home, yet afraid to, I waited until
everyone else said they had to leave. Once home, I stared at the
record player. I wanted to play something but I don't know what
won't remind me of you: my spirit soared with Fairport Convention, and suddenly a sound, a tone—my insides dropped as if in
an elevator, on a roller coaster. I gasped, tears ran from my eyes. A
memory had encompassed me, attacked me before I even remembered it. That's what I'm in a panic about.

I turned on the TV and imagined you meeting the sneaker lady
near the library. Both of you would eat at the Greek Restaurant
we've eaten at so often when there was the Japanese movie festival
at the Regency Theatre. We met there three days in a row when
they played *The Human Condition*. You're going, with coffee to go
and buns, to see Montgomery Clift and Marlon Brando in the Rebel
Series.

*

I walked into the dining room here, appearing brave, at least normal. But no one knows me here, can tell whether I'm a sick person, a half person, whether this is me, the way I am when I'm well.

"Can I sit here?" I asked, my hand on the back of a chair. Everyone introduced himself; I recall none of the names. I think of you feeling well enough to kiss women while I feel too sick to respond to conversation, to brave the nausea at the thought of physical contact.

"What do you write?" asks the man sitting next to me.

"Fiction," I say. "I don't write poetry."

Then I find out that almost everyone at the table is a poet. Introductions over, they delve into dinner conversation.

"Coprophilia means what?" someone asks.

"Love of shit. Coprophobia is fear of shit. But what is hatred of shit?"

"I bet you don't know what coprophagia is?"

There is silence. I want to answer. I recall my biology.

"Shit eating," I say, happy to contribute, hoping to belong now. Yet I realize, through subsequent conversation, that poets' trains of thought are farther from mine than those of any other kind of person, including filmmakers, film editors, writers, or painters— except for, maybe, composers of opera or modern atonal music.

The poet who is sitting so close to me that I can't see her tells the handsome man across from me to put the laundry in the dryer. It seems they're a couple, both poets, who live together outside this place. I'm surprised a couple has come here together to work. I fear I'll never meet someone like you again, whose trains of thought run so wonderfully with my trains.

I recall how I hugged Elizabeth spontaneously outside her studio. Maybe after her boyfriend leaves, she and I will become lovers. Now, for the first time, I realize how important, how binding, how magical alliances can be. I always prided myself on being independent, had a misconception of myself as someone who loves to be alone. I've always read about people who remain together from childhood, bound, always knowing. Finally I understand, but it's too late. It's taking me a long time to get to know myself.

*

My first night here I went to my room early. Unable to face conversation yet, I finished unpacking and took a bath. I was tired because we'd been up so late the night before, when you came to pick up my keys. We made love, long and wonderfully as usual. At least I can recall only the very best. That's the strangest quality of my memory now; it's all in your favor. I vaguely recall the unhappiness but never think about it. I spend my time regretting the very finest things we had. You cried a lot that night before I left (I'm not sure for reasons that would make me feel better), and while we made love you shouted, "You're mine, still mine." I pretended I didn't hear. I thought, how ridiculous to say that now, but I didn't want you to stop.

I try to read *Our Mutual Friend* by Dickens and *Dona Flor and Her Two Husbands* by Jorge Amado, two of the fattest books I could find, to alleviate panic in empty moments, but can concentrate on neither. Reaching a moment I think it possible to fall asleep, I shut the light, after fiddling with the unfamiliar and unyielding switch, by turning the bulb. Then I can't fall asleep.

I think of jerking off. I think you'd be in a situation right now, on a Saturday night, in which you wouldn't have to jerk off to fall asleep. I picture you in someone's apartment on the Upper West Side. It's not the sneaker woman, but one you told me about previously. After a few dates and your libido, it would be hard to imagine you not making love with her by now.

My clitoris is covered by pubic hair still matted from my underpants, which, you know, unless I'm going to have sex, I wear to bed. I'm not in the mood to give myself a long and relaxed pleasure; I want to peak, then fall asleep. I raise my hips, touching myself round and round on the most sensitive spot. I never even attempt to arouse myself more slowly, by touching all around, putting my fingers in my vagina, having a fantasy. I feel a hardening under my sliding and relentlessly moving finger. It feels, at first, like a little worm. "Oh, yes," I say, "little worm. Oh, yes, you're getting hard," as if turned on by the fact that I'm turning myself on, as if that little worm, little snake, is someone else's.

Suddenly, I'm aware that the ringing I hear is the telephone downstairs. I rise quickly and go out onto the balcony in my nightgown. A man is sitting in the lounge but I don't know who because I'm not wearing my glasses.

"It's the office phone," he says.

I realize I'm in my nightgown. "Oh," I say, and go back into my room. It hasn't occurred to me that someone might call the office number when the office was closed. The phone would just ring and ring; there would be no way to answer. As I'm new and have given everyone both the booth and office numbers, I'm sure it's for me. Even though you've seen me off this morning, I imagine you're calling from my apartment. You want to reach me but can't get through. I can't bear to let you need me and not answer.

I sigh so I can breathe better. For one second as I inspire a full breath, a thought grows in the small space of new air. Let him need me, I think. Then the anxiety returns.

*

After that I can no longer jerk off. I wish I'd brought my vibrator, the one you got me, but it buzzes and I don't want anyone up here to hear it.

*

The night Roberto and I went to dinner together he took me home We sat on my couch.

"Can I see your vibrator?" he asked.

"Who told you I had a vibrator?" I laughed, not recalling that we'd probably discussed it sometime when we were with Lorraine.

"I don't know, I just guessed," he said, taking out a second cigarette. We discussed it more, but I didn't go get it, somehow feeling that it was too intimate an object to bring out for a male friend. I wondered whether it was scaly with dried secretion, as, exhaustedly, after using it, I let it drop into my drawer.

"How does it feel?" he asked.

"It's weird. At first it's strange. I had to get used to it. First of all it buzzes, and since buzzing had never been in my lexicon of turn-ons, it was distracting. Second of all, it wasn't sexual to me right away because nothing in real sex vibrates in quite the same way."

"That's interesting," he said. I recited all this in a most matter-of-fact, thoughtful manner, eliminating any sign of seductiveness from a possibly provocative situation. As an afterthought I showed it to him, the way one displays a pet, a cute child, a new lover. He looked at it, felt it, turned it on. He put it near his face and rubbed it along his cheek.

It crossed my mind that perhaps he wanted a sexual situation, a seduction, but I was too sick with longing for you to think about it. I couldn't anyway, just because Lorraine was in California and I, the former wife of Roberto's friend, was free—Roberto, who reminds me so much of you because you and I introduced him to Lorraine when she was miserable trying to forget someone else. Now it feels strange to see their relationship endure beyond ours. It wouldn't have been good anyway. It's Lorraine he's having a relationship with, Lorraine who's engaged his emotions, as he would put it.

He took out a third cigarette. "I'll leave after this one," he said.

*

Peeling an orange reminds me of you, walking through grass reminds me of you, the feel of my sheets reminds me of you, coffee reminds me of you, my clothing reminds me of you, newspapers remind me of you, sounds, smells, colors . . .

This morning I had a chill. My nipple hardened in my thin scarlet silk shirt. My small breast became rounder, the nipple stuck out. I caressed it gently, thinking, Hsueh-tung would love that. You'd touch it and gasp.

I'm not sure that what I miss about you is something that you ever gave me or a fantasy. Or what you never gave me. I am sure, though, that you taught me what I wanted and that I wanted it from you. I tried to get it, but unsuccessfully. I keep imagining now that perhaps I asked too much, was too rigidly demanding. Why couldn't I accept less, be happy with what I (we) had? Was I happy? Was I miserable? It's almost impossible to remember.

What I hated was the time we slept on the floor because it was so hot, two years ago. You said our relationship was horrible and I was surprised because I thought it was stormy but wonderful. That's only a fragment of the times I pieced together the puzzle of how you thought a relationship should be. Needless to say it was frighteningly different from my idea. Why couldn't you accept mine? I would have liked to be the incarnation of your ideal partner, but I couldn't. Not even after I learned what that was. I couldn't control myself. When I was upset I confronted you, always, in ways that made you feel bad. I tried to learn the way you wanted me to communicate with you but I couldn't. It seemed to me the only way you wouldn't feel incapable was if I said nothing. Paradoxically, after you'd decided to move out, and began to treat me differently, I did it. But then, I always said you made our relationship that way because you needed this ending, the ending had to be, it was the only way you could do it, because I know you were in love with me, but couldn't accept me. Now I can't stand the thought of your giving someone else what I want, what I never knew I wanted until I knew I wanted it from you, and until I couldn't get it.

Even though you may not be able to give that to anyone, I think you realize now that you need it too and you may be too hasty to give it to someone else. I wanted you to believe, to be able to say, "She's my life, she's important to me, I chose her. When you couldn't tell your family about us, when you asked my daughter to let you use her room so you could pretend to be our roommate when your mother came from Hong Kong for a visit, when your brother asked you to dinner on New Year's Eve and you went alone, pretending to be a person who is not attached, always available to their call, only their needs, I knew you hadn't decided that for yourself. Despite the fact that you told me "yes, yes."

*

The day before I came up here, Carole and I were having coffee at the Bagel. Behind us was an Oriental woman feeding her adorable infant rice pudding. I was jealous of her, her baby, her husband who wasn't even there, everything I imagined about her life. I wished I were she or that she were I. I wished that was our baby, that we had a baby. Perhaps I should have done everything I know to keep you. You made me feel that you could have been happy that way too, a willing victim of a fate you didn't have the courage or stupidity to choose. But I couldn't do that. I already have my children. I might have had a baby with you, but I really wanted you to choose, to decide, to want. I was also afraid that if you weren't happy with that life you'd try to get even with me in some obscure way. Now I regret the baby we didn't have, wish I'd trapped you. I know, knowing you, it would have bound us forever. I'd have belonged to you then, to your family, the way I wanted, needed, and you would have belonged to me, the way I let you. Each month when I got my period I knew you were as relieved as I was. But I thought you were a little sorry too, as I was. I may have imagined it.

*

I can't write this without crying. My eyeglasses are spattered with tears, my eyes rimmed with salt. There's a bed here in my studio for me, the invalid, to lie on. There's a woolen cover to wrap myself in. It's chill and rainy. At first I lay there. I read, I slept, I wept. I wanted to work on a story but I found myself talking to you (to myself), still attempting to tell you my thoughts, share this place with you, make everything clear about how I feel. My last memory of you was in the bus station seeing me off, getting me coffee, holding my heavy bag. Coming on the bus despite an angry driver, to say a last goodbye, as if we were together and I'd be coming home to you. Now every time we say goodbye it's a different goodbye. One where I'm left alone again and again.

I felt funny in my studio in the woods at first. I kept hearing cars but didn't know where the road was. I had the feeling I was being watched. I knew someone would be delivering lunch and didn't want to be seen sleeping. I jumped up every time I heard a car. I was incapable of doing anything but read and think of you. After jumping up at every sound of a car, I was finally woken by the sound of a car motor. I realized that that was the lunch and someone had probably seen me sleeping. Later, everyone I spoke to said they'd slept in their studios. I pictured the person delivering lunch to all these artists, supposedly applying themselves day and night so much so that they couldn't be disturbed even long enough to have a lunch hour, and seeing us all sleeping. I had then one of those moments when I feel normal or perhaps, because it's so momentary, a memory of what I feel like normally. Like when the sky is dark and heavy, filled with gray voluminous clouds that suddenly move a bit, expand, allow a bit of clear sky to show through.

*

When Roberto took me to dinner that night, he tried to make me feel better. He really believed what he said because of his experience. I recall the time he referred to, nearly three years ago— when he, scared of Lorraine (like me, older than him with two kids) got a letter from an old lover, a young blond medical student who had no children. She wanted to try to work something out. Roberto was in love with Lorraine, but he was scared. If I can be in love with Laura instead, he thought, it will be better for me. Lorraine cried during the entire three months. It was I who accompanied her to get her abortion, not Roberto. He tried, but he couldn't fall in love with Laura. When he did live with Lorraine, he realized that besides needing to he wanted to. That's different from us. I wanted us to; you were scared. You knew you needed me, though.

When you said, "It will be a good experience for me," instead of "I love you and want to live with you," I should have known. I did know in a way. You don't have to be a fortune teller.

At first I didn't understand Roberto. He's so vague sometimes. He said something about jumping into the water and swimming farther than you can, being stupid.

"It isn't only Hsueh-tung's choice," he said, "it's yours too." I had been pretending that you left me for reasons of your own, despite the fact that I told you we couldn't live together any longer without commitment. That's still the way I want to believe it, so I got angry at Roberto.

"He never accepted that I'm older than he, have children, am a writer, have been divorced," I repeated. I can't believe anything else anymore. When you told that parable about destructive relationships and waking up one day to find both your arms gone (and I know how much your arms mean to you), I was crushed, devastated. Was I really that destructive to you?

"When you're in a relationship," I said to you, "you're also pretty destructive to yourself. It's yourself you can't live with."

You thought it would be better to forget me and meet someone you wouldn't have problems with. You said my temperament and yours didn't go well together, yet you loved mine. Everything you wanted you also wanted the opposite of. I loved that about you, but it made you suffer. You could meet someone young, perhaps Chinese, who has no kids and an exciting career. Your dream woman, I called her.

"I'm real," I told you, "and we love each other. I know how much that's worth. You may never find your dream woman. What we have is invaluable. It's worth fighting to keep." You had different ideas. This passion we shared was not so valuable to you, it was scary, painful, impractical. You were taught that marriage meant society and family acceptance, economic betterment, not necessarily love. That's why the Romeo & Juliet theme of lovers unable to be together is so popular in Chinese literature and movies now. You could deal better with losing love than being in love. I felt you slipping away as if I were holding onto your hands at the edge of a roof and first one hand dropped, then the other let go. Leaning back a bit in horror, I watched you fall.

*

In spite of the fact that it's not modern to be possessive, I feel that you're mine, I'm yours. Your sperm, your *ching* is part of my blood still. I picture you with the sneaker woman, the other woman, others. I piece things together from things you told me. What makes it worse is I have nothing to tell you. So I told you that lie. Soon after you moved, when I wasn't yet feeling too bad except for when I missed you, I thought it possible to live without you, hearing from you often and seeing you too. My one fear was you'd meet someone else soon, have a relationship secret from me and suddenly tell me about it, saying you could no longer see me.

*

You could tell what I wanted that day and gave me a rundown of your time spent away from me, truthful or not, to appease me.

"Did you have a good few days?" you finally asked me.

"Yes, I did," I said. "I went to bed with someone."

"What?" you said, nearly choking. I feel good when (after

the last few weeks of superhuman attempts at control, myself feeling that to oppress you with crying and begging would alienate you further, further make you feel our relationship is sick without giving me what I want from you) I see that I can elicit some emotion in you.

"Who?" you asked.

"What do you care?" I said, "I'm not yours." You put down the menu for a moment, perhaps not able to eat. Good sense prevailed and you chose a dinner after all.

"Matthew," I said, "an old friend."

"What made you do it?" you asked. "I knew you would, but I didn't think it would be so soon. I know it's unreasonable of me to be so hurt, so miserable, but I can't help it. I feel guilty having you comfort me for this, but I have no one else." I loved your misery because it helped me feel I hadn't just been used or cheated by you. It made me feel you cared. I also couldn't bear to see you suffer. Every moment I wanted to tell you I'd only been kidding, but then you wouldn't know what to believe. A joke that elicited so much pain even though I hadn't known it would.

"How was it?" you asked.

"Okay," I said. If it had really happened I would have been able to be more graphic.

"Kathy did this too," you said, "and I felt the same way." You kept comparing how I was acting to how Kathy acted three years ago when you left her for me. You were terrified that I'd hang on the same way, rip emotions out of you. I didn't and I was hurt that you thought I'd be like her. Yet, despite your comparisons, you became angry when I said your leaving me was the same as your running from her when she wanted you to make a commitment to her. But every moment it reminded me, and I felt the same as she did, I know, because I recalled her letter that I had found and read in secret: *I can't believe it, you don't love me anymore, I can't believe it. I don't understand why. When you lie next to me and make love with so much passion and desire, I can't believe it . . . I can't believe it.*

*

"Shall we see a movie?" you asked during dinner in Sheridan Square, the night before I came up here.

"Is there anything playing?" I asked.

"Have you seen anything lately?"

"No," I said, "I haven't had time. Have you?"

"No," you said. "I haven't gone to the movies. I haven't even seen a play or a concert." A minute later you were telling me you'd seen a Newport Jazz Festival concert up at Grant's Tomb.

"Who did you go with?" I asked.

"No one," you said. "I didn't want anyone to think I was a cheap date because the concert was free."

"It's a lovely date," I said, knowing you were lying. Later I pictured you on the grass outdoors, listening to wonderful jazz, your arm around someone, the moon in a corner of the sky. When you like someone new you make a special effort to find something interesting to do; perhaps it was her idea. I never liked jazz. I pictured you holding her hand, taking her home, sleeping over. This very quickly, like two-minute commercials, repeated throughout the evening. But you were with me still, and we made love. It wasn't until I came up here, lying in pain on this cot—the blanket, edged carefully in yellow wool, around my chill body—that I picture it again and again in great detail, both with the sneaker woman and the other.

"I know we can be good friends," you said that time in the restaurant. "There's something pure between us."

"I don't want to be just your friend," I said.

"I know," you said. "I don't want to be just yours either."

Now I'm not sure if I remember correctly. Did you say that?

You once said, referring to my children, "I wish those were our kids. Yours and mine." That hurt me so much because I knew you loved me but wanted me only in an unreal situation, that you never accepted me with the facts of my real existence. It made me wish the same, so I could have you.

"I wish I'd met you nine years ago," you also said many times.

But nine years ago, even though I'd be nine years younger, so would you.

"I wish I'd met you before you had your kids," you said wistfully, "but then I'd still be in high school."

"Never," said Roberto, "has Hsueh-tung been so emotionally engaged before by any woman. He comes from a strange and rigid culture. You have to let him find himself and what he wants." We were eating Chinese food, which reminded me of you.

"I see myself in him," he continued, "I know how pained he is. But don't worry, he's never, never been so emotionally engaged."

"Roberto, you don't understand. Hsueh-tung and I want two different things. He didn't move out in order to see what he needs, how we can make our relationship work by trying different things. The only way he can see a relationship is to find the 'right one' and get married to her and then they'll have the 'right relationship.' He doesn't want our relationship any more, he doesn't want me any more," I said emphatically, trying to remain calm while he looked at me, his eyes white in his black face, reflecting the candle. My eyes sting, but I don't want to blink them. "He wants to forget me. That's the way he wants to deal with it."

"Really?" asked Roberto, dipping a dumpling in soy sauce. "How do you know that?"

"I asked him, Roberto. He told me. After I came home from Florida I realized it. I asked him, Roberto, and he told me I was right. I realized the answer as soon as I understood enough to formulate the question, and he said yes, he felt that was the only way for him."

"You're going to have to be like a fox," Roberto said later, anyway.

"You don't understand Roberto. It's too late."

Roberto couldn't believe it either. He meant well, but he did the worst thing, even though I was guarding against it. He made me feel that you loved me so much that you'd soon realize how valuable, how much I meant to you. Such a fantasy is the worst thing for me when I should be forgetting you, learning to live without you.

Imagining you'd come back realizing that we should be together forever reminds me of Marsha Gross. I may have been eleven, perhaps younger. Every year or so, in the spring, from the time she was seventeen, Marsha Gross would go mad. She'd sit outside and tell stories, with people coming and going all day the way we used to go to movies, about a lover she was engaged to who was going to marry her soon. This man was crazy about her. In one of the anecdotes she related about him, he was carrying her into some house. I realized even at that age, there was something horrifying about her exposing her dreams to friends and strangers alike. After a few days, an ambulance would come and take Marsha Gross away to get better.

*

You introduced Liz to her husband. Their baby must be born by now. Allan and Margaret have a new baby, too. I guess I'll never see them again, or any of your friends whom we shared for a while. You were smarter than I. By not sharing my friends with me, even though I wanted you to, now you don't have as much to lose. After you moved out I read the little card Allan and Margaret sent. It had your name on the envelope, but I knew it was meant for me too, as they didn't know you'd moved out. I was shocked because you hadn't even told me that Margaret was pregnant. It filled me with longing and jealousy, knowing that all these people had with someone, as the years went by, something I couldn't have with you. When Allan called to invite us to a party for his new son I wasn't capable of telling him we'd split up, and I told him you were asleep. He took it for granted, more than I ever could, that I was your wife.

"Are you happy about the baby?" I asked him.

"Radiantly," he murmured.

On the Fourth of July, while watching the fireworks without you, I was crying. No one noticed even though almost the entire building was on the roof. I remembered all the Fourth of Julys we spent together, wonderful and intense, and the movie we made during the Bicentennial. I pictured you way uptown in Riverside Park, your arm around someone new, tentatively, but with excitement. We should be together now, I thought, we should be together now.

Later, when I asked you what you had done, you told me it was raining too hard in Brooklyn to go out. If that were true and not a story you made up to make me feel better, then you were able to think of that July Fourth as just another day, one when you didn't have to go to work, but when you weren't forced by memories of other Fourth of Julys to go see fireworks, to do something, celebrate, remember.

*

"At the office today," you told me, "Maureen asked each of us what building we'd like to be." When I first met you, Maureen had taken a leave of absence for a small breakdown. Was it over a man? I wonder with sympathy I didn't feel at the time. Now Maureen sees you every day and knows I'm no longer part of your life.

"Roberto said he wanted to be Grand Central Station."

"What did you want to be," I asked, getting involved. "A wrecked subway station men's room?"

"No, though that's not bad. St. John the Divine Cathedral."

"That's great. And what did Jonathon Regan say?"

"He wanted to be Citicorp."

"I wouldn't mind being Citicorp," I said.

"And Delongo, remember Delongo? He wanted to be—" I began to cry at the thought of Delongo, whom I met only twice at the most, once at an office party.

"I'll never see those people again," I said, feeling expelled. While talking I'd felt almost as if I were sharing the event, only to realize I was forever left out.

*

The day you moved out I didn't feel like this. I knew there was some danger but never realized what I'd feel like. Moving was hard work. It was strange for me to realize then that we were such good friends, that I understood you so well that I was helping you move, carrying your boxes filled with the belongings that had been loved, magically endowed and so hated by me, memories of your past that I didn't share, things I thought beautiful, the garbage you'd collected, some of which you finally discarded recently.

When we were finished, Roberto picked up Lorraine in the large rented truck. She and I tried to fit together on the little seat while you sat in back with my boys. We went to get clams at Sheepshead Bay, where you now live. Afterward we drove to your new apartment and we went in again so Lorraine could see it too. We sat there for a while looking out the window, getting the feel of your new neighborhood, watching your new neighbors. Then we got in the car, but without you. You stood next to the house and we looked out and waved goodbye. It felt strange leaving you there. I tried not to feel anything and was successful. I watched Lorraine's profile as we squeezed on the tiny seat. Please don't say anything, I thought, and she didn't. The ride home was completely silent, the entire event covered in gauze like a movie in soft focus.

*

It's hard to believe that if you ever read this you won't feel what I'm feeling as I write it, or that even now you don't feel the way I do. But because we're not together I'll be forced to recall only my version of memories, forever be embroiled in my own inescapable way of thinking.